ROBERT LUDLUM'S™
THE
TREADSTONE
RENDITION

THE BOURNE SERIES

Robert Ludlum's The Bourne Sacrifice (by Brian Freeman)
Robert Ludlum's The Bourne Treachery (by Brian Freeman)
Robert Ludlum's The Bourne Evolution (by Brian Freeman)
Robert Ludlum's The Bourne Initiative (by Eric Van Lustbader)
Robert Ludlum's The Bourne Enigma (by Eric Van Lustbader)
Robert Ludlum's The Bourne Ascendancy (by Eric Van Lustbader)
Robert Ludlum's The Bourne Retribution (by Eric Van Lustbader)
Robert Ludlum's The Bourne Imperative (by Eric Van Lustbader)
Robert Ludlum's The Bourne Dominion (by Eric Van Lustbader)
Robert Ludlum's The Bourne Objective (by Eric Van Lustbader)
Robert Ludlum's The Bourne Deception (by Eric Van Lustbader)
Robert Ludlum's The Bourne Sanction (by Eric Van Lustbader)
Robert Ludlum's The Bourne Betrayal (by Eric Van Lustbader)
Robert Ludlum's The Bourne Legacy (by Eric Van Lustbader)
The Bourne Ultimatum
The Bourne Supremacy
The Bourne Identity

THE TREADSTONE SERIES

Robert Ludlum's The Treadstone Transgression (by Joshua Hood)
Robert Ludlum's The Treadstone Exile (by Joshua Hood)
Robert Ludlum's The Treadstone Resurrection (by Joshua Hood)

THE BLACKBRIAR SERIES

Robert Ludlum's The Blackbriar Genesis (by Simon Gervais)

THE COVERT-ONE SERIES

Robert Ludlum's The Patriot Attack (by Kyle Mills)
Robert Ludlum's The Geneva Strategy (by Jamie Freveletti)
Robert Ludlum's The Utopia Experiment (by Kyle Mills)
Robert Ludlum's The Janus Reprisal (by Jamie Freveletti)
Robert Ludlum's The Ares Decision (by Kyle Mills)
Robert Ludlum's The Arctic Event (by James H. Cobb)
Robert Ludlum's The Moscow Vector (by Patrick Larkin)
Robert Ludlum's The Lazarus Vendetta (by Patrick Larkin)
Robert Ludlum's The Altman Code (with Gayle Lynds)
Robert Ludlum's The Paris Option (with Gayle Lynds)
Robert Ludlum's The Cassandra Compact (with Philip Shelby)
Robert Ludlum's The Hades Factor (with Gayle Lynds)

THE JANSON SERIES

Robert Ludlum's The Janson Equation (by Douglas Corleone)
Robert Ludlum's The Janson Option (by Paul Garrison)
Robert Ludlum's The Janson Command (by Paul Garrison)
The Janson Directive

ALSO BY ROBERT LUDLUM

The Bancroft Strategy
The Ambler Warning
The Tristan Betrayal
The Sigma Protocol
The Prometheus Deception
The Matarese Countdown
The Apocalypse Watch
The Scorpio Illusion
The Road to Omaha
The Icarus Agenda
The Aquitaine Progression
The Parsifal Mosaic

The Matarese Circle
The Holcroft Covenant
The Chancellor Manuscript
The Gemini Contenders
The Road to Gandolfo
The Rhinemann Exchange
The Cry of the Halidon
Trevayne
The Matlock Paper
The Osterman Weekend
The Scarlatti Inheritance

ROBERT LUDLUM'S™
THE TREADSTONE RENDITION

A NOVEL SET IN THE
JASON BOURNE UNIVERSE BY JOSHUA HOOD

HEAD
OF ZEUS

An Aries Book

First published in the US in 2023 by G.P. Putnam's Sons,
an imprint of Penguin Random House LLC
First published in the UK in 2023 by Head of Zeus,
part of Bloomsbury Publishing Plc

9 7 5 3 1 2 4 6 8

A catalogue record for this book is available from
the British Library.

ISBN (HB): 9781803285818
ISBN (XTPB): 9781803285825
ISBN (E): 9781803285795

Printed and bound in Great Britain by
CPI Group (UK) Ltd, Croydon CR0 4YY

Head of Zeus
5–8 Hardwick Street
London EC1R 4RG
www.headofzeus.com

PROLOGUE

TANGI VALLEY, AFGHANISTAN
AUGUST 2011

Alpha Team was sucking gas. The twelve-man team of Afghan soldiers and Green Berets had been roaming the mountains of the Wardak Province in central Afghanistan for days now, tracking a group of insurgents responsible for shooting down an American CH-47D Chinook resupply helicopter just weeks before. All thirty-eight people on board the helicopter had died, including thirty American military personnel—the worst loss of American lives in Afghanistan since Operation Enduring Freedom had begun a decade earlier. Lieutenant Adam Hayes and his men had been tasked with finding the Taliban fighters who'd fired the rocket-propelled grenade, and they and an escort squad from the

Afghan National Army had been searching tirelessly, their bodies beaten down by the unrelenting Afghan heat and the fifty-plus pounds of body armor, weapons, and ammunition strapped to their backs.

But despite the pain, Hayes knew they were closing in on their prey. He'd pushed his men hard, and had no intention of letting up until his team had avenged the loss of those thirty-eight lives.

His team sergeant had other ideas.

"Boss, we're going to need to call a halt," the sergeant told him over the radio, as the team trudged slowly up a steep, rocky trail. *"The Afghans are out of water."*

Hayes muttered a curse, wiping his face against the sleeve of his desert BDUs. "What, Mike, again?"

"Roger," the sergeant replied.

Hayes cursed again. Turned back the way they'd come in time to see one of the ANA regulars shuffling up the trail, the stock of his AK-47 dragging in the dust.

You've got to be shitting me.

As more of the soldiers came into view, Hayes could see clearly they were struggling. Breathing heavily, open-mouthed, every step looking like they were wearing concrete boots. They'd chosen a hell of a place to shut down, though; with the ridgeline on their left flank and a craggy rock face to their right, this place was Ambush City. It was not the kind of terrain Hayes wanted to hang around in for long.

But as the team leader, he was responsible for the safety and well-being of both his men and the Afghans assigned to him, and Hayes could already sense that the ANA fighters were losing their trust in him. The Americans were motivated—seventeen Navy SEALs had died in that Chinook attack—but the locals required a little more finessing.

Besides, it wouldn't do to lose a valuable fighter to dehydration and heat exhaustion. Not here, miles from anything remotely resembling safe ground.

Fuck.

Realizing he had no choice, Hayes depressed the push-to-talk button on his plate carrier and keyed up the radio. "All right, Mike," he told his sergeant. "Find us a place to stop."

Two minutes later, they came to a halt in a narrow clearing, and while the rest of his men set up a hasty perimeter, Hayes gathered their extra canteens and moved to the rear of the formation to wait for the Afghans.

Dropping to a knee next to a boulder, he fished the hydration tube from the inside of his plate carrier and stuck the valve between his lips. The first pull came out of the tube warm as bathwater, but it was still wet, and with the amount of dust coating the inside of Hayes's mouth, that was all that mattered. While he swished the water around in his mouth, his team sergeant broke off from the ANA men he'd herded into the perimeter and came over to retrieve the canteens.

"How are they already out of water, Mike?" Hayes asked him.

"Boss, you've got me," the sergeant replied. "I checked all their canteens this morning and they were full."

3

"Do you think they're pouring it out? Trying to slow us down?"

"No, I don't think they'd do that. Do you?"

Hayes wouldn't have believed it, but he remembered the warning he'd received from a Special Forces major back in Kabul.

The Afghan regulars are worthless. Half of them would rather be fighting for the Taliban than helping us take back their country. And the rest are a bunch of fucking cowards.

It sounded like a shit sandwich to Hayes, and the major had agreed.

Keep your hand on your pistol and your head on a swivel, he'd told Hayes. *Because the moment you let your guard down, one of these* savages *will put a bullet in your back.*

The warning had rung hollow at the time—Hayes knew there were plenty of good men among the Afghan ranks, and good fighters, too—but now, with an unknown enemy lurking behind every ridge, he was beginning to wonder if he'd put too much trust in the ANA team's commanding officer.

Only one way to find out.

"Where's Captain Nassim?" Hayes asked his sergeant.

The sergeant shrugged. "Last I saw, he was chewing someone's ass over by that boulder."

"All right. Get the men hydrated and ready to move." Hayes stood. "I don't want to be here any longer than we have to."

While his team sergeant gathered the canteens and carried them back to the Afghans, Hayes went in search of Abdul Nassim, the Afghans' commanding officer. He found the captain standing toe to toe with his platoon sergeant, eyes angry as he jabbed the man in the chest.

"The men running out of water is *unacceptable*," Nassim told the sergeant. The man made to argue, but Nassim cut him off with the wave of a hand. "I will deal with you later," he snapped. "You're dismissed."

Hayes waited until the platoon sergeant was out of earshot, then approached Nassim. "Rough day at the office?" he asked, pulling a Nalgene bottle from the pouch on his plate carrier and handing it over.

Nassim pursed his lips. "They're all rough," he replied. "And I have *plenty* of water."

"Can't have too much out here," Hayes said. "Not in this heat, anyway."

"A fair point." Nassim took the bottle, but instead of drinking stepped closer to Hayes, his dark eyes serious. "My men are *not* cowards, Lieutenant Hayes."

"Never said they were."

"Maybe *you* haven't, but your colleagues back in Kabul—"

"Aren't here, Captain," Hayes told him. "As far as I'm concerned, every man on my team is grateful for your help tracking down these assholes who killed our friends." He met Nassim's eyes. Smirked. "We just wish your people would quit drinking your water so fast."

Nassim glanced at him. Smiled a weary smile. He unscrewed the top of the Nalgene, and after drinking his fill, handed it back. "You are different than most Americans I have worked with."

Hayes was about to respond when a trickle of shale and

crushed earth from the ridgeline to his left grabbed his attention. It was a little thing, a variance most men wouldn't have even noticed, but after five months in the aptly named Valley of Death, Hayes's senses had learned to pick up on such things.

Instantly on guard, he raised his M4 skyward, studying the ridgeline through the Trijicon ACOG scope mounted to the rail of the rifle.

"What is it?" Nassim asked. "What do you see?"

Hayes ignored him, and panned across the rock face, senses straining for anything out of place. But there was nothing, and Hayes began to wonder if he was overreacting.

Suddenly, a flash of flame burst out from a pile of rocks maybe twenty yards from Hayes's eyeline, followed a split second later by the guttural roar of a Soviet-made PKM machine gun.

"*Contact left!*" Hayes shouted, flicking off the safety catch of the M203 grenade launcher mounted beneath the barrel of his M4. He pulled the trigger, the *thoop* of the 40mm grenade leaving the launcher anemic compared to the hellfire roar of the machine gun.

But the grenade hit its mark, and while the explosion silenced the gun, there were more fighters hidden in the rocks, and soon the defile was echoing with the chatter of AK-47s and the screech of RPGs leaving their launchers.

Desperate to get out of the line of fire, Hayes was looking for cover when he took a 7.62x54mm round to the plate carrier, the impact sending him staggering backward. At first there was no pain, just the hiss of the air from his lungs and the sudden imbalance in his legs. Then he felt it, the burning thunderclap through his nerve endings and the spreading warmth across his skin.

Shit, I'm hit.

The thought had no sooner crossed his mind than a second round found his helmet, and then he was on the ground. Bullets sparked off of the rocks around him, showering his face with fragments of lead and slivers of stone.

You're going to die here, he realized. His movements sluggish, his thoughts a crawl. The whole world strangely muted, the firefight already fading out around him. *This is it.*

There was no time to feel scared, or angry. There was barely any pain, even. Just an overarching sense of guilt, of failure.

You let down your team. And those thirty-eight men who died in that helicopter.

You let down your country.

There was nothing Hayes could do about it now. He couldn't make his muscles move, couldn't stand and run or even crawl. He was a sitting duck out here, he knew; sooner or later, one more Taliban bullet would find him, and that would be the end.

And then, he was moving. Not by his own volition; someone was dragging him. Rough, over the rocks and the dirt, away from the line of fire. Toward safety.

Hayes craned his neck back. Saw Abdul Nassim above him, gripping tight to his plate carrier, his mouth set in a thin line of determination. The face of the ANA captain was the last thing Hayes would remember seeing, before the whole world cut to black.

1

The CIA-contracted Mi-17V raced over the ridgeline, the pilot chomping hard on the stick of gum as he cleared the ridge and dove for the spiderweb of wadis—water channels, bone dry in the summer heat—that crisscrossed the valley floor. Like everyone else aboard the helicopter, he was all too aware of the valley's reputation as a Taliban stronghold, and with the American withdrawal from Afghanistan already underway, the last thing he wanted was to get shot down in Indian country.

The pilot had been desperate for a way out of this mission ever since they'd taken off from the CIA compound in Kabul, but with the target area rapidly approaching, he knew he was running out of time.

He was beginning to give up any hope of aborting when a quick look at the instrument panel showed both the oil pressure and the RPM gauges dangerously close to the red, a clear sign that he was pushing the aged Russian helo too hard. The prudent move would be to ease up, decrease the power, but instead, the pilot sensed the chance for a last-minute reprieve. He reached for the collective, wondering how much more throttle it would take before something on the aircraft finally failed.

He wouldn't get the chance to find out. As he began to increase power, a silver-haired man stepped into the cockpit from the helo's cargo bay, the lights of the instrument panel glinting off of the pistol in his hand.

Dominic Porter wasn't a maintenance officer, but after ten years in the Navy SEALs and another decade as a CIA paramilitary officer, he'd logged more hours in the air than most pilots. From fresh off the assembly line UH-64 Black Hawks to the Eastern Bloc relics favored by third-world dictators, he'd spent enough time in darkened cargo holds to know the good sounds from the bad.

It had taken Porter about five seconds of listening to the high-pitched roar of the Mi-17's turbine to know that something was seriously fucked.

He was on his feet in an instant, his hand on the butt of his Glock 19 as he squeezed past the squad of heavily armed mercenaries packed in around him.

"What is it?" the team leader asked.

But Porter ignored him, not sure if he was being paranoid or if Ground Branch had stuck him with another spineless pilot. The moment he stepped into the cockpit, he could smell the pilot's fear over the caustic burn of aviation fuel and transmission fluid that permeated the cabin. Sweat streamed down the pilot's face as he white-knuckled the controls.

His eyes darted to the instrument panel, and the red-lined gauges he found there confirmed what he'd suspected since taking off from Kabul thirty minutes prior: the pilot was trying to sabotage the mission.

Fucking coward.

Before the pilot could register his presence, Porter drew his pistol and jammed the barrel hard into the man's neck, the cold press of steel against warm flesh sending the man stammering over the internal comms.

"*Wh-what the hell*—"

"Back it down," Porter told him. "Now."

The pilot stared at him, his pupils wide as eight balls.

"Back it down. Or you're a dead man."

But the man was vapor-locked, his mind flatlined by the 9-millimeter pressed to his throat.

Porter turned to the copilot, who'd to this point only watched, wordless, as the drama played out. "You've got the controls," Porter told him, and without waiting for the man's reply, turned back to the pilot, backhanding him across the face with the barrel of his Glock.

The pilot slumped forward, blood gushing from his flattened nose, and the helicopter dipped crazily toward the craggy outcroppings below, the terrain avoidance radar toning loud in the cockpit.

"Get him off the stick!" the copilot shouted.

Porter holstered the pistol and grabbed the unconscious pilot by the back of his flight suit and hauled him off of the controls. He pushed the man's limp body against the firewall, and expertly unhooked his harness. Once the copilot had regained control of the aircraft, Porter jerked the pilot from his seat.

Porter threw the man back into the cargo hold and motioned a thick-necked mercenary forward. "O'Malley, drop your gear and get in the pilot's seat," he ordered.

O'Malley frowned, confused by the order, but like every man in the mix of contract mercenaries and Afghan commandos in the cargo hold, he'd been handpicked by Porter for the mission at hand. Aware he was being paid handsomely to obey without a moment's hesitation, he dutifully dropped his kit and climbed into the right-hand seat.

"What the hell is this?" the copilot asked.

"An insurance policy," Porter replied.

"I don't understand."

"Just fly the fucking bird." Porter turned to O'Malley. "Make sure this man doesn't forget why we're here."

Then he was back in the cargo hold, pausing to snatch his HK416 and helmet from the nylon bench. He slung the rifle across the front of his blood-spattered plate carrier and strapped the helmet tight over his head, then moved to open the troop door. He held up his hand to the men around him, all five fingers extended. *"Five minutes."*

———

At forty-three, Porter had almost two decades on the men around him, but their cocky smiles and easy confidence as they stretched and double-checked their weapons and gear reminded him of when he'd first come to Kabul as a twenty-four-year-old Navy SEAL with bright eyes and an eagerness to make a difference.

"Loyalty to Country and Team" was the code he'd lived by, and that loyalty was the reason Porter and so many of his brothers had returned to Afghanistan, again and again. But somewhere during the twenty-year war, Porter had lost faith in the mission. He'd grown tired of risking his ass for a country and a people that at best didn't seem to want his help, and at worst tried every way they possibly could to kill him.

Osama bin Laden was dead. The lives of innocent Americans back home were no longer at stake here, not the way they'd been when Porter had first arrived in-country. Still, the war dragged on, and Porter could see no real benefit to it except to line the pockets of the weapons manufacturers back home who kept feeding the machine, sending young American lives to be slaughtered thousands of miles from their homes.

Somewhere along the way, Porter had grown sick of risking his life and getting nothing in return. He'd given twenty years to this godless place. He was damn sure going to walk away with something for his trouble.

"*One minute,*" the copilot announced.

Porter raised his index finger and the men pushed themselves to their feet and shuffled toward the rear of the helo, past the door gunners hunched expectantly behind the pair of M134 miniguns mounted behind the cockpit.

Ordinarily, Porter would have preferred to land short of the target and close the distance on foot, using the cover of darkness and perhaps an orbiting AC-130 gunship or a CIA drone to mask their approach. But this little excursion was in no way a sanctioned hit, and Porter didn't have any air assets to protect his men. If something went wrong, this was going to have to be a down and dirty fight.

"Target building coming up," the copilot advised over the radio. "Looks like we've got a welcoming party out front."

"I see 'em," the door gunner said, spooling up the minigun.

"Light them up," Porter told him. Knowing that the Taliban fighters gathered below wouldn't be expecting the ambush—and that even if they were, there wasn't a hell of a lot they could do about it now.

The pilot brought the helo in low and fast, and Porter braced himself against the strut watching the first tracers come coiling up from the ground like a multicolored snake. In retaliation, the door gunner mashed down on his trigger and the minigun roared to life, flame spitting from its six rotating barrels. The gunner hosed the rooftop, the two-hundred-round burst of 7.62x51mm bullets from the minigun cutting through the fighters like a flail, sending a cloud of torn flesh and bone drifting down to the street below.

The gunner relaxed the trigger. "All clear."

A second later, the pilot pulled back on the stick and the helo flared like a stallion, the downdraft from the rotors sending a wall of dust and debris tumbling over the collection of mud-brick buildings and terraced gardens built into the side of the mountain.

Porter leapt from the helicopter the moment the rear wheel touched the earth, the impact of his boots against the hard dirt sending a lightning bolt of pain through his knees. The sudden surge of pain might have sent another man to the ground, but Porter's adrenaline was pumping, and he made himself ignore it.

He hooked right and brought his rifle up to his shoulder, the exhaust from the turbine hot as a blowtorch on the back of his neck. He held his breath and started toward the target building just as a man stepped out of the alley with an AK-47.

The fighter lifted the rifle at Porter, but before he could fire, Porter was already on the trigger of his HK. He fired twice, the pair of Black Hills 77-gram hollow points punching through the other man's sternum at 2,700 feet per second.

The impact rocked the fighter back on his heels, the clatter of the rifle to the ground muted by the roar of the Mi-17 lifting skyward.

Porter held security on the alley and waited for his team to catch up, studying the target building out of the corner of his eyes. Compared to the rest of the village, the aluminum façade of the target looked like something from another planet.

But Porter had seen enough of the modular buildings being unloaded from the backs of C-17s to know they weren't from another world; they were from Texas. Each one custom-built for the Provincial Reconstruction Teams who thought they could buy the people's loyalty by providing infrastructure to the more rural areas.

This one had been set up as a medical clinic. And though it had been installed here to help Afghan citizens, civilians, and perhaps the odd member of the Afghan National Army, Porter knew the equipment inside was now being used to treat Taliban fighters instead. And while Porter couldn't have truly cared anymore, one way or the other, there was one particular patient inside who he very much wanted to see.

The rapid-fire chatter of another AK from one of the target's windows brought him quickly back to the present. But before he could lift his rifle onto the target, one of his men sent a 40-millimeter high-explosive grenade arcing through the window, the explosion killing the fighter and blowing the glass out of every window on the west side of the building.

"Ten minutes," Porter told the mercenaries over the radio, starting his stopwatch.

For most teams, it was an impossible time hack, but Porter had spent the last year drilling his men for just this moment, and the commandos worked through the lethal ballet with a confidence born of thousands of repetitions.

The point man moved to the window on the left side of the door and grabbed a frag grenade from his kit. He pulled the pin and released the spoon, hesitating a couple of seconds before tossing the grenade through the window.

There was a panicked shout from inside the building, followed by the resounding boom of the grenade, and the crash as a mercenary booted down the front door. Then the team was flowing through the breach, Porter pausing to activate the GoPro attached to his helmet before following them in.

With most of the wounded inside the clinic confined to beds, the assault was over almost before it had begun, and Porter's men made light work of the few combatants inside still able to lift a weapon. Leaving Porter with nothing to do but record the bedridden Taliban begging for their lives.

Porter had seen the atrocities the Taliban had committed on their comrades in Kandahar—seen the pinched faces and thousand-yard stares of the refugees fleeing north to Kabul. There would be no quarter.

While Porter filmed, his men walked calmly between the beds, dispatching the wounded fighters with double taps to the chest. For the few who managed to drag themselves to the back of the building and lock themselves into the surgical rooms, his men used frags.

"*Sir.*" A voice behind him. One of the mercenaries—one of the younger guys, Spinarski. "I think we found the target," he said, meeting Porter's gaze with worried eyes. "But it looks like someone got to him first."

2

orter followed Spinarski through the ruins of the clinic. Past the beds of lifeless bodies that lay in bloody rows down the length of the small building, to a row of private rooms at the rear. There, two more mercenaries waited, their HK416s pointed down at the floor, their expressions as troubled as Spinarski's.

All three men watched Porter as he looked past them through the doorway, as his eyes took in the scene that awaited him.

For most of the men on the Mi-17 tonight, this hit was supposed to be just one last kick at the Taliban before everyone went home, a last-second, garbage-time, moral victory for the good guys that would remind the enemy that American soldiers still weren't to be fucked with, no matter if the war was over or not. One last hit to celebrate on the plane ride back Stateside, end the war on a positive note. One last good battle story to tell your buddies at the bar.

Only Porter and a few of his men knew the real reason they'd come here tonight. To *this* medical clinic, in *this* part of Afghanistan. Only a few of Porter's men knew they'd come here for the man who lay dead in the bed in front of Porter.

The dead man's name was Akhtar Mansour, and he was Taliban, but not a fighter. No, Mansour was a bagman, a money guy. And though Dominic Porter desperately wanted him dead, he'd expected to have to be the one who pulled the trigger.

But someone had gotten to Mansour first. The bagman had been stabbed to death; he'd bled out where he lay, beside the dialysis machine that Porter knew was the reason he came here, three times a week, from whichever hole in the desert he called home.

"What the hell is going on here?" Porter asked his men. His mind struggling to compute the implications of what he was seeing. "Who found him?"

"I did, sir," Spinarski said. "He was long gone before I even opened the door."

"Get the rest of the team out of here. I don't want anyone seeing this. Not until we figure out what the hell we're dealing with."

He crossed to Mansour's body. The bagman wore a tunic and trousers, his head wrapped in a white turban. As Spinarski closed the door to the private room, Porter pulled on a pair of latex gloves and proceeded to pat down Mansour's

19

body. The man was rail-thin and bony beneath his clothes; Porter found a holster for a sidearm at his hip, but no pistol, and nothing else.

Porter removed the dead man's turban. Unfurled it and let it hang over the floor, but nothing fell out of the folds of cloth. *Maybe it's your lucky day,* he thought. *Maybe this bastard screwed some other haji's wife and tonight just happened to be the night he got what was coming to him.*

Porter searched the rest of the room. The tables with syringes and gloves and swabs, the cabinets full of clean towels, saline solution. He saw signs of a struggle, the tubes of the dialysis machine ripped out of Mansour's arm, dangling and forgotten, the bed lying askew and the bedclothes torn and disheveled.

A knock at the door. Spinarski. "Sir?"

"Not now," Porter called back.

Spinarski pushed the door open an inch. Peered in. "Sir, you're going to want to hear this."

Damn it.

Porter scanned the room one more time. Then he turned to the door and followed Spinarski back out into the carnage of the main room. The mercenary gestured with the barrel of his rifle to a figure on the floor, a few feet away. A man in his thirties, wearing medical scrubs. The floor around him pooled with fresh blood.

Maybe Taliban, maybe not. But either way, he was helping the bastards.

The man was alive, Porter saw. Barely. As Porter watched,

he groaned, opened his eyes, and reached, feebly, toward Porter.

"He says he's a doctor," Spinarski told Porter. "Says he knows what happened to Mansour."

The dying man nodded. Drew one hand, weakly, across his throat. "Killed," he whispered, in English.

Porter crouched down beside the man. "Yeah, no shit someone killed him," he said in Pashto. "I want to know who."

The dying man took a shallow, ragged breath. Winced from the pain. "A man," he said. "Older than . . . me. Army, I think. Afghan. Not white."

"What else?" Porter asked. "Why was he here? Who was he?"

The dying man tried to shrug. The effort clearly exhausting, and painful. "He took something." He coughed, wincing again. "I think . . . a computer drive. Small."

Porter felt a jolt of electricity through his body. This was bad. "Where did he go? Who the hell was he? What kind of computer drive?"

But the man on the floor had no more answers. He coughed again, weaker this time. Stared up at Porter, his eyes beseeching. "Please," he whispered. "Help."

Porter ignored him. "Search this village," he told Spinarski. "Round up every man you find. We're not leaving until we find out who did this."

Spinarski frowned. "Sir—"

"Find him," Porter told him. "And burn this fucking place to the ground."

While the team got to work, Porter slung his rifle over his shoulder and went outside for a cigarette. He stepped into the alley and shook a Marlboro Red from the pack, his mind replaying the words of the dying doctor inside.

This was very bad. God knows what Akhtar Mansour had carried with him to the clinic. What he'd brought that could implicate Porter and his men.

That's what you get for doing business with the fucking Taliban, jackass.

It had started as a way to get paid. A little end-of-war bonus for Porter and a few of his most trusted operatives. Hell, the Taliban were going to get their hands on most of the Afghan Army's equipment soon enough anyway; why not sell them a little bit of American overstock?

Porter had made sure that the weapons he sold wouldn't be traced back to him. That they wouldn't be used on American troops. Hell, he wasn't even sure half of the shit was operational. But the money he'd received in return sure spent like real American dollars.

Anyway, the war was over at this point. Within days, Porter knew he and his men would be headed home. All that remained was covering up the evidence, burying the haji bastards who knew what he'd done.

Hence the unsanctioned hits. Hence the visit to Akhtar Mansour's dialysis appointment. Hence the twenty-five or so dead Taliban in the clinic, a perfect cover for what was, in essence, an ass-covering mission.

Except some bastard had gotten to Mansour first. And there was no telling what he'd pulled from Mansour's body.

A flash of light from beside Porter snapped him back to full alert. Porter dropped the cigarette and spun, his rifle snapping to his shoulder. Through the optics, he saw a man with a phone in his left hand running toward the end of the alley, but before he could get a shot off, a pistol appeared in the man's right hand, the muzzle already spitting fire.

Porter fired blind, managing to get a shot off before the first of four bullets came snapping overhead. He threw himself to the ground, fully expecting the white-hot burn of a bullet finding flesh. But the man had rushed the shots, and the bullets sailed harmlessly overhead.

By the time Porter was back on his feet, the man had disappeared down the end of the alley, the only indication that he'd ever been there a cloud of pistol smoke lingering in the air.

"We've got a squirter," he informed the rest of the team through the radio. "South side of the building."

Then he was running, his boots slapping against the hard earth as he sprinted after the man. The man had been holding a phone; Porter was sure of it. The flash meant a photograph, and a photo meant evidence that Porter and his team had been here. And neither Porter nor the CIA needed that.

With his adrenaline back flowing full bore again, Porter made the end of the alley. He forced himself to slow at the corner, stepped wide, and panned around the edge of the building with his finger tensed on the trigger of his rifle, ready to take the shot the moment he saw his target. But the street beyond was empty, the only sign of life an Afghan commando at the far end.

"Anyone see him?" Porter asked over the radio.

"No," came the response.

Shit.

Porter hurried down the alley, his eyes searching the packed earth for any sign of the target. But just as he reached the Afghan commando midway down the street, he heard the distant beat of the helo, followed by the copilot's voice over the radio.

"We've got hostiles coming in from the south," the copilot advised.

"Hold them off," Porter replied. "I still need more time."

The pilot coughed. "Uh, sir," he said. "We can try it your way, but there's a lot of heavily armed people heading your way, and they look angry. I think we need to scram while the going is good."

Shit.

Only thing worse than that picture getting out into the world, Porter thought, *is the whole lot of us dying in this godforsaken place.*

Still, he hesitated, unsure of what to do. Then the commando pointed to Porter's helmet. "You have his face—yes?" the man asked.

Porter reached up, felt the GoPro camera still strapped to his helmet. Still recording. "Yeah," he said. "I have his face."

"Then we need to get out of here," the commando said. "While we still can."

The man took hold of Porter by the plate carrier. Pulled him forward, toward the sound of the helo's rotors, rapidly approaching. Porter resisted for an instant. Then he followed the commando.

Shit.

3

I t was a short sprint to the far end of the street, but Porter struggled to keep pace with the younger commando. He'd barely covered fifty meters, but by the time he reached the corner of the last building, Porter's lungs were on fire and his legs were beginning to cramp.

The younger man waited for him to catch up, then motioned for him to take the lead. But Porter shook his head, his non-firing hand digging into his pocket for the baggie of Tramadol. He'd come to rely on the opioids more and more during his time in-country, and lately, he'd been popping the pills like candy.

War was a young man's game.

"You go," Porter told the other man, swallowing two of the pills. The commando pretended not to notice the Tramadol, or didn't care. Wordless, he nodded and stepped out from behind the corner, leaving Porter to cover the intersection while the commando ran back toward the clinic and the waiting helicopter. A few seconds later, the man called back that he was set, and it was Porter's time to move.

Still out of breath, Porter peeled from the corner and forced himself into a painful jog. The commando had taken up position behind a low wall, and Porter hurried past the man, eyes searching for cover of his own.

He found what he was looking for in the rusted hulk of a car on the left side of the road, and he quickly ducked behind the trunk, his knees screaming. From his new position, Porter could see the Mi-17 on the ground, and the blink of his team's infrared strobes through the cloud of dust as they clambered aboard.

Just might make it, he thought.

Porter turned back to the street and brought his rifle to bear. "Set!" he called back to the other man.

At his signal, the commando left his position and was racing toward Porter and the rusted vehicle when the first Taliban gun truck hove into view behind him, the gunner behind the Russian PKM machine gun mounted to the rollbar swinging his weapon toward the running man.

With no time to shout a warning, Porter stepped from cover, flicking the selector on his rifle from safe to full auto. He feathered the trigger and sent a pair of controlled bursts toward his target, but his rounds pinged harmlessly off the turret shield welded to the top of the cab.

Porter hammered through the magazine, maintaining his rate of fire until the gunner swung the PKM in his direction.

The machine gun roared to life in a blaze of yellow, and time seemed to slow as the 7.62x54mm bullets came snapping down the road. Porter tried to escape the line of fire, but his legs suddenly seemed impossibly heavy.

The bullets snaked across the road, sparking off the gravel, showering Porter with shards of rock and dirt. He cursed and threw himself to the ground, rolling out of the line of fire and pulling a fragmentation grenade from his kit.

"Covering fire!" he shouted.

While the commando engaged the truck, Porter ripped the pin free and released the spoon that triggered the frag's five-second fuse. Most people couldn't wait to be rid of a live grenade, but instead of throwing it, Porter let it cook off—waiting a long three seconds before lobbing the frag toward the truck. His aim was true, and the grenade hit the hood, bouncing up the windshield and into the cab, where it exploded in a wash of flame and frag.

The concussion caught the gunner full in the chest and sent him tumbling from the back of the truck, but even as he fell, he squeezed one last burst from the PKM toward the commando, and Porter was helpless to do anything but watch as the gunner's final rounds sent his man spinning to the ground.

Porter broke cover and rushed to the man's side, pausing to rip a smoke grenade from his kit and toss it down the road. "I have a man down!" he shouted into the radio. "Pilot, I need you to slow down these gun trucks and then pick us up at the alternate LZ."

"Affirmative," the copilot replied.

While gray smoke billowed from the cannister, Porter went

to work on the commando, ignoring the snap and hiss of the bullets past his head. He ripped open the trauma kit attached to the front of his body armor and pulled out a tourniquet. With the ease of hundreds of repetitions, he looped it around the man's shredded thigh and tightened the windlass.

The commando screamed in pain and tried to squirm away, but Porter used his knee to hold the man down, and continued to tighten the tourniquet until the bleeding finally stopped. Then he turned his attention to the ragged bullet hole that puckered the man's left arm.

"We can't stay here," he said, packing the wound full of gauze. "And I'm not carrying your fat ass, so you'd better figure out a way to walk."

The man nodded weakly, his face ashen from the loss of blood, but when Porter hauled him to his feet, there wasn't so much as a whimper of pain.

Good man.

While the helo worked over the convoy with its miniguns, Porter and the wounded soldier began the painful shuffle to the alternate landing zone on the south side of the village. By Porter's estimation it was only a hundred meters, but halfway there, the man went limp against Porter, a sudden dead weight in his arms.

Unconscious. Blood loss.

Cursing, Porter began to drag the man toward the LZ. He hadn't made much progress when the Mi-17 flashed overhead and settled into a low hover, twenty meters away. The copilot came up on the radio, his voice shaky but determined.

"You've got two minutes, then we're leaving."

Even though he'd left one of his own on board to make sure the copilot did as he was told, Porter knew the man wasn't bluffing, knew he wouldn't think twice about abandoning them here to save his own skin. Porter dug deep, summoning the last of his strength to drag the unconscious commando the last twenty meters.

The pain was all-consuming, and his muscles screamed for him to stop, but Porter shoved it away and kept moving, never feeling the spray of warm blood from the man's loosened tourniquet.

It was a battle of inches, and with each shaky step that he took, Porter could feel himself fading. *Just keep moving,* he told himself. Then he was at the ramp, feeling strong hands close around his shoulders, pulling him into the rear of the helo.

Once inside, he collapsed on the floor, completely exhausted, unable to do anything but lie there and watch the team's medic begin working on the wounded man. He felt the motion of the helicopter beneath him as the pilot coaxed the Russian bird skyward.

If Porter had learned anything during his time in Afghanistan, it was that helicopters were at their most vulnerable during takeoff and landing, which is why they usually traveled in pairs. But without a gunship to protect their exfil, the Mi-17 was a sitting duck, and as it wobbled skyward and the pilot shoved the nose forward, the transition from vertical to level flight seemed to take hours.

It was a helpless feeling, but finally, the pilot got the nose down and the throttle open, and with a final *fuck you* from the miniguns, the Mi-17 was racing across the valley. Porter let out the breath he hadn't realized he'd been holding and looked up, any momentary relief vanishing at the sight of the medic beating on the wounded man's chest.

"Stay . . . with . . . me!" the medic shouted in Pashto.

But all it took was one look at the man's sallow face and the growing puddle of blood pooling on the floor of the cargo hold, and Porter knew the man was gone.

Dead, he thought. *Forfeited, and all because of some nosy Afghan motherfucker with a camera.*

The anger cut through his exhaustion like a shot of epinephrine. Porter unclipped his GoPro, ejected the micro-SD card from the base of the camera, and retrieved the micro Quik Key reader from the pocket of his assault pack. He pressed the card into the slot on the back and plugged the reader into the data port of his CIA-issued phone. Brought up the video and hit the fast-forward button, scanning quickly through scenes of slaughter from inside the medical clinic.

There was a grim satisfaction to how effortlessly efficient the operation appeared on his screen, blazing forward in twice normal speed, but that satisfaction was narrow and short-lived. There was a man dead. And another man out there with a picture of Porter, and some sort of computer drive to boot. Akhtar Mansour was a diligent record-keeper, Porter knew. The contents of that drive could very well contain enough evidence to destroy his whole team.

Right now, all that mattered to Porter was finding the face of the man who'd killed the bagman. He watched the screen until the video showed him stepping outside of the clinic again, then hit the pause button and advanced slowly through the rest of the footage, studying each frame until the face of the man with the phone appeared in the center of the screen.

The picture was blurry, the man's face partly obscured by shadow, but there was enough there, Porter knew, that a technical operative with an image enhancer and access to the right databases could make a positive identification.

Got your ass, Porter thought, staring down at the screen. *Now it's just a matter of time.*

4

Abdul Nassim knew he wasn't safe. Knew he might never be safe again. The Americans were gone, but what did that matter? They'd seen his face. They'd seen him take their picture.

And they must have known by now that he'd gotten to Akhtar Mansour first.

Nassim had not expected the Americans, whoever they were, to come by helicopter. He'd not even been certain when they would come. He had been following Mansour for nearly a week, hoping that whoever was doing business with the Taliban deputy would show themselves eventually. Hoping that Mansour's partners hadn't packed up already and gone home.

Nassim hadn't expected the helicopter, and he hadn't expected the attack. He hadn't planned to kill Mansour, either, but when the gunfire had started outside the clinic, the older man had sensed his opportunity and leapt at Nassim's Beretta, knocking it away and lunging for Nassim's throat. It had been all Nassim could do to fend the older man off. All he could do to scramble one-handed for a weapon while Mansour fumbled beneath his tunic for his own pistol.

His fingers had closed on a pair of scissors resting on a side table. He'd gripped them tight and swung at Mansour just as the Taliban deputy withdrew the gun, and he'd swung and swung again, until the pistol lay abandoned on the floor, and Mansour motionless in his bed.

By the time Mansour went still, the helicopter outside had landed, and Nassim could hear small-arms fire erupting all around the clinic. He'd searched Mansour's body. Found only a wallet, and inside, a slim thumb drive. He'd taken the drive and then made his escape, bumping into a Taliban doctor at the door as he fled Mansour's room.

Nassim had no idea what might be on the thumb drive. He'd hoped it would be enough to implicate Mansour and whoever had come to find him at the clinic. To finally unmask the American traitors who'd sided with the Taliban, selling surplus weaponry that the enemy had used to murder ANA troops.

He'd decided he needed more proof. Knew he couldn't count on the thumb drive alone, knew the Americans would need as much evidence as possible before they would believe him over one of their own. Knew he needed the face of the American traitor, his name. And that's why he'd lingered outside of the clinic instead of just taking the thumb drive and disappearing into the night, like any smart man would have done.

Instead, he'd snuck back to the hospital, as close as he dared. Caught the American operative unaware, surprised him with the flash. It wasn't even a good picture, Nassim realized later. It showed nothing of the massacre. Nothing of the clinic, or what remained of it. It showed the man's face, yes, but grainy. And without context, what did it matter? Who would care?

The American cared. The American cared, and that's why it mattered. Because the American had seen him, too. And Abdul Nassim knew he'd just painted a target on his own back. A target on the backs of his family.

Nassim had known from the start it was a fool's errand to chase Akhtar Mansour. Very few people in Afghanistan had time to care anymore about the activities of a low-level Taliban bagman, even if he was rumored to be meeting with American operatives. Even if more and more of the Taliban fighters waging war against the Afghan Army seemed to be armed with American gear—and not just the old, abandoned stuff the United States was leaving behind. Nassim had heard stories of Taliban with Javelin missile launchers, and he was pretty sure the Marines weren't just leaving those lying around unguarded.

Nassim had heard enough rumors that he'd decided he needed to know the truth. And though the war was over and he should have been preparing his family—Freshta, his wife, and his daughter, Zarah; Payam and Bilal, his sons—to escape from Afghanistan, Nassim had pushed forward with his search. Especially when he'd learned that Akhtar Mansour had met with an American a few months back, in Kabul—or so said the rumors, anyway.

None of Nassim's former colleagues in the ANA cared enough to investigate. Everyone was too busy trying to get out of the country. And truthfully, Nassim had promised Freshta that tomorrow he would bring the family to Kabul, where the Americans still held control of the airport, where possibly he could negotiate their way out. The hour was getting late in Afghanistan. And Freshta knew that the Taliban would take a dim view of her husband, an ex-ANA captain who'd worked so closely with the Americans.

They would go, tomorrow, and pray that the Americans welcomed them. That they would show gratitude for Nassim's assistance in the war, and help him and his family make lives somewhere new.

They would go tomorrow. But first, Nassim had learned that Akhtar Mansour's kidneys were failing. And he'd learned where Mansour came, three times every week, for treatment.

Nassim had gone alone. Driven the long hour to the medical clinic, with instructions to Freshta to leave with the neighbors tomorrow if he didn't return. It was a risk driving anywhere these days; just being out on the road was enough to wind up in the Taliban's crosshairs.

As it turned out, Nassim had stayed clear of the Taliban. He'd talked his way into the clinic by claiming he needed asthma medication for his youngest son, had prevailed on a sympathetic and distracted doctor to let him inside. A truckload of injured Taliban fighters had just arrived, and the clinic was a chaos of pain and urgency. Nassim had found Akhtar Mansour's private room without anyone taking notice.

And then the Americans had come. Just as Nassim had locked the door and begun to introduce himself to Mansour. Just as the older man's eyes had gone wide, and he'd reached for the pistol beneath his tunic.

Nassim had stilled him with his own Beretta M9, aimed square at Mansour, center mass. "Shh," he told the Taliban deputy. "I'm only here to talk."

Mansour had visibly relaxed. Smirked at Nassim. "I'm afraid you've chosen an inopportune time for a conversation."

Nassim held the M9 steady. "Just a few simple questions. And then I'll leave you in peace."

"You don't know what you are barging into," Mansour replied. "This will not end well for you, I promise."

"You are buying weapons from an American traitor," Nassim told him. "What is his name?"

Before Mansour could reply, both men heard the *thump* of the helicopter's rotors in the distance. And the Taliban bagman's smile had widened. "You can ask him yourself," he told Nassim. "He'll be here shortly."

Nassim had frozen. Listened to the helicopter approach and realized he was suddenly in a seriously bad situation. Could tell from the look on Mansour's face that the other man knew it, too.

"Tell me his name," Nassim repeated, more urgently. But Mansour only grinned.

And then, somewhere outside, the helicopter's minigun roared to life. And Nassim had just enough time to register the surprise on Mansour's face before the Taliban bagman was leaping for the Beretta.

He'd snuck out of the clinic with Akhtar Mansour's thumb drive. Waited as the Americans massacred everyone inside, torn between wanting to run and wanting to see just who it was who'd been double-crossing his countrymen. He'd waited until the gunfire died down, and then he'd caught sight of the American stepping out into the alley, and raised his phone and took the man's picture. He'd realized his misjudgment the instant the camera flashed, lighting up the back alley and the American's face. He'd run without thinking, picturing the rifle behind him, its owner drawing a bead on his back. He'd expected to die in the dirt in that alley. Had pulled his own gun, his old Beretta M9, fired wild just to buy himself some time.

That he'd made it out of the alley seemed like victory. He'd known he wouldn't survive the night. Not in this village, crawling with highly trained hostiles. The American would force his men to search every building. Sooner or later, Nassim knew they would find him.

He'd hid in the shadows. Willing himself to stay silent. Trying not to even breathe. Listening to the shouts of the Americans nearby, searching for them. Hearing the sound of the helicopter overhead, and then hearing something else, too—trucks.

He'd been saved by the Taliban. Ironic that he'd fought so long beside the American Army, killed the Taliban with them, and now he was thanking God that the enemy had chosen this moment to mount an ambush. Nothing seemed right-side up in Afghanistan anymore. Especially not after tonight.

Nassim waited in the shadows as the Taliban drove the Americans away. Waited until the sound of the helicopter rotors disappeared somewhere across the valley. Until even the trucks had sped off again into the night. Then, cautiously, he crept out of the narrow alcove, the dust of the firefight still settling on the road. Fresh bullet holes on the concrete beside him, blood in the dirt.

He went back to the clinic. Or what remained of it, anyway. The building nearly destroyed by gunfire and frag grenades, walls charred by smoke that still billowed out from within. Here and there, the villagers stood, dazed, in groups or alone, looking in at the wreckage.

There *had* been Taliban in the clinic, Nassim knew. But he knew the American operative had come for Mansour. Mansour had known it, too. He just hadn't expected the operative to come in with his guns blazing.

It wasn't safe to stay here. Nassim knew the American would be back. But as he stood at the smoldering ruins of the clinic, gazing in through the windows at the dim flickering flames inside, Nassim replayed the events of the night in his mind, and realized something that made the panic rise in his throat like bile.

The American had a camera, too.

Nassim opened his phone. Brought up the picture. Stared, and knew he was already dead.

The American wore a GoPro on his helmet. The American had been filming.

The American had a photo of *his* face, too. And Nassim had worked with the Americans long enough to know that once the right people had your face, they could find everything about you.

Your name.

Your address.

Your family.

The places you would go to hide.

Quickly, Nassim turned away from the clinic. His mind swimming, his whole body numb. He forced himself to walk through the village to his vehicle, a Toyota Prado SUV. Fumbled with the keys as he turned the ignition. Seeing his wife's face in his mind. His daughter. His boys.

The Americans would find him. This much was certain. They would be waiting for him in Kabul, at the airport; it's the first place they would expect him to go. And there was no hope in going to the Taliban for help; he'd spent his career killing them, as many as he could.

There was no one, Nassim knew, he could trust.

No one he could turn to—except, perhaps, one man.

Driving one-handed, Nassim pulled out his phone. Scrolled through his contact list until he found the number he wanted, the name of the one person in the world who Nassim believed could help.

5

MUMBAI, INDIA

I t was 8:20 in the evening, and Adam Hayes stood in the lobby of the InterContinental Mumbai, his tie as tight and unfamiliar as a noose around his neck. Outside the hotel, lightning flashed across the horizon, the sudden strobe illuminating the squall building over the Arabian Sea. It wasn't the storm that concerned Hayes, though, but the doughy night manager standing behind the hotel's front desk.

It was Hayes's third day in Mumbai, and with the summer monsoons raging, his view of the city had been limited to what he could see from the hotel's windows. The forecast called for clearer skies tomorrow, but all the same, Hayes knew that the only chance he had of escaping the hotel and experiencing some of the local culture was if he figured out what in the hell was up with the hotel's security system first.

Prior to coming to Mumbai, Hayes had sworn he'd never become a contractor—never use the skills he'd honed in service of his country to fatten his wallet. But that had changed three months ago, when his wife, Annabelle, had surprised him in their bedroom, tears streaming down her face and a pregnancy test in her hand.

"We're going to have another baby," she'd said.

Her words had struck him dumb, and he'd stood there barely trusting himself to speak. "A-another baby? Are you sure?"

Annabelle had grinned. Showed him the test stick, the telltale double lines. "I took two," she told him. "They were both positive."

A sudden rush of pure joy had hit Hayes like a slap to the face. Unable to speak, he'd taken Annabelle by the waist and lifted her into the air, both of them crying as he spun her around the room, neither of them able to do much more than laugh through the tears, through the kisses.

It was only later, when the emotion had worn off, that Hayes had realized the obvious: *I'm going to need a job.*

With his experience and contacts, he had access to the world's top private military companies, and if he'd wanted, he could have named his price at any of them. But he'd promised Annabelle that he'd stay out of trouble, for the sake of their family, and that meant finding a job that *didn't* involve killing people.

So far, he'd been true to his word, but standing there in the lobby as the clock on the wall ticked down toward the bottom of the hour, Hayes wondered if his vow was about to be put to the test.

Like all of the premier hotels on Mumbai's Marine Drive, the InterContinental had been designed to focus first on the comfort of its guests, not their security. But that focus had been forced to change on the night of November 26, 2008, when ten members of the Lashkar-e-Taiba terrorist group beached their inflatable speedboats on Mumbai's southern peninsula and slipped ashore, armed with Chinese-made AK-56 assault rifles, 9-millimeter pistols, and grenades.

Once on the ground, the attackers had formed up into four kill teams and set off to hit their predetermined targets. At 9:30 on the night of the twenty-sixth, the first team entered the historic Chhatrapati Shivaji train station and opened fire on the passenger platform. The second team hit the trendy Leopold Café roughly twenty minutes later, and while they opened fire on the westerners sitting on the restaurant's outside patio, the largest team stormed the Taj Mahal Palace hotel, a symbol of India's wealth.

The siege that followed lasted three days, and when the Indian Special Forces finally regained control, one hundred and seventy-five people were dead. The attacks served as a wake-up call to both the city of Mumbai and the nation as a whole, and following those four deadly days in November, security became the hospitality industry's watchword.

But while the corporations that ran the hotels had the financial means to make the necessary changes to their operations, when it came to the execution, they were severely lacking. Enter Simon Monroe, former MI6 station chief and current CEO of Ramparts Overwatch.

For a meat eater like Hayes, who'd been trained to hunt down and kill his nation's enemies without leaving a hint of his presence, accepting a job with the Hong Kong–based security firm was a massive step in the wrong direction. It was mind-numbingly boring work, better suited for a mall security guard than a former Treadstone operative. But it was honest work, and the paycheck was twice as large as anything he'd made during his time in the military. And even though the job meant plenty of time away from home, Hayes knew that Annabelle slept better at night knowing her husband was, more or less, safe.

You gonna pay attention, or what? the voice asked.

The voice wasn't real. It was a synthetic echo from the government-issued mind job the doctors at Operation Treadstone had used to turn him into a genetically modified assassin. But real or not, it had a point, and Hayes forced himself to focus on the man behind the counter.

The problems at the InterContinental had begun the previous year, when a glitch in the hotel's firewall allowed unknown parties to access the hotel's registry and steal the credit cards stored in guests' files. Enraged, Simon Monroe had sent his best techs to Mumbai to investigate, and while they were unable to find the offending source code, they assured the owners that they had fixed the glitch. But the breach that followed proved them wrong, and the two after that set Ramparts Overwatch on the verge of losing one of its largest clients.

Despite assigning his best minds to the task, Simon

Monroe was nowhere near a solution—until Adam Hayes joined his team. It hadn't taken Hayes very long to suspect that the security experts crammed into Ramparts Overwatch's Hong Kong conference room were barking up the wrong tree.

"We've closed all of the network ports, updated the firewall and the encryption keys for the system," the team lead had complained. "And we still can't seem to figure out how they're getting in."

"That's because you're looking in the wrong place," Hayes had replied, looking up from the documents spread across the table in front of him. "They have a rat."

"How do you figure?" Monroe had asked.

"Look at the time stamps from the breaches," Hayes had said. "They're all at night, somewhere between eight thirty and nine. Someone on the night shift is compromising the firewall."

Two days later, he had been on a flight to Mumbai, the personnel record of every employee at the hotel stacked on the tray table in front of him.

Follow the money.

Hayes wasn't a numbers guy. All that the bank statements and credit reports in the files did was give him a headache. But his time in the field had taught him how to read people, and there was something about the night manager that pinged his radar.

At exactly 8:30, the night manager walked away from the front desk. Hayes gave him a slow five count, then started after him, slipping silently across the lobby and following him through a security door.

He let the door hiss closed behind him and waited for his eyes to adjust to the gloom. Ahead of him, down a short hallway, the night manager was swiping his keycard across the reader outside of the security offices, and the moment he stepped inside, Hayes was moving, hurrying down the hall as silent as a wraith to grab the door before it closed. Slipping inside, he found the night manager sitting at the terminal, fingers flying over the keyboard—and the look on the man's face told Hayes everything he needed to know.

"What are you doing here?" the man demanded, making to cover his computer screen.

"Playing a hunch," Hayes replied. "And it looks like I'm right."

The manager moved to stand, but before he had a chance, Hayes had him by the collar, his muscles tensing as he lifted the man out of the chair and shoved him face-first into the wall.

"You've got one chance to tell me everything," he said, twisting the man's arm into a hammerlock. "If I even *think* you're lying, I'm going to break your arm. Got it?"

"O-okay, okay," the man stuttered. "I'll tell you. No lies."

"Good. Now, talk."

Ten minutes later, Hayes stepped out of the security office, leaving the night manager zip-tied to the office chair, Ramparts Overwatch's Hong Kong headquarters notified, and Mumbai Police on their way. Hayes didn't bother to wait for the authorities; he returned to the lobby and crossed to the bank of elevators, the jet lag and pressure of the previous days finally catching up with him.

He stepped into the car and punched the button for the fourth floor, the doors hissing closed as he went to work on the tie that still constricted his throat.

Thank God that's over.

By the time the elevator settled on his floor, the tie was in his front pocket, and with his collar unbuttoned, Hayes felt like he could finally breathe again. He stepped out of the car and started down the hall, his mind on the cold beer waiting for him in the mini-fridge and the detailed report he would have to send to Hong Kong before turning in. He slipped his keycard into the reader and stepped inside, the posh voice of the BBC anchor greeting him from the television in the corner of the room.

Pushing the door closed behind him, Hayes threw the security latch and dug the tie from his front pocket, tossing it on the bed before snagging a bottle of Kingfisher from the mini-fridge. He twisted the cap free, dropped into the leather recliner by the window, and took a long pull from the bottle.

After spending the last eight hours on his feet, the relief was immediate, and Hayes cursed himself for not grabbing his laptop off of the bedside table before sitting down.

Get your ass up and go get it, the voice in his head chided.

"Nah," Hayes told it. "I think I'm just going to sit here for a second."

Pussy.

Like all of the modifications the Treadstone doctors had

done to his mind and body, Hayes's synthetic consciousness was designed to keep him alive and fighting when most men would have given up and died, and Hayes appreciated that very much.

What he *didn't* appreciate was that it didn't come with an off switch.

Hayes turned his attention to the TV in time to catch the tail end of the breaking news ticker crawling across the bottom of the screen: *Medical clinic burns in Eastern Afghanistan, dozens dead: report.*

He frowned, waiting for the rest of the story, but the picture was already shifting from the BBC newsroom to a weary reporter standing on a Kabul street corner. The man began talking about the "speed bumps" in the American withdrawal plan, but Hayes found his eyes drawn to the line of refugees in the background.

He studied them, the expressions of bleak desperation on their faces betraying the seriousness of the situation on the ground.

What the hell did we think was going to happen? he thought, draining the rest of his beer and setting the empty on the table.

He tried to watch the newsfeed, but suddenly his eyelids were impossibly heavy. He fought it, knowing that he still had work to do, but soon realized it was a losing battle and turned off the lamp before letting his eyes drift closed.

The pull of sleep was seductive, and he lay there, savoring the chair beneath him, the soothing monotone of the news anchor's voice. Thirty seconds later, he was asleep, his mind a whirlwind of hotels and firefights in the desert.

Hayes wasn't sure how long he'd been out when the rattle of plastic on wood brought him back to the land of the living.

What the hell is that noise?

He opened his eyes, the strobing white light from his phone hitting his dilated pupils like an icepick, the phone vibrating across the table as it rang. A glance at the clock on the dresser told Hayes it was almost midnight, and he wondered who was calling him this late.

Annoyed, he rescued the phone from the edge of the table. Swiped across the screen to answer. Before he could speak, a man's voice came blasting from the speaker.

"Adam—" the man spoke in Pashto, fear evident in his tone. *"My family and I are in serious trouble. You have to get us out of here!"*

6

The voice hit Hayes like a double shot of adrenaline, and he leapt to his feet, his sleep-fogged mind struggling to keep up with the rapid-fire Pashto blasting from the speaker.

"He's seen my face; he will kill me and my family if you don't get us out of here."

Finally, Hayes's mind caught up enough that he recognized the voice. Abdul Nassim.

"Nassim, you have to slow down," Hayes told him. "Just breathe for a second, and then tell me what happened."

But the Afghan was too keyed up to listen, and instead of answering, he continued to repeat the same lines, begging Hayes to help him until he'd run out of breath. Hayes paced the room, listening to Nassim's muffled sobs, trying to quell his own mounting sense of unease. As a Treadstone operative, he'd been trained to keep his emotions in check—to maintain a clear mind and a cool head no matter how tense the situation. But the fear he could hear in his old friend's voice was impossible to ignore.

"Just breathe, Nassim," he said, keeping his voice calm. "In through your nose and out through your mouth."

On the other end of the phone, Hayes could hear Nassim gasping for breath. "O-okay," he said, finally.

"You good?"

"Yes . . . I—I think so," Nassim replied.

"Good. Now tell me who's trying to kill you."

Hayes waited while his friend gathered himself. Wondered what could possibly have gone wrong to have set the other man into such a state. He'd never known Abdul Nassim to panic, not even in the face of near-insurmountable danger.

Something was different here.

"I have been investigating a rumor," Nassim told him. "Some of my former colleagues in the National Army suspect that the Taliban must be buying weapons from the Americans. Good quality equipment they are using to kill our people."

He paused. "I learned that a man named Akhtar Mansour has been meeting with the Americans. I went to find him at a medical clinic in Maidan Wardak, a Taliban clinic. But it wasn't the Taliban I needed to worry about, Adam."

"Then who?" Hayes asked. "What happened?"

"The American traitors arrived in a helicopter as I was attempting to interrogate Mansour. They attacked the clinic."

"Wait. Why would these Americans attack the guy they're supposedly doing business with?"

"I do not know for sure. But I know that Mansour was not expecting an attack."

"Okay," Hayes said. "And you wound up in the middle of it."

"I escaped, barely. I managed to take a thumb drive from Mansour before I left him. I am hoping it will show proof of what I confirmed with Mansour tonight. That this American and his friends are betraying their supposed allies in my country. But Adam—they saw my face. They *know* that I know."

Hayes felt suddenly unsteady on his feet. Unmoored. He backed his way to the leather chair in the corner and dropped into it, his mind a jumble of a thousand different thoughts.

"Why would you put yourself in danger like this, Nassim?" he asked, finally. "The war is over. Even without all of this, it's not safe for you there."

There was a long pause, and when Nassim finally spoke, there was a new wariness to his voice. "It's not so easy to ask a man to give up on his country. Especially when he can see injustice that wants to be fixed."

Damn it.

Since leaving Treadstone, Hayes had realized that if he wanted any semblance of a normal life, he would have to learn to control the beast they'd implanted in his brain. Master the rage that had once fueled him, lest it break free and devour him and everything he loved. Usually, Hayes was up for the task, but Nassim's words had cut him to the core, and like an errant shovel stabbed into a forgotten minefield, the results were explosive.

"Spare me the hero shit, Nassim!" Hayes said, shouting

now, his voice echoing loud off of the walls of his room. "Your *life* is more important—Freshta's life. Zarah, Payam, Bilal. My God—those Taliban will kill you if they find out who you are. You need to take your family and go somewhere else, now."

"That's easy for *you* to say, Adam." Nassim's voice was strangely calm in the face of Hayes's anger. "For you, leaving Afghanistan was as simple as getting on a plane when your deployment was over. For me, good or bad . . . Afghanistan is my home."

The rebuke was well aimed, and it sliced through the rage that had been ballooning in Hayes's chest like a knife. Deflated, he sunk back in the chair, rubbing his hand over his face.

"Shit—I'm sorry, Nassim," he finally managed. "Tell me about the man who attacked you. Tell me how I can help."

"He was an American. Special Forces. He brought a team, in a helicopter, and they murdered everyone in the medical clinic. Taliban and civilians. But I believe they were coming to kill Akhtar Mansour, specifically."

Hayes frowned. "Because Mansour was buying weapons from them."

"You said it yourself, Adam, the war is over. These Americans are going home. Perhaps they are simply cleaning up behind themselves. Eliminating any evidence of their betrayals. I can't say for certain. But it was an American who came to meet Mansour—and I have the picture to prove it."

"You got a picture of the guy?"

"Yes. Hold on, and I'll send it."

At the chime of the text alert, Hayes took the phone from

his ear and switched the call to speaker before opening the text. "I got it," he said, selecting the file and trying to make sense of the blurred image on the screen. The quality of the photo was so distorted that all he could make out was a fuzzy silhouette standing in an alleyway, the face, body, and clothing too degraded to tell if he was looking at a woman or a man.

It was a mess, and Hayes was initially doubtful that the image would provide anything of value, but as he stared at it, the picture became clearer. The distinctive desert tiger-stripe BDUs and the weathered rifle that hung around the man's muscled neck chiseled away at Hayes's earlier skepticism. Replaced it with a coiling knot of dread.

The man was American, all right. And from what Hayes could tell, he looked like bad news.

"I don't know what's on this thumb drive," Nassim told Hayes. "I don't have a computer to access the files. But I'm hoping they will prove that what I'm saying is true."

There's no time, the voice said. *If Nassim is even halfway near the truth, this dude will come looking for him, and he won't stop until Nassim is dead.*

You can worry about the evidence later. Just save Nassim's life.

"Nassim," Hayes said. "I need you to forget about that thumb drive for now and just concentrate on staying alive. I want you to listen to me and do *exactly* what I tell you."

"Okay . . . okay."

"As soon as we end the call, I need you to destroy your phone. Take out the SIM card and destroy it, then remove the battery and beat the phone to pieces with a hammer or something."

"Okay. Then what?"

"Get your family and take them someplace safe. Buy a new phone before you get there, and make sure you pay cash. Got it?"

"Yes."

"Good. Now, while you're doing that, I'm going to call in some favors. Figure out how to get you guys out of there."

"What if he finds us?"

"That's not going to happen," Hayes said. "I give you my word."

"I'm trusting you, Adam," Nassim said. Then he hung up.

Hayes dropped the phone on the bed, a wave of exhaustion crashing over him. His nap in the chair had done little to recharge his battery, and he felt a sudden urge to crawl into bed and go back to sleep.

But the voice wasn't having it.

You can sleep when you're dead, it barked, loud as a drill instructor. *But right now, we've got a mission to plan.*

Hayes rubbed a calloused hand across his face, his tired eyes drifting to the window, the ambient light of the city a dim glow through the half-opened curtains. He got to his feet and walked over to find Mumbai still shrouded in darkness, the rain still falling heavily on the streets below.

It had been ten years since Hayes's last deployment to Afghanistan, but despite the passage of time, the mere thought of going back unlocked fears he'd thought long repressed. He tried to cut it off, tamp down the dread twisting deep in his guts, but before he had a chance, it was racing up his spine like a flame up a fuse.

The panic attack came out of nowhere, the spurt of adrenaline that accompanied it sending his heart double-timing in his chest. Hayes closed his eyes and tried to control his breathing, but the sudden tilt of the room on its axis told him it was too late. The vertigo sent his stomach rushing into his throat, and he spun away from the wall and stumbled toward the bathroom, the sudden revolt of his body more terrifying than anything he'd seen in war.

Hayes choked back on the sour mix of bile and beer that scalded the back of his throat, then staggered into the bathroom, his socked feet struggling to find purchase on the slick tile floor. He grabbed the towel rod and tried to steady himself, but his weight was too much for the drywall screws securing it to the wall, and it ripped free in his hand. Then he was falling, the back of his head banging hard on the edge of the sink when he went down.

The impact starred his vision and he lay on the ground, the tile cool against his fevered skin. There was a part of him that wanted to stay down, to curl up into a tight ball and wait for the storm raging inside of him to blow itself out. But lying there on the floor, all Hayes could think about were Nassim's parting words, echoing in his mind like a tape on an endless loop.

I'm trusting you, Adam.

7

I t was still dark when the Mi-17 settled on the helo pad at the CIA's compound outside of Kabul, and Porter climbed down from the cargo hold, his plate carrier stained with the blood of his dead commando. While his men loaded the body bag into the bed of the mortuary affairs pickup, Porter instructed O'Malley to make sure the team was ready to roll out on a moment's notice, and then started across the flight line to the row of modular buildings that served as his home.

Known as Eagle Base, the two-mile compound lorded over the plain like a grayscale sentinel, its satellite arrays and signal intercept towers a reminder to all nearby that the CIA was always watching. For Porter, Eagle Base had always been the Agency's city on a hill, the beacon of American exceptionalism that would guide Afghanistan into the twenty-first century.

But walking through the center of the camp, the usually brilliant white of the stadium lights muted a dull gray by the smoke of the classified documents being stuffed into the compound's incinerator, Porter knew that whatever hopes anyone back home *might* have had for the country were dead.

Shaking off the melancholy that came with that grim realization, Porter continued to his trailer, his mind circling back to the Afghan who'd taken his picture in Wardak. Prior to landing, he'd emailed the image he'd taken from the GoPro to one of the targeting officers in the tactical operations center, or TOC. The man owed him a favor, and Porter considered walking over to check on his progress, but decided against it. The visit would invite the inevitable questions about why he'd gone to Wardak Province in the first place, and Porter wasn't in any mood to answer them. He continued to his trailer.

Like all of the special operators in the war, Porter lived on reverse cycle, sleeping during the day so that he and his men could hunt at night. But with the adrenaline from the raid still pumping through his veins, Porter was too amped to sleep. He cleaned his guns and topped off his ammo instead, and when he was done, he headed to the adjoining bathroom to take a shower.

He stripped out of his clothes and waited until the water was scalding hot before he stepped into the stream. He washed his hair and then went to work on his skin, scrubbing himself clean of blood and dirt and gun oil. By the time he was finished, the water was cold and his skin raw, but despite using nearly half a bar of soap, Porter still didn't feel clean.

He doubted he ever would.

Toweling off, he headed back into his room, pausing to pop an Ambien and slide the Glock 19 under his pillow before cutting the lights. Porter lay on his back and stared up at the darkened ceiling, the ancient window air-conditioning unit wheezing like an asthmatic as it struggled to ward off the Afghan heat.

He needed to find the man with the phone. Needed to retrieve Akhtar Mansour's thumb drive to ensure that no word of what he'd done made its way back to Langley. His mind fought the Ambien, computing worst-case scenarios and contingencies until the drug finally won, dragging him into a black, uneasy sleep.

And then he was awake again, jolted upright by the sound of someone hammering on his door. Porter had the Glock in his hand before he realized he wasn't dreaming, the sweat-soaked sheets bunched around him. He kicked free of the covers and swung his feet to the floor, his mind struggling to pierce the fog of the Ambien hangover.

"I'm up," he muttered.

But the banging continued, and Porter's head swiveled first to the door and then to the clock on the far side of the room, but the sunlight streaming in through the chink in the olive drab blanket he'd tacked over the windows blocked his view.

Boom, boom, boom.

"I'm *up*," Porter called. "Just cool it a sec, would you?"

Stepping into his BDUs and shoving a pistol into his waistband, Porter grabbed a pair of dusty Oakley sunglasses from the bedside table and pushed himself to his feet. He slipped the sunglasses over his bloodshot eyes and shuffled across the room.

"All right, goddammit. I'm coming."

He unlocked the door and wrenched it open, the blazing mix of heat and sun hitting like a flash-bang to the face. Porter blinked the stars away, recognized the man standing there as the targeting officer from the TOC who he'd asked to track down the mystery photographer in Wardak.

"Sorry to bother you, bro," the man said, his eyes red-rimmed from staring at a computer monitor all night. "But there's a problem with your guy."

"What *kind* of problem?" Porter asked, stepping aside so the other man could step into the relative cool of the trailer. He closed the door behind them.

"We just got word from on high—the director just called a halt to all kinetic strikes not in *direct* defense of the Afghan Army," the man told him. "Which means the CIA is now officially done killing terrorists in Afghanistan. It's over."

Porter stared at the man, stunned. "So that's it," he said finally. "We're not even pretending we care about winning this fight anymore."

"I guess not," the man said. "It sucks, too, because if I'd had just a little more time, I could have called in a Predator drone on this guy you asked me to find. Get you a little pay-back for the man you lost out there last night."

"You ID'd him?" Porter asked, suddenly hopeful.

The officer nodded. "Got a hit on a military identification and managed to link it to a file at the Afghan Ministry of Defense, but before I could pull the file, the boss came in and shut everyone down."

"You have a name, though."

"Nassim, Captain Abdul. Assigned to the 201st Corps out of Kabul. But that's all I could dig up; everything else is locked away in the file." The man stifled a yawn. "I'm really sorry, man. I wish there was more I could do, but it sounds like it's closing time around here."

Porter thanked the man anyway. Walked him to the door of the trailer. Waited as he stepped back out into the blinding light, the suffocating heat. When the man was gone, Porter returned to his bed, repeating the man's name in his head.

Abdul Nassim.

I'm coming for you, Captain.

8

MUMBAI, INDIA

Hayes stood, unsteady, from the bathroom floor. Splashed water on his face at the sink and stripped out of his sweat-soaked clothes before stepping gingerly into the shower. He centered himself under the showerhead and twisted the knob all the way to the left, the blast of ice-cold water against his bare skin like knives stabbing into him, seizing his lungs in his chest. Hayes gasped for breath, his body instantly forgetting the panic that had gripped it just minutes before, but his mind not so quick to relinquish the shame. Like everyone else in the military, Hayes had been forced to sit through the PTSD classes before getting out, and like everyone else he'd rolled his eyes whenever the doctors talked about the need for routine mental health screening.

In Hayes's mind, post-traumatic stress had always been a problem for the guys on the other side—for the people who'd made the mistake of standing in his way and had to suffer the consequences. He'd never had a problem with PTSD himself, had always figured he was immune. But six months earlier, Levi Shaw, director of Operation Treadstone, had sent Hayes on a routine mission to Haiti that ended with Hayes's family almost being killed in front of him.

The panic attacks and nightmares were quick to follow, and soon Hayes was spending every night staring up at the ceiling—the worst moment of his life replaying over and over in his mind like a horror reel on an endless loop.

Now who's immune?

"F-fuck . . . you," Hayes told the voice, shivering but unwilling to step out of the cold.

His body screamed for mercy, but Hayes stayed in the shower until his skin was numb and the voice was silent, before finally cutting the water and stepping out.

Hayes picked up one of the Turkish cotton towels from the floor, a hint of a plan forming in the back of his mind as he dried off. As a singleton operative with Treadstone, he'd been trained to sneak into denied territory, and was well acquainted with the inhospitable environments and overwhelming odds that would be waiting for him in Afghanistan. The only difference was that during his time at Treadstone, he'd had the backing of the United States government, and the combined resources of the Department of Defense, Central Intelligence Agency, and National Security Agency at his disposal.

Back then, money, fake papers, weapons, and transportation were never more than a phone call away. But Hayes was a civilian now, and not only had he traveled to Mumbai on his own passport, but the only weapon he had was the ceramic knife hidden in the buckle of his belt.

He would need help; that was obvious. The only question was: who could he trust?

You're going to need to call the director.

Hayes had met Levi Shaw for the first time in a dusty exam room at Bagram Airbase in Afghanistan. According to Hayes's commanding officer, he'd been sent back north to Kabul because the Department of Defense was worried about the toll the endless war was taking on the Special Operations community, and had mandated "health and welfare exams" for all currently deployed teams.

Hayes did as he was told, but as he climbed aboard the Chinook that would take him to Kabul, he figured he knew what was happening. It had been a month since his close call in the Tangi Valley and while Hayes knew they'd been lucky to emerge unscathed from the ambush, the rest of the team took it as a good omen. More eager than ever to destroy the enemy, they'd ventured deeper into the mountains after Hayes's recovery, tracking the Taliban on their home terrain, killing them where they hid.

The missions were dangerous, the team pushing its luck, but Hayes and his Alpha Team had initially pulled them off without incurring casualties. Then, with three months before the end of the deployment, things began to get bloodier. The insurgents were still dying, but Hayes and his team lost a man of their own, too. And then another.

Now, on board the transport helicopter, Hayes wondered if the DoD had grown tired of the cowboy games and was sending him to Bagram for a Section 8—a catchall regulation that allowed the military to get rid of soldiers seen as mentally unfit for duty. But once the helicopter landed, and Hayes was ushered into the dusty exam room where Levi Smith waited, he began to have his doubts.

The director of Treadstone was "Doctor Smith" at that point, and he'd introduced himself as a DoD psychologist, though he'd given Hayes no clue about the reason he was here. Before then, Hayes's contact with military doctors had been limited to the physicals required for him to attend Ranger School, and Special Forces Selection, and both of those times he'd been examined by pleasant, soft-spoken men who looked like they spent most of their time indoors.

Doctor Smith, on the other hand, was rawboned with predatory gray eyes that put Hayes instantly on guard. Hayes watched the psychologist from across the table, his instincts telling him that something about the man wasn't right.

But what?

Hayes didn't know, and might have brushed the feeling off as paranoia, until Smith bent down to retrieve a folder from the leather attaché case on the floor and Hayes caught the outline of a pistol holstered at the man's belt.

"So you're a doctor, huh?" he asked.

Smith set the folder on the table. Opened it. "That's right."

"That Glock 19 on your hip, they issue that at the hospital?"

Smith looked up, met Hayes's eyes, the coldness in his gaze dropping the temperature in the room by ten degrees. Hayes held his stare and tried to read the man's intentions, but Smith's face was as empty as the Afghan desert.

"Only one reason to bring a gun to an exam like this," Hayes said, finally. "Are you here to kill me?"

Finally, some emotion from the doctor: a smirk. "No, Lieutenant Hayes," Smith replied. "I came to offer you a job."

Hayes's time in the military had taught him the benefits of traveling light, and after dressing in his hotel room, he stuffed his wet clothes into a trash bag he'd found in the bathroom, and retrieved the Arc'teryx carrier duffel he'd purchased before the trip. He stuffed his laptop, clothes, and toiletry bag inside, and zipped it up.

Hayes used the self-checkout feature on the TV, pulled on a dark blue baseball cap, and stepped out into the hall. A minute later, he was riding the elevator down to the lobby.

The car settled on the ground floor with a muffled thud. Hayes stepped out through the open doors and walked into the lobby, where he found the front desk empty. Taking advantage of the moment, he bent over the counter and fished a paperclip from a basket next to the computer. Crossing the lobby, he straightened one end of the paperclip, and when he stepped outside, used it to open the SIM card door of his Ramparts Overwatch-issued iPhone. He plucked the SIM card out of the tray, retrieved the Purism Librem 5 from the side pocket of his bag, and inserted the card into the new phone.

Compared to the iPhone's clean lines and brilliant display, the Librem 5's slate-gray case and thick bezel was downright utilitarian. But Hayes hadn't shelled out fifteen hundred bucks for the phone because he liked how it looked. No, he'd bought the Librem because the external kill switch on the side allowed him to disable the phone's Wi-Fi signal, cellular data, and satellite navigation abilities—a feature that made the device virtually untraceable, should he find himself in a position where he needed to truly disappear.

Hayes powered up the phone and pressed a Bluetooth earbud into his ear, the gutters that lined Marine Drive foaming as the city's overburdened sewer system worked to suck the ankle-deep water from the roadway. The rain had lessened somewhat, though it still fell around Hayes, and he tried to shield himself under canopies and awnings as he walked, dialing a number on the phone's screen from memory.

The line connected, and a recorded voice began speaking in Cantonese. "Thank you for calling Sterling Mercantile and Trust," it said. "If you know your account number, please enter it now, or stay on the line for more options."

Dodging the coffee-brown puddles that had seeped onto the sidewalk, Hayes typed in his twelve-digit account number, waiting for the beep before ending the call. He returned the phone to his pocket and turned right onto B Road, keeping his head down to avoid the pan of the cameras mounted to the eaves of the buildings around him.

He followed the road east, toward Churchgate Train

Station, half of him hoping Shaw wouldn't call him back, the other half wondering what in the hell he would say if Shaw did. To call Hayes's relationship with the director *strained* was an understatement, but it hadn't always been that way. In fact, when Hayes had first joined Treadstone, he'd found himself looking up to the man in charge, believing in the nobility of both Levi Shaw and his mission.

The years since had given Hayes plenty of cause to doubt both. But extricating Abdul Nassim from his current predicament would be a lot easier with the director's help.

The earbud began to trill in Hayes's ear. Hayes hesitated, knowing it was Shaw and still frozen by indecision.

Look, it doesn't matter how you feel about Shaw, the voice counseled. *We need him for this. Leave your ego at the door.*

Hayes answered the call. "Levi."

"Well, if it isn't the prodigal son." The director was clearly still angry with him; Hayes could tell. "How's the weather in Mumbai?"

That Shaw knew his current location shouldn't have surprised Hayes, but he felt his guard raise nonetheless, and he quickened his step. "You flagged my passport."

"Seemed like the prudent thing to do." Shaw chuckled. "There's no telling what kind of trouble a man with your skill set could get into, son."

"Prudent, my ass," Hayes replied. "You're spying on me. I'm not one of your assets anymore."

"Just doing my job. We *built* you, remember? This country has a vested interest in making sure you keep your nose clean."

Hayes gritted his teeth. Said nothing. Beside him, an open alley yawned, a row of dumpsters sending the stench of rotten food and stagnant water out into the street. Turning his stomach.

"What can I do for you, Adam?" Shaw asked. "I assume you didn't make contact for a restaurant recommendation."

"I need a favor," Hayes told him. "An old friend of mine is in trouble in Afghanistan. I need to get him out."

"Join the club," said Shaw. "This withdrawal is a shit show. This old friend—is he American? Or native?"

"He's ANA. Saved my life in-country ten years ago. Now he needs me to go back and get him."

"How noble of you," Shaw replied. "Adam—I don't know if you've been watching the news, but we're pulling people *out* of Afghanistan right now, not putting them in."

"I'm not asking you to start another war here. I just need a plane and a new set of papers."

"So does everybody else, I'm afraid. And right now, our priority is getting Americans out of there. Not risking more of our lives to save theirs." He sighed. "Your friend will get his chance. Washington has promised to do everything in its power to do right by our Afghan allies. It's just going to take time."

"He doesn't have time," Hayes replied, the blood rushing hot to his face, his fingers turning bone white as he fought to tamp down his frustration. "He's being hunted, Levi. By Americans. One of *us*."

Now, it was Shaw's turn to be on guard. "What do you mean?"

"He stumbled onto something he shouldn't have," Hayes told him. "An American operative selling weapons to the Taliban. They'll kill him to keep his mouth shut."

"That's quite a story," Shaw said. "Can your friend prove any of this?"

"He has a photo of the operative outside of a Taliban clinic in Maidan Wardak Province. He believes the operative was there to meet with a Taliban money man, but things somehow went sideways. He managed to pull a thumb drive from the money guy before the shit hit the fan but doesn't have access to a computer to analyze it."

"Or our guys were just there to kill Taliban," Shaw said. "I heard what happened in Wardak. Officially, Washington isn't willing to confirm any involvement. But unofficially, Adam, nobody around here is too broken up about a building full of dead insurgents."

"My guy swears it's not that simple," Hayes replied. "I believe him. And I'm asking for your help."

Shaw sighed. "In three days there won't be any more Americans in Afghanistan, Adam. Everyone's pulling out. I promise, whatever your friend thinks he saw, every single man and woman wearing stars and stripes over there is more concerned with getting home than hunting anyone down. He'll be fine."

Hayes paced the empty street, a lion in a cage, his hold on his temper growing weaker by the second. "What the hell happened to you?" he asked. "You were one of the good guys, once, weren't you? Or was I wrong the whole time?"

Shaw sighed. "Look," he said, his voice suddenly tired.

"I'm sorry about your friend. I really am. But this is not the time, and Afghanistan is definitely not the place for another one of your crusades. I can't help you; I'm sorry."

Hayes stifled the urge to hurl the phone into the rain. Forced himself to steady his breathing.

"Fine," he said. "Forget I ever asked. I'll do it myself."

Then he hung up.

9

Hayes stepped back out into the street and turned east again, a cool breeze blowing the mist against his face but doing nothing to quell his anger.

So that's not happening, the voice said. *Now what?*

Hayes wasn't sure, but he knew the first order of business was to get out of Mumbai, and with that thought at the forefront of his mind, he crossed the street and headed toward Churchgate Station. After a quick scan of the departure boards inside, he moved to the bank of automatic ticketing machines on the far wall and paid cash for a second-class ticket to Vile Parle. Then he hustled up the stairs to the platform, where a twelve-car train sat waiting to depart, the final boarding call booming from an ancient PA system mounted to the ceiling.

Through the grimy windows, Hayes could see that most of the coaches were still empty at this early hour, and he stepped aboard the nearest car and made his way to the rear. He pressed his back against the wall and then they were moving, the station sliding away as the train slowly began to pick up speed.

Hayes leaned his head against the wall and closed his eyes, forcing his mind back to his conversation with Shaw. Without a DoD-sanctioned flight to Kabul, Hayes knew he would need a new way to get into Afghanistan. The most logical course of action was to fly into Peshawar, Pakistan, and then use the old mujahideen smuggling route to sneak across the border. The only hiccup in the plan was the flag that Shaw had put on his passport, which would also be visible to Pakistan's Inter-Services Intelligence. Hayes knew that without a new set of papers, he ran the risk of being detained by the ISI the moment he tried to clear customs.

You're going to need some new papers. But where in the hell are you going to get those?

Acquiring a quality set of forged papers required time and money. Unfortunately, Hayes was currently short on both. What he *did* have, thanks to his time at Treadstone, was a half-decent network of connections in the region.

Most of the men Hayes had used during his time as an international assassin were disposable assets, low-level pieces of shit: black market privateers, back-alley informers, and foreign intelligence burnouts who had the tendency to get drunk and play Russian roulette with fully loaded automatics.

Scum.

But hidden among the human detritus saved on the Librem

5's encrypted hard drive, Hayes found *one* man with the access and means to provide a set of documents good enough to fool the ISI. His name was Seth Brooks, and as a member of the State Department's Bureau of Intelligence and Research, he had the resources and contacts to get Hayes into Afghanistan. More important, Brooks also had a vested interest in making sure America's withdrawal from the country wasn't scarred by a rogue asset from within.

The only question was, would Brooks be willing to help after what happened in Beirut?

Oh, he'll help you, all right, the voice muttered. *He'll help hide your body after he puts a fucking bullet in the back of your skull.*

That was ten years ago, Hayes thought. *There's no way he's still pissed about that.*

You launched *the man off a fucking building.*

Technically, Hayes had only shot him; it was the 124-gram Federal hollow point to the side of Brooks's knee that had sent him tumbling off of the side of the building. But thinking back on that fateful day, Hayes doubted Brooks would be one to appreciate the nuance of the situation.

Still, he was Hayes's only shot. And given the near legendary animosity the State Department was known to hold toward the CIA, Hayes was hopeful that Brooks would see the merit in forgetting any past history if it came with the opportunity to screw over the Agency.

I think this could work, Hayes thought.

And I think you need to get your head examined.

Well, Hayes thought. *No argument there.*

Fifteen minutes later, he walked into Chhatrapati Shivaji Maharaj International Airport, his shirt soaked with sweat from the short walk from the station to the terminal. Wanting to clean up, he ducked into the bathroom, washed his face, and after drying it with a paper towel, proceeded to the SpiceJet ticket counter.

It was a two-hour flight to New Delhi, and after takeoff, Hayes got on the in-flight Wi-Fi and used his credit card to rent a car. Then, with his transportation secure, he turned his attention to how he was going to get Brooks alone, and willing to talk.

The address he had for the State Department man was in the upscale neighborhood of Vasant Vihar, and after discovering that the house had just been purchased in April, Hayes hoped one of the real estate agencies would still have the listing photos up on their website.

Luck was on his side, and within five minutes he'd found what he was looking for in Sotheby International's recent sales list. Hayes skipped the photo gallery in favor of the guided video tour, and after hitting the play button, settled back in his chair.

The video opened with an aerial drone view of the neighborhood and the smog-laden sky beyond. After a quick pan of the tree-lined avenue and the community park across the street, the camera dropped to street view and centered on a two-story bungalow with pillbox-gray walls and an ochre roof, surrounded by a five-foot security fence.

The virtual tour took Hayes through the gate and into a concrete portico with a high wall to his left and a glass wall and stout wooden door to his right. The exterior shots were limited to the pool and the rectangle of green grass at the rear of the house, before continuing through the door.

Upon entering the house, Hayes was greeted by a large open den, the shimmering blue of the pool visible through the floor-to-ceiling windows that made up the wall. The shot was meant to draw the viewer into the space, and the videographer had done such a good job that for a moment Hayes found himself forgetting the reason *he* was taking the tour. So much so that when the camera panned back to the stairs and started up to the second floor, he almost ignored the voice in his head when it told him, *Go back.*

Instantly on guard, Hayes backed up the video and reviewed it frame by frame, wondering what he'd missed. The video inched forward, and he studied it closely, still not sure what he was looking for.

Then he saw it: the white security panel on the wall beside the stairway.

His way in.

10

NEW DELHI, INDIA

The rain followed Hayes to New Delhi, the sky jet black and the wind rattling the skybridge as he deplaned with the other passengers. On his way to the rental counter, he was waylaid by the mouthwatering smells coming from the food court, and he stopped to grab something to eat.

Properly fueled on airport chicken tandoori and Thums Up cola, Hayes continued to the rental counter and gave his confirmation code to the attendant. The man brought up his reservation, and after trying and failing to upsell him on the trip insurance, handed him the keys.

Hayes stepped outside into the lot, the rain slapping hard against his skin as he navigated the maze of cars parked outside. He'd hoped for a midsize SUV—something with enough power to get him out of trouble if his meeting with Brooks went sideways—but the attendant had explained, apologetically, that the only car available was the burnt-orange Maruti S-Presso hatchback that Hayes now found waiting for him.

What the hell is this? the voice demanded. It looked more like a toaster than a getaway vehicle.

His Danner hiking boots already half-soaked from the short trip from the rental desk to the car, Hayes resigned himself to the tiny hatchback and squeezed himself into the driver's seat. His body heat caused the windows to fog, and he turned the defrost all the way up, bracing from a sudden blast of the sickly-sweet air purifier the rental agency had thoughtfully installed.

Brooks's house was in the diplomatic area, five miles east of the airport, but before he paid the State Department man a visit, Hayes needed a new set of clothes, and a few pieces of kit. The clothes were the easy part, and activating the Librem's VPN, a quick Google search found Hayes a thrift shop a few miles south of his location, where he purchased a pair of dark jeans, a navy-blue hoodie, and a worn but serviceable raincoat. Finding what he needed to bypass Brooks's security system, on the other hand, took a little bit longer.

To break into the man's house, Hayes would have to jam the door and window sensors long enough to gain entry, but to do that, he would need to know the sensors' operating frequencies. Normally, finding such specific data among the myriad alarm makers across the globe would have taken thousands of man-hours, which was time that Hayes didn't have.

Thankfully, the technician who'd installed the alarm had

been kind enough to leave the manufacturer's sticker affixed to the front of the alarm panel, and with that information in hand, all it took was a quick search of the company's U.S.-based website to find the FDC-required compliance documentation that came with each model. With that information in hand, all that was left was to find a handheld radio that operated on a higher frequency than the window sensor, and then Hayes would be in business.

Another Google search showed three electronics stores in the area, and Hayes pointed the Maruti toward the closest, the hatchback's 1.5-liter engine struggling as he attempted to merge onto traffic on National Highway 48. The car drove like an overwhelmed go-kart, and with every jarring pothole, Hayes was sure he was going to lose a tire. But worse than the fear of the flat was the geyser of water and the gusting slipstream that threatened to swamp the car every time a transport truck roared past. By the time Hayes arrived at the Shri Sai shopping center and parked outside the electronics store, he was soaked with sweat, the muscles in his arms and back aching from trying to keep the tiny car on the road.

Maybe we should stick to surface roads from now on, the voice suggested.

With his new coat to protect him from the rain, Hayes hurried into the electronics store, where he bought a Baofeng UV-5R two-way radio, a bag of cheap plastic zip-ties, and a box of latex gloves. His final stop was at a corner market for a case of bottled water and a box of protein bars, and then he was back on the road, heading northeast to his target location.

Like Mumbai, New Delhi was in the midst of a growth spurt, and with the population on the rise, the need for residential housing was at a premium. But unfortunately, while people were a renewable resource, land was not, and with the availability of suitable building sites growing smaller by the minute, local developers had resorted to packing houses into the remaining space nearly on top of each other.

For Hayes, whose sprawling ranch in New Mexico covered an area twice the size of Vasant Vihar, the three-foot alley that separated Brooks's house from his neighbor seemed downright claustrophobic. But while he couldn't imagine living in such stifling confines, the upside of the situation was that the tiny, cramped alley provided the perfect avenue for what he had planned.

With his infil route identified, Hayes went in search of a place to stash the car. After finding what he was looking for at a dental clinic two blocks away, Hayes stuffed the radio, zip-ties, gloves, and a bottle of water into his pocket, and climbed out of the car, pulling the hood of the raincoat over his head as he followed the sidewalk north. He moved back to Brooks's alley and, finding it clear, ducked beneath the overgrowth of banana trees that lined the narrow passageway.

After the gagging sweetness of the car's air freshener, the dank scent of wet earth and rotting banana leaves was a welcome respite. When Hayes was sure there were no motion sensors on this side of the wall, he wrapped his arms around one of the slimmer trees and started up the trunk.

He paused at the top, and still not seeing any visible

intrusion devices, grabbed the security spikes and hoisted himself over.

Landing softly on the other side, Hayes pulled on the pair of latex gloves and then crept across to the portico he'd seen from the video. The rain had picked up, and by the time he made the doorway, rivulets of water were running off the hood of his coat.

Hayes shook it off and pulled out the Baofeng, checked to make sure the radio was set to the correct frequency, and removed a set of lock picks from his wallet. He dropped to a knee, the stamped concrete cold through his jeans as he studied the deadbolt.

The lock was a Medeco Maxum, a Grade 1 pain in the ass whose hardened steel inserts and rotating pins would have convinced most burglars to try their luck elsewhere. But most burglars weren't Treadstone graduates; sixty seconds after inserting the pick into the cylinder, Hayes had the bolt sliding open with a solid *thunk*.

Now for the moment of truth, the voice said.

The door swung open on well-oiled hinges, and Hayes stepped inside, his eyes searching out and finding the security panel in the dark. He closed the door behind him and waited, heart hammering in his chest, ready to run if the system sensed his incursion, but the light on the panel stayed green.

You're in.

Hayes locked the door behind him and started toward the den, his boots tracking water across the tile floor. A quick scan of the ground floor found a bathroom just short of the den, and he stopped at the doorway, intending to find a towel to erase the puddles he was leaving in his wake. He stepped inside and was reaching for the light switch when he heard a faint clicking coming from the hallway.

Instantly on guard, Hayes drew the ceramic blade from his belt and used the mirror to check his backtrail. Finding the outside door still closed, he eased out into the hall and was turning toward the den when a large Doberman emerged from the shadows, its throaty growl freezing Hayes in his tracks.

11

Seth Brooks sat at his desk, the receiver of the Sectéra
vIPer universal encrypted phone pressed to his ear as he
listened to the man on the other end of the line. As the
senior Diplomatic Security Service agent for the New Delhi
consulate, Brooks's primary function was as security attaché
for the American ambassador, a role that required him to stay
abreast of all emerging threats in the region.

It was an exhausting job, one that usually kept him in the
office until well after the rest of his staff had gone home for
the day, but with his daughter's final soccer match of the year
set to kick off in less than thirty minutes, Brooks had planned
on calling it a day early, for once.

Unfortunately, Mason Vonn wasn't getting the message, continuing to blather incessantly on the other end of the phone about how quickly the situation on the ground in Kabul was deteriorating.

"Mason," Brooks finally broke in. "I know you guys are having a hard time, but unless there's something that you need from me, I really have to go."

A pause. "Fine," Vonn said.

Thank God, Brooks thought.

But Vonn wasn't done. "Do you remember those two Taliban attacks I was telling you about a few weeks ago?" he asked. "The two madrassas they hit in Logar?"

Brooks sighed. "What about them?"

"Last night someone hit a medical clinic in Wardak." Vonn lowered his voice. "But get this: according to the DoD, this time they used a helo."

"A helicopter? Since when do the Taliban have air support?"

"Since never, as far as I know. So this morning I had a little look through some of yesterday's flight logs. And it turns out the fucking CIA had an Mi-17 in that same area last night."

Brooks sat forward, suddenly interested. "What are you saying?"

"I'm saying that while I'm busting my ass trying to keep this whole country from imploding, some of the boys from Eagle Base are out playing cowboy."

"That sounds like the CIA," Brooks replied. "But why are you telling me this? I'm still in India, Mason, in case you've forgotten."

Vonn hesitated. "Honestly, I was kind of hoping that you'd ask Jolene about it."

"Jolene?" Brooks blinked, the mention of his ex-wife throwing him off-kilter. "Why would she know anything about this?"

"Because I saw her in Kabul two weeks ago," the man said. "So I figured she might know who authorized the raid."

Now Brooks was totally lost.

"Kabul? That's impossible," he said. "Jolene was in Istanbul two weeks ago. I drove her to the airport myself."

"Well, she must have cut her trip short. Because two weeks ago she was at Eagle Base, running psych evals on the paramilitary guys."

Brooks swallowed. Tried to come up with a logical response. Was still searching when his secretary stepped into the office, tapping her watch. "You're going to be late."

Shit. Daisy's soccer match.

"Listen, I've got to go," he told Vonn, jumping to his feet and grabbing the holstered Glock 19 from his desk.

"What about Jolene?"

"What about her?" Brooks asked.

"Will you ask her about Kabul?"

Damn it, Mason. "Yeah. Sure," Brooks said. "Whatever."

He ended the call. Pulled his ID card from the reader and looped the lanyard around his neck. "I've got my mobile with me, so if the ambassador needs anything, just give me a call," he told his secretary. "I'll see you tomorrow."

It was a short elevator ride down to the parking garage

and the dark blue Audi S8 waiting in his spot. Brooks dropped behind the wheel and stabbed the start button with his index finger, the sedan's powerful engine purring to life.

He backed out of his spot and threw the car into drive, the squeal of the tires echoing off of the walls of the garage as he maneuvered the car up the ramp and past the security gate. Brooks waited until he was out on the street and then stepped hard on the gas pedal, the Audi's twin-turbocharged V-8 shoving him back in his seat as the tires searched and found purchase on the slick pavement.

For a man on a government salary, the big German sedan had put a serious dent in Brooks's savings, but when he'd bought it, he hadn't been thinking about the money. He was thinking that as a freshly divorced middle-aged man who'd reached the peak of his career, he needed to get busy living before it was too late.

Up ahead, Brooks could see the traffic slowing around the university, and he cut the wheel to the right and turned onto Dr Jose P Rizal Marg, his mind still trying to process what Mason had told him.

That the CIA was up to their old tricks was no surprise, but what had caught him off-guard was that Jolene had lied to him about her trip to Istanbul.

Why would she do that?

Brooks turned the Audi into the parking lot of the American Embassy School, nosing into an empty spot next to Jolene's emerald-green Land Rover, determined to get the truth from his ex-wife one way or another.

He climbed out of the car and hurried across the parking

lot, angling for the bleachers that lined the edge of the soccer pitch. Halfway there, his knee began to tighten—that old familiar twinge—but Brooks ignored it and was stepping up onto the grass when Jolene intercepted him.

"Nice of you to show up, Seth," she said, her brown eyes glaring daggers. "If you're serious about being a part of Daisy's life, the least you can do is show up on time. It's important to her."

"I'm sorry, Jolene," he told her, lifting his hands in surrender. Feeling himself start to wilt under that glare, as usual, and as usual, hating himself for it. "You're absolutely right. I should have been here sooner."

Jolene glared at him for a moment longer. Then, mercifully, her gaze softened and she relented, gracing him with a tiny nod.

As a former college soccer standout, Brooks loved watching his daughter play, and usually when Daisy was on the field the rest of the world seemed to slip away. But this time, Brooks was so distracted by Jolene's lie about Istanbul that he barely saw the play on the pitch at all.

"What's wrong with you?" Jolene asked, after a tidy play by Daisy that Brooks completely failed to register. "Where are you, Seth? Because you're sure not here."

Brooks blinked. Back to the present. The bleachers, the match. He glanced at his ex-wife out of the corner of his eyes. "Kabul," he said.

He could sense Jolene's confusion. "What?"

"You were in Kabul. Eagle Base. You told me you were going to Istanbul."

Jolene laughed. "Seth, darling," she said. "We're not married anymore. That means you don't need to care about what I do with my time. And frankly, you shouldn't."

She had a point, Brooks knew. But she'd *lied*.

He said nothing. On the pitch, Daisy collected the ball at the top of the box and launched a shot on goal that sent both of her parents to their feet in anticipation, then back down to their seats again a moment later, when the keeper easily parried the strike.

Neither Brooks nor Jolene spoke for a minute. Then, finally, Jolene shifted.

"How'd you find out?" she asked.

Brooks glanced at her again. She wasn't looking at him, her eyes on the pitch. "Mason Vonn."

"Mason Vonn." Jolene scoffed, shaking her head. "The walking, talking embodiment of why we lost the war."

"What happened in Kabul, Jolene? Mason said the Agency brought you in for psych evals." Jolene said nothing, so Brooks pressed on. "But why now, when everyone's getting out of there? And why the secrecy?"

Jolene still didn't answer. Her eyes fixed on the pitch, on Daisy, on the match. Brooks studied her. Waited. Back in his field agent days, he'd been trained to conduct an interrogation, to look for the little lies that people told when they wanted to hide the truth. He'd dealt with white-collar stuff, mostly. Forged visas and stolen documents. Nothing that gave him an edge when it came to his ex-wife's doctorate from Harvard.

No, Jolene had always been much smarter than him. But

worse than that, as the chief psychologist for the CIA's Near East division, her job was dealing with people who lied for a living. Brooks knew he was woefully out of his depth. He figured he always had been with Jolene.

"You know what? Never mind," he said, finally. "Mason was just curious. He asked if I knew. But you're right, Jolene; it's none of my business."

Beside him, Jolene seemed to deflate. Then, without looking at him, she reached over and took his hand, surprising him with the firmness of her grip. She still wouldn't make eye contact, was still watching the match.

"I'm sorry I lied about Istanbul," she said. "I was trying to protect you."

"*Protect* me? Jolene, why—"

She turned to him. Silenced him with her gaze, her troubled eyes.

"It's the wild west in Afghanistan right now, Seth," she said. "Just believe me; there are things happening there that you don't ever want to know about."

He wanted to ask more. His mind bursting with questions. But Daisy had the ball again, was dribbling toward the keeper, and Jolene launched up out of her seat again, cheering their daughter on. Letting go of Brooks's hand to clap when Daisy deftly directed a pass to a teammate who buried the ball in the back of the net.

Jolene cheered until she was hoarse, and Brooks joined, half-hearted, as Daisy's teammates mobbed each other. The moment was gone, he knew. He'd get no more out of Jolene tonight.

After the match, Brooks took the long way home, the conversation with Jolene replaying in his mind endlessly. Just as he'd expected, the goal had snapped Jolene out of whatever had convinced her to open herself up to him. She'd talked mostly about Daisy after that—their daughter's grades, her friends. The match. And if Brooks had tried hard enough, he could almost pretend it was just like the old times.

What does it matter what she was doing in Kabul? She's not your wife anymore, partner. It's not your concern.

Still, he was curious. And, damn her, the feel of her hand in his was still familiar enough to hurt.

By the time he reached his house and pulled through the gate, Brooks had nearly pushed Kabul out of his mind again, though it was admittedly much harder to forget the warmth of his wife's touch, the smell of her shampoo. The way Daisy's eyes had lit up, seeing her parents spending time together without another world war breaking out.

You're just lonely, old man. Get a grip.

Brooks guided the Audi beneath the portico and climbed out, his attention shifting from Jolene and Kabul to the steak he'd left marinating in the fridge, and the bottle of Absolut chilling in the freezer. Unlocking the door, he stepped into the darkened house and fumbled with the wall switch, frowning when the light didn't come on.

What the hell?

Figuring the storm must have knocked out the power, he silenced the alarm and called for the dog. "Apollo, where are you, boy?"

His voice boomed up the stairs and he waited, expecting to hear the eager clatter of the Doberman's claws on the hardwood floor above as the dog came rushing down to meet him. But beside the distant rumble of thunder, the house remained silent.

"Apollo," he repeated. "C'mon and let's go outside."

When there was still no answer, Brooks went to the kitchen, set his pistol and keys on the granite countertop, and grabbed his Maglite from the drawer. Flashlight in hand, he left the kitchen and was heading back to the stairs, wondering how in the hell he'd ended up with a guard dog who was afraid of a little thunderstorm—when the glow of his open laptop from the darkness of the den stopped him cold.

Confident that he'd left the computer in his upstairs office, Brooks stepped into the den, his confusion turning to fear when the beam of his flashlight swept across the half-dry boot print stamped in the middle of the rug.

His hand dropped to his waist, but instead of the pistol, his fingers found nothing but air. *Shit.* Remembering he'd left the Glock on the kitchen counter, he turned and hurried back into the hallway, feeling a bright burst of pain as his bad knee collided with the doorjamb.

The sudden agony nearly knocked him to his knees, but

Brooks stayed on his feet, the pistol the only thought on his mind. He hobbled into the kitchen, the beam from the Maglite splaying across the counter, revealing the holster where he'd left it—but no Glock.

"Looking for this?" a voice asked, behind him.

12

NEW DELHI, INDIA

Holding the pistol on Brooks, Hayes walked across the kitchen to the breaker panel on the wall. He flipped the fuse he'd tripped earlier, and the house lights blazed to life.

The fear in Brooks's eyes turned to immediate anger, the instant he recognized Hayes. *"You,"* he snarled. "What the hell are you doing in my house?"

"Take it easy." Hayes held the gun level, hoping the threat would be enough to keep the State Department man from trying anything rash. "I'm not here to hurt you. I need your help."

Brooks stared at him, incredulous. "You ever heard of a fucking telephone?"

"Call me paranoid, but I didn't figure you'd answer."

"And what about Apollo? You figure killing my dog was the best way to get back in my good books?"

Hayes blinked, thrown off momentarily. Then he laughed. "I didn't kill your dog, Brooks." He snapped his fingers. Whistled. After a moment, both men heard the telltale click of the dog's toenails on the tile floor, and an instant later, the Doberman appeared, wagging his tail, unharmed—though the steak hanging down from his jowls had seen better days.

"You asshole," Brooks told Hayes. "That was my dinner."

"Guess you're ordering in tonight," Hayes replied. "I needed something to get him to like me."

Brooks's shoulders sagged. He turned off the Maglite and placed it in a drawer before shuffling over to the fridge. "This day just keeps getting better and better," he muttered, pulling a bottle of vodka from the fridge.

"Nice place you've got here," Hayes said.

Brooks ignored him and pulled a glass from the cabinet. He poured himself a healthy dose from the bottle, gulped it down, and then poured another before finally turning back to Hayes. "What is it you want?"

Hayes set the Glock on the table and studied the man, wishing Brooks was a killer or a terrorist—anything that would justify what he was about to do. But Seth Brooks wasn't a killer; he'd proved that in Beirut. And Hayes had seen the photos of the man's daughter displayed proudly in his den. From the rest of the house, it was obvious that Brooks lived alone, but it was just as obvious that he was nothing more than another State Department suit. Harmless.

Still, Brooks had access to what Hayes needed to get Abdul Nassim out of Afghanistan, which meant he was going to help Hayes whether he wanted to or not.

"I have a friend in Afghanistan," Hayes told him. "An ex-ANA captain. He's in trouble, and I need you to help me evacuate him and his family."

"ANA personnel are eligible for the special asylum program," Brooks replied, finishing his second drink. "All he has to do is fill out the packet. You broke into my house for *that*?"

Hayes shook his head. "There's no time. Asylum will take months. Years. My friend won't survive a week unless I get him out of there."

Brooks glanced mournfully at the steak hanging from Apollo's jaw, the dog happily devouring the meat, the floor beneath him a puddle of drool. He reached for the bottle instead. "Everyone wants out of Afghanistan," he said, the slight slur in his voice a sign that he was already feeling the effects of the booze. "What makes this guy so special?"

"He saved my life," Hayes said. He paused. "And—he saw something. Something he shouldn't have. Something *we* did."

He pulled his phone from his pocket. Brought up the photo Nassim had taken. The gunman outside of the medical clinic. "Wardak Province, last night," he said. "This guy and his buddies showed up at a Taliban medical clinic. There was a firefight, but my friend thinks it was supposed to be a back-channel meeting that went sour. He's pretty sure this guy is selling American weapons to the Taliban."

Brooks took the phone. Stared at the picture. Hayes watched his eyes go wide.

"CIA," Brooks muttered.

Hayes frowned. "What?"

"The CIA had a helicopter in the area last night." He paused. "My wife—my ex-wife . . ."

Hayes waited. But Brooks had trailed off. Shook his head clear. Rubbed his bleary eyes. He focused on Hayes again.

"I don't know what this is about," he said, handing Hayes his phone back. "But I know it's not something I want to get involved in."

"I'm not asking you to get involved," Hayes replied. "I'm asking you to get me into Afghanistan."

"And if I don't?"

Hayes shrugged. "Then I guess I'll find my own way in." He looked hard at Brooks. "And once I get my friend and his family out, the first place I'll take him is to a press conference with every major news outlet I can find, where I'll explain how a State Department official stayed silent to protect a traitor within the CIA." He paused. "Or maybe he was protecting his ex-wife."

One look at Brooks's face and Hayes knew he'd gone too far. "You leave her name out of this," the bureaucrat shouted, reaching for a knife from the butcher's block on the counter and brandishing it drunkenly in Hayes's direction.

Hayes took a step back, lifting his hands. "Put that damn thing away before you hurt yourself."

"Go to hell," Brooks said, advancing, unsteady. His speech slurred. The knife wavering in his hand. Hayes suspected the man was more of a danger to himself than any real threat at this point, but he needed to keep Brooks alive and uninjured for what happened next.

Neutralize him, the voice said. *Before someone gets hurt.*

Hayes circled around the island in the center of the kitchen, searching for a nonlethal weapon. With no time to be selective, he reached for the lip of a farmer's skillet hanging on a rack above the island, but before he could get the handle free of the hook, Brooks was circling the island after him, the blade of the knife glinting dangerously in the light.

Hayes let go of the skillet and reached higher to take hold of the rack itself. Pulling hard, he tore the rack free of the ceiling and brought it crashing into Brooks's path, burying him in an avalanche of pots and pans.

The knife skittered free as Brooks fell to the floor. Calmly, Hayes kicked it aside. Dropped to one knee beside Brooks, who lay gasping, flat on his back, on the floor. "So will you help me or not?" he asked.

Brooks stared up at the ceiling. His eyes swimming. His chest heaving. "We do this my way," he said, finally. "None of that cowboy shit you pulled in Beirut."

Hayes smiled. "Wouldn't dream of it," he said, reaching out his hand to pull the State Department man to his feet.

13

KABUL, AFGHANISTAN

Dominic Porter stepped out of the Afghan Ministry of Defense building and slipped on a pair of dark aviator sunglasses. He started down the stairs, not noticing the droplets of blood staining the personnel folder in his right hand until he'd almost reached the sidewalk.

Shit.

Folding the file in half, Porter continued to the street, his eyes locked on the pair of Afghan military policemen standing outside the guard shack. He forced himself to stay calm, fought the urge to run, get the hell out of there before someone in the building discovered the dead clerk he'd stuffed under the desk in the records office.

But Porter kept his movements nonchalant, offering the

guards a casual nod as he passed their position. Then he was out on the street proper and aiming for a dusty Land Cruiser parked on the far curb, so close now that he could smell the smoke coiling from the cigarette pressed between his driver's lips.

The driver—an Afghan commando named Ikram—saw him coming, and by the time Porter dropped into the passenger seat, the truck was already in gear.

"Get me the hell out of here."

Ikram did as he was told and they pulled away from the curb, the dank stench of the Kabul River rolling thick into the cab. Porter kept his eyes glued to the rearview mirrors, fully expecting to see one of the military police pickup trucks come racing after them, but the cops never came, and a few moments later they were turning onto Ebn-e Sina Road, Kabul's midday traffic closing around the Land Cruiser like a steel blanket.

Porter hadn't wanted to kill the man, but he'd needed the file and had hoped that his CIA credentials and the usual bullshit song and dance about mutual aid would be enough to get his hands on it. Unfortunately, the clerk in charge of the archives had turned out to be a stickler for procedure, and Porter didn't have time to wade through the red tape. It wasn't ideal that the clerk had to die, but Porter had what he needed, and really, that was all that mattered.

Another dead body in Kabul was hardly going to make the evening news now, anyway.

Porter reached for the pack of Eighty Eight Milds stuffed into the cupholder, felt his driver's eyes on him as he shook out a cigarette.

"You're bleeding," Ikram said, nodding to the crimson smear staining the knuckles of Porter's left hand.

Porter lit the cigarette. "Not my blood," he replied, taking a deep drag of the smoke.

The cigarettes were from South Korea and more cardboard than tobacco, but it was the nicotine, not the taste, that Porter was after. He inhaled again greedily and blew the smoke out the open window, his eyes dancing over the cityscape.

With an elevation of 1,790 feet above sea level, Kabul was one of the highest capitals in the world. It was also one of the oldest. But even with the formidable peaks of the Hindu Kush mountains guarding its flanks, the city's proximity to the Silk Road had made it irresistible to invading armies, and throughout its violent history, Kabul had been conquered and reconquered so many times that the population had learned to grieve in fast-forward.

Porter knew that the Afghan ability to adapt was key to the population's survival, but still, the sight of the freshly whitewashed window advertisements outside of the beauty salons, and the sudden reappearance of the pale blue burkas among the jeans-and-T-shirt crowd moving along the sidewalks made a stark, and sobering, reminder of what the country would once again lose, just as soon as the American withdrawal was complete.

Porter turned away from the window. Opened the folder in his lap and thumbed through the neatly typed pages, looking for anything that would help him locate his quarry. He found what he was looking for near the back of the file, in the section that listed Adbul Nassim's home of record, and next of kin.

Just as Porter had thought, most of the addresses were in Maidan Wardak, but Porter ignored them, knowing there was no way the man would stick around there after what he'd seen at the clinic. No, the man wasn't stupid, which meant he would already be on the run. But where would he go?

The most obvious choice would be to head east, Porter figured, try to get across the border into Pakistan, but traveling through the Khyber Pass wasn't an easy task, and Porter knew Nassim would need a place to lay up before making the journey.

Porter found what he was looking for on the next page, when he found an address for Nassim's father in Jalalabad, roughly ninety miles east of Kabul.

There, he thought. *That's where he'll be.*

Nine months ago, he would have simply labeled Nassim a high-value target and then called in a strike by a Predator drone on the man's hideout, leveling the building with a couple of Hellfire missiles. But the Agency wasn't game for such simple solutions anymore, Porter knew, which meant he was going to have to do the job himself.

Or better yet, keep his hands clean and find someone else to do his dirty work. But who?

Porter mulled it over as his driver navigated the traffic-choked streets. The Land Cruiser had nearly made the outskirts of town when it hit him: Muhammed Ghul.

As the commander of the Taliban's elite Blood Unit, Ghul had been on Porter's radar since 2016, when Afghan National Army units stationed in the Helmand Province began taking heavy casualties while trying to push the Taliban from the area. According to the commanders on the ground, the tactics and sophistication of the attackers signaled that the men they were fighting were not the run-of-the-mill Taliban.

"This is a special group," one of the men said. "Like ghosts in the night."

Porter hadn't believed the hype. Like most everyone else at Eagle Base, he figured the Afghan regulars were just being cowards. But after a team of commandos from Kandahar were wiped out during a night ambush, he'd changed his mind. Porter had been hunting the Blood Unit and its commander ever since, and while there had been some close calls, Muhammed Ghul had somehow always managed to evade him.

Porter closed the folder and looked out the window, the hint of a plan forming in the back of his mind. Prior to the American withdrawal, getting close to someone like Ghul would have been impossible, but with the Taliban blitzing north across the Afghan hinterland, Porter was confident that times had changed.

Unfortunately, finding Ghul was only part of the solution. Porter knew that for his plan to succeed he was going to have to convince the Taliban commander to kill Abdul Nassim. It was a risky move, one that would require him to leave Kabul without a quick reaction force or dedicated air cover to back them up if they ran into trouble.

The thought went against everything Porter had learned

during his time as a paramilitary officer. But Porter was a gambler, and he looked at the situation in the simple terms of risk versus reward. Sure, there was a chance that Ghul might kill him instead of agreeing to the partnership, but compared to the certainty of what would happen if Langley found out about his betrayal, Porter figured it was the only play he had left.

14

Adam Hayes was asleep in the main cabin of the State Department C-37 when the muted thump of the flaps alerted him to the plane's imminent descent. He jolted upright in the oversized leather chair, instantly awake and all too aware of the man staring at him, startled, from the seat on his right.

"What the hell is the matter with you?" Seth Brooks demanded.

Hayes rubbed his eyes. "You're going to have to be more specific."

"Waking up like that." Brooks gestured. "Like you're ready to kill someone. It's creepy."

"If you're still alive, it means you're not the target." Hayes reached for his window shade. "So you have nothing to worry about."

Located in the valley of Peshawar and flanked by the towering Spīn Ghar and Hindu Kush mountains, Peshawar was one of the oldest cities in Pakistan. With settlements dating back as far as three thousand years ago, the ancient border town sat at the crossroads of India and South Asia. It was ancient when Alexander the Great swept through in 325 B.C., and thanks to its proximity to the famed Khyber Pass, the area over the centuries established itself as an important trading hub. Fueled by the influx of goods and gold, the metropolis had earned the nickname Crown Jewel of Bactria. But looking down at the cityscape, Hayes wasn't fooled by its gilded history. No, to him Peshawar was just another border town, a wild and unruly place known for its deep distrust of foreigners.

Realizing that even the smallest slipup on his part could have potentially deadly consequences, Hayes turned his focus to the aircraft's steady descent into Bacha Khan International.

"What's the plan when we hit the ground?" he asked Brooks.

Brooks cleared his throat. "Well, after you clear customs—"

"Customs? You told me you were handling that."

"No, I said I would *try* to get you a diplomatic passport." Brooks shrugged. "I tried. No dice. So you'll talk your way through customs, and then we'll go see my contact and find out if he knows anything about the guy in your friend's picture."

Great.

The C-37 was the Air Force designation for the civilian Gulfstream V private jet, and while it was a much smoother ride than the C-130 transport that Hayes had flown in the last time he'd come to Pakistan, the distinctive blue and white livery of the State Department aircraft guaranteed he wasn't getting into the country unnoticed.

A yellow tug was waiting for them on the ground, and the pilot followed it to a hangar on the south side of the field. Inside the hangar were a pair of black Chevy Suburban SUVs and a handful of men in black suits and wraparound sunglasses, but it was the sole customs official in his olive-drab uniform who held Hayes's attention.

Damn you, Brooks. This had better work.

Hayes was the last off the plane, and by the time he made it down the airstair, the dour-faced customs agent had both his passport and his luggage. While Brooks and the rest of his detail climbed into the back of one of the Suburbans, the customs agent gestured to Hayes that he should follow him.

"This won't take long," the man said, starting for the door.

From the outside, Bacha Khan International Airport looked austere and outdated, its faded blue signage and sandblasted concrete walls looking more like Soviet-era housing than a major transport hub. But following the customs agent inside, Hayes was surprised to find the interior had recently been renovated, the tired linoleum flooring and flickering fixtures replaced by gleaming sandstone tiles and warm track lighting.

"I like what you've done to the place," he said.

The customs agent's expression became even more sour, if that were possible. "A waste of money."

Well, this guy's a barrel of laughs, the voice muttered.

Hayes followed the agent to a dimly lit booth on the far side of the immigration area. The man set his luggage on one of the stainless-steel tables, wiped the sweat from his brow, and turned his attention to the passport.

"Mr. Robert Ash," he said, reading the name off of the document. "What is the purpose of your visit to Pakistan?"

Hayes kept his eyes on the man. "I am a contract employee with the U.S. Department of State," he said, using the legend he and Brooks had come up with the night before.

"And how long will you be staying?"

"Four days," Hayes replied, his eyes drifting to the section of glass next to the stout metal door on the far side of the hall.

For most travelers, the mirror was just a mirror, but Hayes had been in the game long enough to know that sitting on the other side of the two-way glass were members of Pakistan's Inter-Services Intelligence, trained to keep men like him from doing exactly what he was trying to do now.

As far as legends went, Hayes figured his story was good enough to pass a cursory inspection, but he knew that it wouldn't hold up long under the practiced eye of the ISI agents. For most people in his position, the natural reaction was to start talking, try and distract the customs agent from the task at hand. But Hayes avoided the urge, kept his mouth shut and his head down to avoid the camera perched over his right shoulder. While he waited, his mind slipped back to

Annabelle and the call he'd made after taking off from New Delhi.

Considering he was on his way to sneaking into a war-ravaged country and attempting to rescue Abdul Nassim without getting his head cut off, the phone call should have been a trivial thing. But as he had dialed the number of his ranch in New Mexico, Hayes had realized he would much rather face the Taliban than explain to his pregnant wife why he wasn't on his way home as scheduled.

Annabelle had answered on the third ring, her voice muted by the screaming of their son, Jack, in the background. "Mommy, I want some *chiiiiips*!"

Yeah, this is going to suck.

"You can't have any chips; it's almost dinnertime," Hayes had heard Annabelle tell Jack. "Now go watch TV while I talk to your father."

"But I want—"

"*Jack,*" she snapped, her mom voice in full effect.

There was a moment of silence, and Hayes imagined his son slinking out of the room. Smiled at the thought of Jack's hangdog expression. Suddenly, he missed his family more than words.

"Adam," Annabelle had sighed. "*Please* tell me you're on your way home."

Hayes had said nothing, unwilling to lie, but not ready to face the consequences of the truth. "Not exactly," he said.

"Not *exactly*?" Annabelle's voice had been sharp. "What does that mean, Adam? What are you mixed up in now?"

Being married to a government-conditioned assassin

wasn't exactly easy, Hayes knew, and the fact that Annabelle was still with him after everything that Treadstone had done to their family spoke volumes about her character. Which wasn't to say she hadn't paid a price.

No, both Annabelle and Jack had suffered for Hayes's loyalty to his country. But while the marriage had never been easy, it had always been honest. And true to that tenet, Hayes knew he had to tell Annabelle the truth.

"Nassim and his family are in trouble," he'd said. He'd explained the situation as best he could. Told her about the frantic call and the picture of the man at the clinic. "Going to Afghanistan is the last thing I want to do right now," he'd told his wife. "But I owe Nassim my life."

There had been silence on the other end of the line, and as the seconds ticked by, a familiar question slipped, unbidden, into his mind. *Is this the call that is going to finally end our marriage?*

"You know what this means, don't you?" Annabelle had asked, at last.

"No," he'd replied. "What does it mean?"

"It means that when this little girl shows up, Adam, you have the late shift. Any feedings or dirty diapers after eight p.m., that's *all* you."

He'd laughed despite himself, the sudden relief like a heavy weight lifted from his chest. "Baby," he said, "I don't deserve you."

The metallic *cha-chunk* of the customs agent's stamp on his entry visa startled Hayes back to the now, and he looked up, his eyes darting to the stainless-steel door by the mirror.

Finding it clear, he turned his attention back to the customs agent, who handed him his passport. "Have a pleasant stay, Mr. Ash."

Hayes thanked the man. Slipped his passport into his back pocket and shouldered his bag as he stepped past the booth. He started for the exit, the familiar tingle up the back of his neck telling him that he was being watched. A wave of paranoia came rushing up his spine, but he pushed it down, and continued to the baggage area where he used the safety mirror hanging above the carousel to check his backtrail.

The customs agent hadn't moved, but sat in his booth with a phone pressed to his ear. For all Hayes knew, the man was talking to his wife, or the shawarma delivery boy, but his instincts told him otherwise.

You're blown.

15

It was midnight in Georgetown, and inside the redbrick row house that served as the nerve center for Operation Treadstone, Levi Shaw sat ensconced on his Chesterfield, grateful at last for some peace and quiet. With the situation on the ground in Afghanistan rapidly deteriorating from bad to worse, Shaw had spent most of the day at the Pentagon, bouncing from one intelligence briefing to the next.

Officially, he was there to assist the DoD decision makers as they tried to make sense of what was happening in Kabul. Unofficially, most of his time had been spent watching a roomful of four-star generals playing pass the buck, and by the time his driver dropped him off at the row house, Shaw had a massive migraine.

He climbed the steps, swiped his ID card over the reader, and then punched his security code cypher lock. The magnetic lock disengaged with an audible click, and Shaw pushed the door open and followed the hall to the stairs that led up to his office.

A few minutes later, he was comfortably installed on the sofa, a lowball of Blanton's in his right hand. Shaw took a sip of the bourbon and kicked off his shoes, the low light from his desk lamp reflecting in his dark eyes.

What a waste of a day.

In many ways, the political backstabbing and lack of accountability he'd witnessed that day was indicative of the way America had waged its longest war. But beneath all the bluster and bullshit, Shaw knew there had been one unifying emotion that each man in the room had shared. Guilt.

And it was that thought that he was trying to trace to its logical conclusion when the encrypted laptop on his desk dinged to life.

What now? Taking another sip of the bourbon, Shaw pushed himself to his feet and walked across to his desk.

Fighting a wave of exhaustion, he set the lowball on a coaster and typed in his ten-digit password to unlock the computer, the flashing red border around the XKeyscore program immediately grabbing his attention as the laptop booted up. According to the National Security Agency, XKeyscore was a program that allowed the United States to legally obtain information about foreign intelligence targets. But Shaw knew the reality of the situation was far more nuanced.

In essence, XKeyscore was a search engine on steroids, a

system designed to allow unlimited digital surveillance on any person anywhere in the world. All it needed was a target, and in Shaw's case, the current target was Adam Hayes.

Hayes, whose passport photograph had apparently just been scanned by a customs agent at Bacha Khan International Airport in Peshawar, Pakistan—under an assumed name, but Adam's picture nonetheless.

Damn.

Shaw reached for the encrypted phone on his desk and dialed a number. The line connected and began to ring. Once. Twice. Three times. As the line trilled in his ear, Shaw found himself hoping she wouldn't answer, but he knew his luck would never be that good.

On cue, Lisa Barton, director of the CIA, answered the call. "What is it, Levi?"

"You were right," Shaw told her. "Adam Hayes is in Peshawar."

A pause. "You're sure?"

Hayes studied the picture on his laptop screen again. It was definitely Hayes. "Yes, I'm sure. What do you want me to do?"

"You? Nothing," the director said. "I'm going to have someone I trust reach out to our contact at the ISI, have him keep an eye on Hayes until we can figure out what's going on."

"Is there any truth to it, Lisa?" Shaw asked. "What Hayes believes happened in Wardak?"

"Are you asking me if my guys are selling weapons to the Taliban?"

Shaw said nothing.

After a beat, Barton sighed. "Look, this is the first I'm hearing of it, but . . ."

"That doesn't mean it's not happening."

"We're looking into it; I assure you. But it's chaos over there. And as you well know, Langley can be a tough place to get answers—even for me." She paused. "Can Hayes get himself into Afghanistan?"

"Adam could get himself to the moon if he had to," Shaw said. "Are you suggesting we let him try?"

"I want to know if he's right," Barton said. "If I have a rat in my house, then I'd better start cleaning. But I'd prefer not to move unless I know for certain."

"This is a dangerous game we're playing," Shaw said.

"It's only dangerous if we lose," Barton said. "Whatever Hayes does, it doesn't come back on me, understand? We never had this conversation."

"Of course."

"Let's just hope your boy hasn't lost a step, Levi. Call me when he figures this out." She ended the call.

16

PESHAWAR, PAKISTAN

Hayes pushed through the airport's security door and stepped outside. Where the atmosphere inside the customs terminal had been reserved, the scene waiting for him beneath the arched loggia that led to the street was pure chaos. The shouts of the vendors hawking their wares and the thick acrid bite of cigarette smoke from the cabbies lounging against the railing all threatened to overwhelm Hayes's senses.

Welcome to Pakistan, the voice said.

Keeping his head down, Hayes threaded his way through the crowd and followed the concrete pavers out to the street. He stopped at the curb, his paranoia turning quickly to anger when he saw the pair of shiny black Suburbans and the three men dressed in khaki 5.11 pants and navy-blue blazers waiting for him in the loading zone.

You've got to be shitting me.

To most people back in the States, the scene would have barely registered, but here in Pakistan, both the trucks and the men screamed *American*. And Hayes had been hoping to stay a little more discreet.

He started toward the trucks, his eyes on a burly man with a freshly shaved head leaning against the first vehicle. "Are you in charge of this crew?"

The man straightened. "That's right. Is there a problem?"

"I think customs made my passport," Hayes told him.

"Impossible. Those docs are clean. I checked them myself."

"Maybe. Maybe not. Either way, we need to get out of here." Hayes moved to the rear of the Suburban and opened the door. Inside, Seth Brooks was waiting.

Hayes climbed in beside him. "Let's go."

The driver pulled away from the curb, guiding the convoy through the airport gate and pausing for a break in the traffic before pulling out onto Khyber Road. He slowed to let the trail vehicle catch up, and when the second driver advised that they were on the main road, picked up speed and joined the flow of traffic. While he drove, Hayes kept his eyes glued to the mirrors. The driver glanced back at him in the rearview.

"I told you, those docs are pristine," he said. "There's no way we're burned."

"Yeah, well, we've got a tail," Hayes replied. "Dark blue sedan. Three car lengths back and closing."

The driver swore. "You want me to shake them?"

"Not yet." Hayes turned to Brooks. "Who did you tell about this meeting?"

"The only person I talked to was Mason Vonn," Brooks said. "And he knows better than to go running his mouth."

"Then why all the heat?"

"Gee, I don't know, Adam. Maybe it's because you broke into my house and forced me to provide you with fake documentation so you could illegally enter a sovereign nation."

During his years spent working as a singleton operative, Hayes's survival had often depended on his ability to read people. To pick up on the microexpressions, the subtle shifts in posture that telegraphed their lies. He studied Brooks's face, searching for any tells that the State Department man had sold him out somewhere.

He's telling the truth.

"Fine," he told Brooks. "But we still have to deal with this." To the driver, he asked, "You got a map up there?"

The driver gestured to the passenger seat. "In the glove box."

Hayes unfastened his seat belt, climbed over the center console, and slid down into the passenger seat. He opened the glove box and pulled out the worn city map he found inside.

"What are we going to do?" Brooks asked.

"I think the *we* part of this exercise is over," Hayes replied. He looked at the driver. "I'm going to need your sidearm."

The man glanced at Hayes, incredulous. Hayes held his gaze until the driver found Brooks in the rearview mirror.

"Sir, I can't just give my service weapon to a civilian. My boss will have my ass."

"Just do what he says," Brooks sighed. "If he wants your gun he's going to get it, one way or another. Save us all the trouble."

The man deflated, but did as he was told, tugging the holstered Glock 19 from his hip and handing it over. Hayes checked the pistol to make sure there was a round in the chamber, and then clipped the holster to his belt. He pulled his shirt over it, and then turned his attention back to the map.

"Take your next right," he said. "Then head south, past the water treatment plant."

The driver nodded, still looking unhappy about the loss of his gun. "Understood."

Hayes picked up the man's radio from the center console. "In a hundred yards, we're taking a little detour," he told the driver of the trail vehicle. "I need you guys to try to box out that blue sedan."

"Roger that," the second driver replied. *"I see them."*

The lead driver turned right onto Babar Road and pressed hard on the gas pedal. The big V8 spooled up and they rocketed down the road toward the water treatment plant.

"Turn here," Hayes instructed.

The driver spun the wheel, the tires screeching as he made another hard right turn. The radio crackled to life. *"First car took the bait, but a white motorcycle just flew past me."*

I knew it couldn't be that easy.

Hayes double-clicked the talk button to tell the man he

understood, and continued directing the driver. "Cut through the alley. Take a left on Bazar Road."

The driver did as he was told, the bumper scraping against the wall as he turned into the alley. "Shit, this is tight."

"Keep going."

Slowly, they maneuvered down the narrow alley and emerged out onto Bazar Road, the traffic beginning to bunch as they neared the market. Hayes waited until the end of the block, and then reached for the door handle, his eyes on the speedometer. He waited for the needle to drop to five miles per hour, then cracked the door.

"Catch you guys on the flip side," he said. Then he was stepping out of the Suburban and onto the street, slamming the door behind him and disappearing into the crowd.

17

Colonel Malik Tahir of the Inter-Services Intelligence sped south on Police Lines Road in his Chinese-made Changan Raeton CC sedan, trying to make sense of the chatter coming over the radio.

"Trail vehicle is slowing down. Give them space."

"I'm switching to lane three. Javid, you've got the eye."

"Good copy."

After spending the previous five years conducting counter-surveillance operations against the Americans in Afghanistan, and the militants in Kashmir, Tahir knew his men were the best at what they did. Still, the ISI colonel knew they'd have their work cut out for them with this assignment.

The call from Tahir's contact in the CIA had been short

and to the point. "An American citizen named Robert Ash has just passed through immigration. The director needs to know where he goes, and who he meets with."

Tahir had paused before answering. To say that the operative's request was unusual was an understatement. Pakistan's relationship with the United States had deteriorated significantly during recent times; in fact, over the last four years it had gone from strained to downright hostile. And while there were many in Islamabad who felt that the newly elected American president would be a more favorable ally to Pakistan, Tahir was a realist, and he knew that once the Americans completed their withdrawal from Afghanistan, nothing would ever be the same.

"Are you there?" the operative had asked.

"I'm here," Tahir had replied. "I was just waiting for you to explain to me why the ISI should bother to help the American government."

"This isn't the American government asking. And the director is not asking the ISI, Colonel. She's asking *you*."

Tahir had said nothing.

"One hundred thousand American dollars," the operative had said. "Cash. Untraceable. Delivered to you, not the ISI."

Tahir had hesitated. As much as he hated the Americans for the violence and instability they'd created in the region, their cash was still king. And his CIA contact had been offering a significant sum.

"Tell me who Robert Ash meets with in your country," the operative had said. "And tell me when he leaves."

"Two hundred thousand dollars," Tahir had countered. "I will need a team of men to do this."

A pause. "Very well. Just get me the information."

Then Tahir's contact had ended the call.

Now, Tahir monitored his team's conversation on the radio as they trailed the American's convoy of SUVs—hardly an inconspicuous way for Robert Ash to enter the country. Tahir didn't know what the CIA wanted with Ash, and he didn't care. He only hoped that the American wouldn't cause too much trouble during his stay in Peshawar, and that he would leave quickly.

The radio squawked to life. "Shit, *they are turning. Javid, you're too close.*"

"*Fazil, do you have him?*"

"*Yes, I've got them,*" a third voice entered the conversation, the distortion of the wind noise in the background telling Tahir that the agent was on a motorbike. "*They are headed south on Babar Road. I'm trying to catch up.*"

"*How far?*"

"*Half a kilometer,*" Fazil said. "*They're going for the bazaar.*"

"*Do not lose them.*"

Tahir stepped on the gas, urging the sedan forward as he tried to predict where the American was going. It didn't take long before he'd come up with an answer.

18

Hayes waited for the Suburban to pull away, and then headed south, pausing beneath the red sandstone gate of the bazaar and glancing back toward the roadway. The dark blue sedan he'd noticed following from the airport now sat marooned amid the chaos of traffic on Babar Road. As Hayes watched, the rear door opened, and two men in traditional knee-length tunics and baggy trousers emerged.

To the uninitiated, there was nothing unusual about the men, but the outline of the pistols beneath their tunics, and the pigtail of acoustic tubing attached to their tactical earpieces instantly made them as operatives. Hayes studied the men long enough to memorize their faces. Then he turned back to the bazaar.

Nestled in the heart of the city, the Qissa Khwani, or "Storyteller's bazaar," was one of the oldest institutions in Peshawar. It was also one of the busiest, which made it the perfect place to drop a tail. With that thought in mind, Hayes hurried deeper into the market, the sandblasted façades of the Indo-Islamic architecture rising around him, giving the impression that he'd stepped back in time.

Dodging the flow of tuk-tuks and motorbikes that zipped past on Qissa Khawai Road, Hayes turned onto one of the side streets and followed it north to a line of cabs waiting on the curb. Glancing back into the bazaar to ensure the two operatives hadn't yet caught up, Hayes hurried to the first of the taxis in line, a lemon-yellow Suzuki hatchback, its bodywork covered in dents and scars from years—and perhaps, decades—of doing battle in Peshawar traffic.

"Take me to the Pearl Continental," Hayes told the driver in Pashto.

The driver, an older, heavyset man, his black beard going to gray, didn't blink. He flicked his cigarette out of the driver's-side window and shifted the Suzuki into gear.

Probably brought plenty of guys like you to the PC before, the voice said. *Between the Suburbans and the meeting spot, you might as well be wearing a neon sign that says "spy."*

Nestled on a hill overlooking the Peshawar golf course, the Pearl Continental was a stately, six-story building frequented by foreign journalists and aid workers—and operatives. Constructed in 1975, the handsome, white stucco building wasn't just the oldest four-star hotel in the area, it was the *only* four-star hotel in Peshawar, and its understated elegance and modern amenities were the reason the CIA had chosen it as its unofficial base in the city.

The only problem was the Agency hadn't exactly bothered to keep this fact a secret, meaning the PC was in many ways the *worst* possible location in Peshawar for a clandestine meeting.

But Brooks had been adamant. Mason Vonn wouldn't meet anywhere but the Pearl. And with Nassim's life on the line, Hayes wasn't in a position to negotiate.

The hotel sat two and a half miles from the Qissa Khwani Bazaar, and the drive took ten chaotic stop-and-start minutes. The driver barely glanced at Hayes in the backseat, and Hayes spent his time monitoring the traffic behind the taxi for any signs of a tail. He saw no one, and knew by the way the driver weaved through traffic, the Suzuki blending in to the sea of other taxis, motorbikes, trucks, buses, and private vehicles on the road that the chances of anyone following were slim.

Confident that he'd dropped the tail, Hayes paid the driver in rupees as the taxi pulled to a stop outside of the Pearl Continental's gates. He grabbed his bag from beside him and stepped out onto the street, the fresh air a reprieve from the suffocating, tobacco-tinged heat inside the taxi. At the gates of the hotel, Hayes leaned against the brick and fished out a pack of Gold Leaf cigarettes, appearing to the casual observer as nothing more than another expat enjoying a smoke while waiting for a ride into the city, but a closer inspection would reveal a man on edge, his gaze constantly shifting behind the Oakley Flak 2.0 sunglasses that covered his eyes.

Hayes stayed there for another five minutes, eyeing the cars that passed until he was sure that he hadn't been followed. Finally, he crushed out the cigarette, hoisted his bag, and started up the drive.

According to everything he'd ever read about the Pearl Continental, the hotel boasted an immaculate lobby, but Hayes had no intention of going through the front door. No, if there was anything he'd learned during his time at Treadstone, it was to never enter a building until you knew how you were going to get out.

With that thought in mind, he turned to his right and followed the service road around to the loading dock. During his brief career working hotel security for Ramparts Overwatch, he'd learned that no matter how stringent a site's security may have been, there was no mitigating the human factor, the seemingly harmless shortcuts most employees took to save time.

As Hayes had hoped, both the hotel's rolling loading bay door and the access door beside it were propped open in preparation for the afternoon's deliveries, and Hayes hustled up the stairs and into the bowels of the building without attracting any attention. Using the exposed ductwork and tangle of electrical and phone wires on the ceiling above him as a guide, he navigated the long, mazelike hallways to the hotel's electrical room. The door was secured by a simple electronic lock, and after studying the panel, Hayes set off to find the tools to bypass it.

Continuing down the hall, he located the laundry facilities. Once inside, Hayes found a rack of freshly cleaned and pressed staff uniforms—each one with its owner's name pinned neatly to the front. Hayes pulled one of the tags free, tucked the safety pin into his pocket, and walked out again.

Back in the hall, he found a folding chair and carried it back to the laundry room. Closing the door behind him, Hayes placed the folding chair in position underneath the room's smoke detector and climbed on top of it to reach up and deftly twist the smoke detector from its mount.

Hayes cracked open the back of the detector and removed the nine-volt battery and its wiring harness. Using his fingernails, he stripped the rubber coating off the wires, connected the safety pin to the positive wire and left the negative bare.

He returned the chair to the hallway, and headed back to the electrical room. Using the safety pin as a ground, he pressed the negative wire to the exposed signal pin on the bottom of the lock. The lock disengaged with a click, and Hayes was in.

Inside the electrical room, Hayes found a bank of computer processors and a row of servers. He pulled his laptop from his backpack and, while he waited for it to boot up, studied the electrical panel. With only a rudimentary knowledge of Urdu, he was unable to read the wiring diagram, but after a few minutes of trial and error, Hayes was able to connect his laptop to the processor responsible for the hotel's CCTV feed, and, a moment later, was clicking through the various cameras that covered the hotel property.

He started with the exterior, searching the grounds for an idea of the hotel's security detail. Then he switched to the lobby, where a quick pan across the marbled hall proved that the travel magazines had all been correct. *Yeah, it's a nice-*

looking place. Finally, Hayes clicked over to the bar where the meeting was supposed to take place.

The man who must have been Mason Vonn sat at a table at the rear of the bar, his back pressed against the wall. He was younger than Hayes had imagined, and from the aggravated drum of his fingers against the table, and the way his eyes barely stilled as they constantly surveyed the room, Hayes could tell that Brooks's contact was very much on edge.

Nervous? Or is there something more at play here?

Hayes supposed he would find out.

Confident there were no surprises waiting for him, Hayes broke down his setup, returned the laptop to his bag, and stepped out of the room. Two minutes later, he was sliding into a chair across from Mason Vonn.

Vonn barely glanced at him before resuming his scan of the bar. "You're late."

"Traffic," Hayes replied.

Vonn snorted. "I heard you picked up a tail at the airport."

The younger man's breath was sour, and Hayes could see the sweat stains underneath his armpits. His eyes still hadn't stopped moving.

Paranoia. Maybe drugs.

Unless it's not paranoia at all.

Stifling the instinct to twist in his seat, follow Vonn's gaze around the room, Hayes reached into his pocket instead. Pulled out his phone. "Brooks said you could identify this man."

"That depends," Vonn said. He ignored the phone.

"On what?"

Vonn gave Hayes a sly grin and leaned back in his chair. "You know, I've known Seth for a long time," he said. "We're close, almost like brothers, but there's one thing I've always been curious about."

Hayes waited. "And what's that?"

"I want to know what happened in Beirut."

Hayes cocked his head, momentarily off-kilter. *What does this guy care what happened in Lebanon? That was six years ago.* According to the file Hayes had studied on Mason Vonn, the man was a burnout, a CIA case officer who'd never quite had the stuffing to run with the big boys in the intelligence community. Sitting across the table from Vonn, Hayes figured the dossier was correct.

But what the hell, if telling this guy some old war stories is what it takes to get across the border to Nassim, then so be it.

"Beirut," Hayes said. "Yeah, okay. Sure."

Conscious of time wasting, Hayes began to give Vonn the executive summary of the operation—a Pakistani national with ties to al-Qaeda. "According to our intelligence, he was there to meet with a local financier, but for some reason the State Department believed he intended to turn himself in."

"Why would they think that?"

Because Seth Brooks tried to play spy, got played instead.

Hayes shrugged. "You'd have to ask Brooks. Anyway, it blew up in our faces. We were lucky that nobody died."

Vonn grinned. "Especially because you shot Seth off a rooftop."

"I was saving his life," Hayes said. "Even if he doesn't see it that way." He held out the Librem again, the picture that Nassim had taken. "Listen, do you know this guy or not?"

Finally, Vonn looked at the phone. Immediately, something clouded his expression. "Yeah, I know him. His name's Dominic Porter. He's bad news."

"Any idea where he is now?"

"Last I heard, it was Eagle Base. But that was a while back." Vonn leaned forward, drank from the bottle of water on the table in front of him. "You want a more updated location, you could try asking Seth."

He set down the bottle. Grinned again at Hayes, an off-kilter smirk that didn't hold much humor. "Better yet," Vonn said, "ask his *wife*."

19

JALALABAD, AFGHANISTAN

The Land Cruiser drove east on National Highway 8, the fading cityscape giving way to vast, open desert. Sitting in the passenger seat, Dominic Porter gazed out at the rocky terrain and tight curves and saw perfect terrain for an ambush. Once again, he wished for a drone—or better yet, a couple of F-18s—to cover his ass if things went south, which they usually did when you ventured out this far beyond the wire.

He watched the GPS on the dash, his stomach growing tighter as the SUV neared the red X that marked their rendez-vous point.

"We should not be out here," Ikram remarked. "It's too dangerous."

Porter was about to respond when the Land Cruiser rounded a curve and the road ahead opened up to a Taliban blockade—two dusty Toyota Hilux technicals parked across the road, Russian PKM machine guns mounted to each bed. "It's a little late for that," Porter said.

Ikram was already reaching for the MP7 submachine gun stashed between the seats. Porter reached out, stilled his hand. "Take it easy." The driver stopped the Land Cruiser as they approached the blockade.

Through the windshield, Porter watched the machine gunner from one of the pickups step down from the bed of the truck to the road, slinging an AK-47 on his shoulder. He started toward the Land Cruiser, his partner in the back of the second Hilux holding his PKM's sights steady on Porter and his driver.

The first man closed the distance to the Land Cruiser. Leaned in through the driver's-side window, studying first Ikram, and then Porter. His eyes were dark, suspicious. He said nothing.

This is where you die, Porter thought. *Some nowhere road in this Stone Age country when you should already be on a plane home.*

The Taliban fighter seemed to look him over forever. Porter was conscious of a bead of sweat dripping down his forehead, ached to wipe it away. Resisted the urge, fearing any sudden move might provoke the man.

Finally, the fighter stepped back. Signaled to his buddies in the technicals to clear the road. "Follow us," he told Ikram in Pashto.

Beside Porter, Ikram shifted the Land Cruiser into gear as the fighter walked back to the trucks. When the trucks pulled off of the road and started farther down the highway, he fell in behind them, and Porter allowed himself to breathe again.

Don't get too comfy, he thought. *That was the easy part.*

They followed the technical along the highway for ten minutes or so. Then, abruptly, the lead Hilux turned off of the pavement onto the desert, following a rocky track that seemed to lead over a small, barren rise, though Porter couldn't yet tell what waited on the other side.

The second truck slowed and followed the first, and Porter and Ikram did the same, navigating the Land Cruiser slowly over the uneven terrain. The desert floor was littered with sharp rocks, any one of which might have punctured a tire, and Porter didn't like the odds of the Taliban offering them a ride back to Kabul if the Land Cruiser were to suffer a breakdown.

He felt suddenly very thirsty.

Beside him, Ikram said nothing as he guided the Land Cruiser along the path and over the hill behind the Taliban trucks. On the other side, hidden from view of the highway, Porter could see a small, mud-brick shack waiting for them, the only man-made object visible for miles, besides the two Taliban technicals and a third truck parked beside the shack's doorway.

The technicals pulled in and parked beside the third truck, and the machine gunner who'd looked them over on the highway gestured that the Land Cruiser should follow. Beside Porter, Ikram complied and brought the SUV to a halt, the engine ticking from the heat as the two men studied the shack, the trucks, the Taliban fighters.

"I should go with you," Ikram said.

"No. Stay with the truck," Porter replied, pressing the earpiece into his ear and turning on the radio hidden inside of his jacket. "If I'm not back in fifteen minutes, forget about me. Just try to get out alive."

Ikram nodded, though he and Porter both knew that if this meeting went sour, neither man was walking away with his life.

Porter stepped out of the Land Cruiser and crossed toward the shack and the handful of men milling outside, his eyes sweeping their faces, searching for the barest hint of treachery, the telltale sign of betrayal that might save his life.

A thick-necked man with an American-made M4 carbine slung around his neck stepped forward and motioned for him to stop. "No guns," he told Porter in Pashto, pointing to the Glock on Porter's hip.

Wanting Ikram to hear the conversation, Porter discreetly thumbed the transmit button sewn into his sleeve and waited for the hiss of static in his ear before pointing to the rifle necklaced around the man's neck. "You have a gun."

"No guns," the man repeated. "Ghul's orders."

"And if I say no?"

"Then you—" The man switched to English. "Fuck. Off."

"Do not give up your pistol," Ikram told Porter over the radio. "To do this is suicide."

Porter could understand the driver's point. Considering Muhammed Ghul's reputation, going into the house with nothing more than the knife clipped to the back of his belt was simply begging for a Darwin Award, but Porter hadn't come all this way to leave empty-handed.

"Fine," he said, slowly removing the Glock from its holster and handing it to the insurgent. The man accepted the pistol and stepped out of the way, gesturing that Porter should enter the shack.

Porter touched his watch as he walked through the open doorway, starting a timer. *Fifteen minutes,* he thought. *Though you'll know long before then how this is going to go.* The interior of the small building was dim, almost dark, after the relentless glare of the Afghan sun. On instinct, Porter took a half step to his left and pressed his back against the wall, his senses straining while he waited for his eyes to adjust to the gloom.

Slowly, his surroundings came into focus, his eyes scanning the room over mud walls, rug-covered floors, and a low sleeping mat in the corner before coming to rest on the shadowed figure in a jet-black turban seated at the wooden table to his right.

Muhammed Ghul.

The sight of the Taliban commander was enough to send Porter's hand to his hip and his fingers reaching for the reassuring contours of the Glock's worn grip, but the holster was empty, and all his hand found was air.

Ghul and Porter studied each other for a long beat. Finally, the Taliban commander shook a cigarette out from a pack on the table in front of him. "Tell me, do your masters at the CIA approve of this meeting?"

"They don't know about it," Porter replied. "I didn't think they'd approve of me having a face-to-face with the guy they've spent the last five years trying to kill."

Ghul scraped a match across the table, the flicker of flame illuminating hard eyes and a patchwork of scars and burns from one of the Agency's near misses. The man lit the cigarette, took a deep drag, and exhaled, the smoke rising lazily to hang beneath the low ceiling.

"To come here alone means you are either very brave or very desperate," Ghul said. "So tell me: what is it that an American spy needs from the Taliban?"

"I need you to kill someone for me," Porter said. He took the photograph of Abdul Nassim from his pocket and set it on the table in front of Ghul. Glanced at his watch as he waited for the man's reaction, surprised to find that he'd already been inside for five minutes. *Tick tock.*

Ghul stuck the cigarette between his lips, squinting at the picture through the smoke wafting around his head. "Why should I help you?"

"The man is Abdul Nassim," Porter told him. "A former captain in the Afghan National Army. He's responsible for killing many of your men. This is your chance at retribution. I'll tell you how to find him; all you have to do is pull the trigger. But I need you to do it quickly."

Ghul continued to study the photograph. "And what has he done to you, that your side wants him dead?"

"That's my business," Porter replied. "You don't need to worry about that. Just think about how much damage he's done to your people. I'm giving you an opportunity to make it right. And I'm willing to pay you to do it."

"How much are you offering, Mr. Porter?" Ghul asked.

"One hundred and fifty thousand dollars. Paid immediately in Bitcoin, untraceable. Just kill Abdul Nassim. And if he happens to have a computer drive on him, I'd love if you could destroy that, too."

"So we're friends now—is that it?"

"No," Porter said. "We're not friends. But it's better to have an intelligent enemy than a foolish ally."

Ghul crushed the cigarette out in the ashtray. Beside the cigarettes was a dusty notebook and a pen. The commander picked up the pen now and toyed with it. "An American who thinks like an Afghan," he mused. "No wonder you've been such a thorn in my side."

"Will you help me?" Porter asked. Knowing his fifteen minutes were nearly up.

Ghul clicked the pen, unclicked it again. "This war makes strange bedfellows," he said. "That much is truth. But whether I help you or not, you'll leave this country soon. And I will have plenty of time to hunt down my countrymen who betrayed us—with or without your help."

Porter opened his mouth to argue. "If it's money you're after, I can—"

Ghul stilled him with a raised palm. "I will kill this man for you, Mr. Porter," he said. "And I will accept your fee. But on one condition."

"What is it?" Porter asked.

Ghul clicked the pen again. Looked past Porter to his fighters at the door, gestured out toward the trucks. The men disappeared. Outside, Porter heard voices. Heard a sharp electronic squeal come through the radio in his ear, then cut silent. A truck door closed. More voices.

And then the door opened, and then Ghul's men returned, bracing Ikram between them. The ANA commando struggled, wide-eyed, but the men held him firm.

"Whoa," Porter said. "What the fuck is this?"

"You've killed many Taliban during your time in my country," Ghul told him. "I need to know that you can be trusted."

One of the fighters stepped away from Ikram. Thrust a pistol into Porter's hand. His own Glock 19, he realized.

"Kill this man," Ghul told him. "Prove your betrayal. And I swear to you, I will hold up my side of the bargain."

Porter looked down at his pistol. Sweat slick in his hands. At the doorway, Ikram fought for his life. Screamed Porter's name.

Porter studied the Glock, and was aware of every eye in the room watching him. Waiting to see what he would do.

20

KHYBER PASS, PAKISTAN/AFGHANISTAN BORDER

Hayes sat behind the wheel of the Toyota Corolla, the compact car's aged air conditioner fighting a losing battle against the stifling mid-morning heat. Up ahead, three men worked hard to push their stalled truck clear of the roadway, while a border guard in a green uniform and battered AK-47 lounged in the shade of a deodar cedar.

With traffic stopped until the men could move the truck, Hayes shifted the car into neutral and engaged the emergency brake. Pushing the earth-brown pakol hat Vonn had given him back on his head, Hayes grabbed a bottle of water from the passenger seat and cracked the cap. He drank deeply, his eyes following the curve of the roadway as it serpentined up through the craggy vastness of the mountains.

Unlike the more accessible caravan routes that crisscrossed the area, Khyber Pass had been used primarily for war. From Cyrus the Great to Genghis Khan, every invading army that had set their eyes on the riches of the Indian subcontinent had traveled this stretch of earth. Rising to a height of thirty-five hundred feet above sea level, the pass was a perilous crossing, and as he sat baking in the sun in his ancient Toyota, Hayes couldn't help but marvel at the determination of those ancient warriors.

Fighting in this part of the world was hard enough with helicopters and tanks, but to do it on foot—carrying everything you owned on your back—was beyond his ability to comprehend.

The air coming out of the vents was doing nothing more than stinking up the interior of the Corolla, and Hayes killed the engine, letting his mind wander back to the previous day's meeting with Mason Vonn—and the conversation with Seth Brooks that had followed.

"Absolutely not," the State Department man told Hayes, *when they'd reconvened after the meeting. "We are not dragging my wife into this mess."*

They met across the street from the Peshawar Zoo, on the grounds of the Peshawar Forest Institute, a leafy and sprawling campus that left plenty of space for anonymity. Brooks was still traveling in that fleet of Suburbans, but Hayes wasn't sure that mattered anymore. It wasn't the ISI he needed to worry about now; it was the CIA.

But even though he'd been married once to the Agency's chief psychologist in the region—and, according to Vonn, was still very much in love with her—Seth Brooks wasn't willing to call in any favors with his former wife, not on Hayes's behalf. Not to help Hayes locate Dominic Porter, at least.

"She's your ex-wife," Hayes told Brooks. "And anyway, don't you think she'd want to know which of the guys on her team of handpicked paramilitary operatives is turning traitor to the Taliban? Wouldn't that be useful information for the next psych eval?"

Brooks went red. "What does it matter to you?" he asked Hayes. "I thought you just wanted to get your friend out." He gestured across the campus to the pockmarked Toyota Corolla parked inconspicuously in the west parking lot—far away from Brooks's Suburbans, the keys already in Hayes's pocket. "I'm helping you do that, Adam. Shouldn't that be enough?"

It should, *the voice said*. This is about Nassim. Not Dominic Porter. If you can get Abdul out without losing your head, you should consider that a win.

The voice was right, Hayes figured. But knowing a CIA paramilitary operative was trying to kill his friend made Hayes kind of want to meet the guy. Have a conversation with him. Or maybe a little more.

"You do realize that by not going after Porter you're basically letting him skate for what he's done?" Hayes asked. "He'll go home with a bank account full of the Taliban's money and a trail of bodies behind him. Doesn't that bother you?"

"That's not my problem," Brooks said, unable to meet Hayes's eyes. "And it's not yours, either."

"But it's Jolene's problem, isn't it?"

"You said it before: she's my ex-wife," Brooks said, and there was finality in his voice. "That means her problems aren't mine anymore."

Back on the road, the men had their truck pushed clear of traffic, and with the vehicles ahead of the Corolla beginning to move, Hayes was reaching for the shifter when a man stepped out of the guard shack to his left and came walking over.

Hayes cursed beneath his breath, his eyes darting to the rearview mirror, searching for a way out, but with a line of cars behind him, Hayes was stuck. *Shit.* Before he could think of his next move, the man was at his window, tapping insistently against the glass and brandishing a badge from the Pakistani Inter-Services Intelligence agency.

He motioned for Hayes to roll down his window, and seeing no other choice, Hayes complied.

"Mr. Ash?" the man asked. "Robert Ash?"

Hayes forced his expression to remain neutral, though inside, he was cursing Seth Brooks again. *Pristine documents, my ass. You were blown the moment you set foot in Peshawar.*

He met the intelligence officer's eyes. "That's right."

"My name is Colonel Malik Tahir," the man said. "Would you kindly pull your car over to the guard house? I would like to treat you to a cup of chai."

"Since when does the ISI buy people chai?"

Tahir smiled, thin. "If you prefer, we can head back to Peshawar. Continue our conversation in my office."

Hayes glanced past the man. Beyond the guard house, the road rose high into the mountains—and on the other side, Hayes knew, was Afghanistan, achingly close. But the ancient Corolla didn't have the gumption for a high-speed getaway, and standing between Hayes and the border were not just Malik Tahir, but at least three border guards with AK-47s.

Hayes sighed. "On second thought, a nice cup of chai sounds wonderful about now."

"Excellent," Hayes replied. "If you'll follow me."

Hayes pulled the Corolla onto a patch of dirt in front of the guard house and cut the engine. Stepping out of the car, he forced a smile for Tahir, and followed him into the guard shack.

It was cooler inside, but the smell of unwashed feet and rotting trash permeated the small building. Hayes almost wished for the heat again.

"Please excuse the mess," Tahir said, ushering Hayes to the sole desk in the room and setting down two paper cups between them. "These men need a lesson in housekeeping."

"I hadn't noticed," Hayes said, sitting down opposite the man, but ignoring the chai. "Now, what can I do for you, Colonel?"

Tahir studied Hayes intently. "Your name is Robert Ash," he said. "You're an employee of the American State Department, and you intend to stay in our country for four days before leaving. Or that is the story you told the customs officer at Bacha Khan Airport this morning."

Hayes was suddenly conscious of the weight of the Glock 19 at his hip, and was thankful he'd taken it from Brooks's security detail that morning. *That pistol might be the only thing standing between you and a lonely death in these mountains,* the voice said.

"How does a State Department employee find himself in the Khyber Pass, Mr. Ash?" Tahir asked. "Surely your work here in Pakistan doesn't allow much time for sightseeing."

This isn't an accident, Hayes realized. The colonel had been waiting for him here. Had known he was coming. "How long have you been following me?" he asked. "And who put you on my tail?"

Tahir smiled. "Long enough that you shook my men outside of the Qissa Khwani Bazaar," he said. "A fine piece of evasion, I must admit. But surely you're aware that the Pearl Continental is notorious as a meeting place for men of your . . . aptitudes."

Curse you, Vonn. That hotel was too conspicuous by a mile.

"You met with a man at the Pearl," Tahir continued. "A man who's known to us to be affiliated with your Central Intelligence Agency. And now you're here, Mr. Ash, high in the mountains, trying to make your way to Afghanistan. Why, I wonder?"

Hayes studied the man, wondering if he was going to have to shoot his way out of this claustrophobic little building. Trying to figure his chances of evading the border guards with their assault rifles long enough to get a head start over the pass.

Tahir smiled, like he could read Hayes's thoughts. "You won't get far," he told Hayes. "Even if you kill me, my men are waiting for you, farther up the road. Your only way forward is to talk."

Hayes wasn't quite ready to give up on the Glock idea just yet. But he figured it couldn't hurt to try it the colonel's way.

"This is a humanitarian mission," he told Tahir. "I represent no nation or government interest. I'm just trying to rescue a friend."

He explained what he knew. About Nassim, about Porter. About the attack on the clinic in Maidan Wardak. The photograph.

"This man saved my life," he told Tahir. "I owe him everything. And now I'm the only chance he has at survival."

"Because an American is trying to kill him," Tahir said. "An American CIA. And you're willing to act against them."

"I don't know what's going on with the CIA," Hayes said. "Frankly, I don't care. I just want to rescue my friend."

He held the colonel's gaze. Waiting as Tahir studied him, mulling over his words. "You know it will be dangerous," Tahir said. "This part of the world—it is not like it was even a year ago, for your people. You will probably die if you go any farther."

"Maybe," Hayes said. "But I have to try."

Tahir pursed his lips. Hayes said nothing, waited for the colonel to make the next move. But when Tahir spoke next, his words nearly knocked Hayes out of his chair.

"It was your CIA who asked me to follow you," he told Hayes. "They know you are not Robert Ash, as do I. They wished to know who you spoke to in Peshawar, and where you went from there, and they are paying me handsomely to report this information back to them." He paused, and met Hayes's eyes. "But they are not paying me to detain you."

Hayes said nothing. *Is he—letting you go?*

"Be careful in the mountains, Mr. Ash," Tahir told him, his expression betraying nothing. "I hope for your friend's sake you're a lucky man."

He pushed back from the desk, and Hayes took his cue to do the same. Stood, and turned for the door, still not quite believing the ISI agent was allowing him through.

"Mr. Ash?" Tahir's words stopped him, and Hayes turned back reluctantly, half-expecting to find himself staring down the barrel of a gun.

But it was only the paper cup that Tahir was holding.

"Don't forget your chai," the colonel told Hayes. "I promise, it's very good."

21

JALALABAD, AFGHANISTAN

The convoy came at dusk, the white flag mounted to the bumper of the lead Toyota Hilux snapping in the wind as it turned off of the highway at the outskirts of the city. Compared to the asphalt that had carried the convoy this far, the roadway was rough, and the spring rains had washed away the gravel the locals used to fill the potholes. But despite the hazards, the driver kept his foot on the accelerator and raced north toward the Kabul River, the pickup bouncing and swaying like a ship in stormy seas as it approached a small collection of low concrete homes in the distance.

In the backseat of the technical, Muhammed Ghul squeezed the door handle, the jostling of the truck sending a lightning bolt of pain rushing up from the gunshot wound in his leg. He'd taken the bullet weeks prior, while fighting the Afghan National Army down south, and his body begged him to tell the driver to slow down. But Ghul was a proud man, and despite the pain that came with each jarring bump, his ego made it impossible to show any sign of weakness.

Never let them see you bleed, he thought, repeating the mantra he'd heard from his commander so many years before.

Shoving the pain aside, Ghul shook a cigarette from the pack of Marlboro Reds and lit it from a patinaed Zippo. He took a deep drag and snapped the lighter shut, his dark eyes dropping to the worn Afghan Commando crest and inscription embossed on the front of the lighter. Like most of the men in the truck, Ghul couldn't read, but before he'd taken the lighter from its owner, he'd asked the dying man what it said.

"It is our motto," the man had gasped. "The Lions of Kabul."

"Lions?" he'd asked.

"Yes, th-that is what they called us."

"It is easy to be a lion when you have the Americans to protect you," Ghul had said, pocketing the lighter and reaching for the Glock 23 holstered on the commando's hip. "But you're all alone now."

The man had cursed at him and tried to fight him off, but Ghul had easily brushed his hands away, stripped the pistol from its holster, and rose to his feet.

"You will die on your knees in the dirt," he'd told the man. "Tell me—do you still feel like a lion?"

The compound sat on the outskirts of Jalalabad, not far from the Kabul River. This was the address that Porter had given Ghul, the home of Abdul Nassim's father. Along with the address, Porter had given Ghul aerial drone photographs and satellite imagery of the Nassim house and its surroundings, a handful of modest dwellings bordering an orange grove.

"I wouldn't expect much resistance," Porter had told the Taliban commander. "Maybe a stray dog or two. The men are all fighting your people in the mountains; it should be just families and maybe some elders waiting for you."

Ghul hoped the CIA operative was correct. Most Afghan men of military age were in battle already somewhere, whether on the side of the ANA or the Taliban. Still, if Adbul Nassim truly was hiding here, he'd expect someone to come looking, eventually. And Nassim was ex-ANA, a captain. Ghul wasn't taking any chances.

Picking up the radio that lay on the seat beside him, he spoke instructions to the men in the three trucks behind the lead Hilux.

"We surround the home," he told the drivers. "North, south, east, and west. Destroy anything that moves."

In the passenger seat in front of him, the fighter checked the magazine of his AK-47. Ghul reached unconsciously for the pistol at his belt.

The CIA operative had paid for blood; he would get what he paid for.

"Show no mercy," Ghul told his men, as the convoy sped closer. "Let no one escape with his life."

Somewhere in the distance, a dog began to bark.

22

JALALABAD, AFGHANISTAN

At first, Nassim believed it was another false alarm. Another wasted burst of adrenaline mixed with fear, another half-frantic scramble for the M4 carbine he still carried with him, the Emerson CQC-6 combat knife he still kept at his hip, long after his fighting days with the ANA were over. He'd heard the dogs barking up the road again—an incessant, infuriating chorus piercing the twilight—and had tried to convince himself that this disturbance, like every other so far, was a dud.

A stray cow wandering on the road. An airplane overhead, somewhere in the distance. It didn't take much to get the dogs riled. And Abdul Nassim was tired of leaping to attention every time the animals set off barking again.

Nassim groaned, forced himself upright from the *toshak* on which he'd been resting in the living room of his father's home. Met his wife's eyes and could see exhaustion there, too. They'd been running for days now, scared for their lives. The fear was taking its toll.

"Probably just the neighbor's children," Nassim said. "You've seen they like to kick their ball until well after dark."

Freshta nodded, but Nassim could see she wasn't convinced. He lingered, torn between trying to reassure her and going to check the window, when Zarah burst in from outside.

"*Trucks,*" she said, breathless. "Many of them, Papa. No headlights."

Instantly Nassim was on his feet. Reaching for the rifle propped against the wall in the corner, already hearing the engines approach. Cursing himself for his complacency.

"Fetch Babajon and your brothers," Nassim told Zarah. "Hurry. Like we practiced."

Wordless, his daughter hurried past him toward the bedrooms at the rear of the house. Nassim checked his rifle. Strained his ears for the sounds of the trucks, praying they still had enough time.

Across the living room, Freshta walked quickly to the front door that Zarah had neglected, in her distraction, to close. Nassim watched his wife glance briefly outside into the day's last light, then close the door and secure the bolt.

She was holding the pistol he'd given her, the American M9 Beretta he prayed she would never have to use.

"Stay behind me," he'd told her, when he'd taught her to

fire. "Let me do the shooting. Save your ammunition until you truly need it."

Left unspoken, but understood, was the grim truth that the time might come that Freshta would need that ammunition for herself, for their children. The Taliban were ruthless, both parents knew. Better to die as a family than let Zarah and the boys be dragged away by the fighters as captives.

Now, Nassim could see the fear in his wife's eyes, but determination, also. *Whatever happens,* he knew, *whoever comes through that door will not get their hands on our babies.*

"Go," he told Freshta, pulling her away from the door. He knelt at the window that looked out onto the front yard, leveled his rifle against the window frame and squinted out into the gloom. Patted the pocket that held the thumb drive he'd taken from Akhtar Mansour, and tried to breathe steady, calm his beating heart. "I'll make sure you have enough time to escape."

The convoy dispersed as it approached the target. The last daylight all but gone now, the only light outside from the windows of the homes in the compound, and a few stars above. The glow from the instrument panels inside of each truck.

The drivers had extinguished their headlights as they approached the target. They'd slowed, but not much; Ghul had instructed them to memorize the geography around Ramze Nassim's home before setting out on the mission.

Now, the trucks separated as they entered the compound, taking up positions around the sides and the rear of the Nassim house. In the lead truck, Ghul's driver headed for the front door, slowing to a stop outside of the low concrete wall that encircled the home.

Ghul drew his pistol, the Glock he'd taken from the dying ANA commando. "No one leaves the house," he spoke into the radio. "Wait for my signal."

He opened the pickup's rear door and stepped out onto the hardpack dirt road. Wincing again as the pain from the gunshot wound seared his leg. Trying to mask the pain so that his men wouldn't see, as they climbed out of the technical beside him, cradling their rifles.

In the rear bed of the Hilux, the gunner swiveled the PKM to face the building's front door, ready to unleash hell on whoever tried to resist what was coming.

Ghul checked to make sure his men were prepared. Then he walked to the gate, his pistol at the ready, studying the building beyond.

A dim light burned in the windows near the door, but Ghul could detect no movement inside. It was too early for the occupants to be sleeping; Ghul wondered if they'd heard the trucks approach. If they realized what it meant.

He wondered if Dominic Porter was wrong—if Abdul Nassim hadn't fled here with his family, but somewhere else instead. It would be Ramze Nassim's bad luck if his son wasn't here; this night would not go well for anyone inside the home.

Ghul locked eyes with the two fighters beside him. Nodded toward the front door. Wordless, the fighters advanced on the home, their AK-47s at the ready. Ghul tensed as the men approached the door, bracing for gunfire. Resistance of some kind from within. But nothing moved, anywhere. The whole compound was silent; even the dogs had stopped barking.

The night seemed to wait for whatever was coming next.

The lead fighter knocked on the front door. Still, there was no movement inside. The fighter knocked again, waited. This time, when nobody answered, he kicked the door in.

In Ghul's experience, this was when people started to panic. As much as a target tried to stay silent, it took nerve to keep quiet when your door was kicked down. When men with assault rifles were suddenly inside your home.

It was about now, Ghul knew, that anyone hidden inside would begin to doubt their hiding place. It was now, usually, that the gunfire began. Or the screaming. Or both.

But nobody fired on the Taliban fighters as they entered the Nassim house. Nobody screamed from within. Ghul lingered outside and listened to the shouts of the men as they searched the small residence. Listened to the crash of furniture being overturned, the tinkle of glass breaking. He heard no voices but his fighters'. Still no screams.

Was it possible Porter was wrong?

As his men searched, Ghul scanned the handful of other homes surrounding the Nassim residence. Here and there, a face silhouetted in a window, quickly drawing back when they realized Ghul saw them. Ghul could sense the fear all around him; the whole compound *reeked* of it. Could sense eyes everywhere, watching him, waiting to run.

"Sir." One of the fighters appeared in Ramze Nassim's

doorway. His rifle slung across his chest, held lazily in one hand. "There's nobody here. The house is empty."

Shit.

"Search every house," Ghul instructed. "Every room. Somebody here knows Abdul Nassim. We will not leave until we know where he is."

23

Gripping the M4 with sweat-slick fingers, Abdul Nassim had shepherded his family—Freshta, Zarah, his two boys, his father—quickly through the orange grove and away from the compound. Flinching when his youngest son had tripped on the uneven ground, stumbled, stifled a cry.

"Bilal," Nassim had whispered urgently, pulling his son to his feet with his free hand, guiding him forward through the dark rows of trees. "We must be quiet now. Please."

The boy was six years old, terrified and disoriented. Nassim could hear his muffled sobs and gasps for breath through the whisper of the branches of the trees around them. Could hear his father's heavy footfalls as he struggled to keep up, his every sharp intake of air.

"Leave me behind," Ramze had urged Abdul. *"I'll only slow you down."*

But Nassim would hear none of it. "This is my mess," he'd replied. "I won't let them hurt you for something I've done."

He wasn't sure he could keep that promise, not forever. But there had been no way he was leaving his father behind to face the American murderer on his own.

They'd escaped from the house just in time, just as the trucks entered the compound. Freshta and Zarah hurrying the boys, Ramze following as quickly as he could on his cane. Abdul bringing up the rear, when he was sure that the others were safe. That he wouldn't need to buy time with the M4 at his side.

They'd snuck across the narrow laneway to the house next door, the home of Shamal Aziz, who'd lost a leg fighting against the Soviets forty years before and very quickly grown disillusioned of war, who'd agreed to help Nassim and his family should the Americans come after them.

Only then, Nassim hadn't been sure it was Americans who'd rolled into the compound. He'd glanced down the laneway as he followed his family into Shamal Aziz's home, caught sight of a white Toyota pickup truck pulling to a stop behind his father's home. A machine gun mounted atop the rear bed, a figure in shadows crouching at the gun.

The Americans didn't use technicals like that, Nassim had known; that was Afghan equipment. When the American murderer did come, Nassim had expected he would arrive in a helicopter, or at least a Humvee.

Who had come looking for them?

There was no time to worry about that. If Nassim's family didn't move quickly, they would find out soon enough.

Shamal Aziz was waiting in his living room. Nassim had only met his father's neighbor a couple of days before, but the old mujahideen had not hesitated to offer to help, after Ramze Nassim had explained his son's predicament.

Aziz was a tall man, unbowed by age or the mortar wound that had taken his right leg many years before. He carried an ancient bolt-action M1891 Mosin that appeared as weathered as its owner, though Nassim was certain that the old rifle was still just as dangerous as the man who held it.

Aziz met Nassim's eyes over the heads of the children. He ruffled Bilal's hair, muttered something to the boy, his voice calm. Then cocking his head to Nassim, he gestured toward the rear of the small house. He didn't have to remind Nassim to be quiet. Any noise now might bring the intruders— whoever they were—to the door.

It would not take long before the intruders found the house next door empty. Nassim hoped to be far away before that happened. He gathered the children and nudged them after Aziz, who led the family to a narrow door that led out to a high-walled rear courtyard. At the opposite end of the courtyard was a metal gate; beyond, the orange grove.

Quickly, silently, Nassim and his family followed Aziz across the courtyard to the gate. As they neared, Aziz held up his hand that they should stop. He went to the gate alone, his rifle at the ready. Peered out into the night. Finally he turned back, found Nassim again, and nodded.

Nassim hurried to the gate to join Aziz. Followed the older man's gaze. Ten yards away was the orange grove: dark and relatively safe, full of places to hide. Twenty yards to the right of the gate was the rear end of one of the technicals, its machine gun aimed directly at the Nassim home, the gunner behind it smoking a cigarette, so close that Nassim could smell the tobacco.

The gun could easily be swiveled to face Aziz's house, Nassim knew, or the orange grove. If the gunner caught wind, he could cut the whole family to pieces.

But there was no time to think of such things. Next door, Nassim could hear shouting. The gunner's radio crackled, the words indistinct. But Nassim knew the men who'd come looking for him would soon broaden their search. The window of opportunity was rapidly closing.

Nassim slipped the gate unlocked. Nodded to Freshta, and stepped aside to let his wife step through. Zarah came next, then Bilal and Payam, and Nassim hardly dared to breathe as they dashed across to the grove, the gunner still focused on the house, oblivious to the escape.

Ramze Nassim passed through the gate next, slower than the children, but again without the gunner taking notice. Finally, it was Nassim's turn. He turned to Aziz. Dared to whisper. *"We have room for one more."*

Aziz shook his head. "They won't hurt me," he replied. "Besides—" He scowled, gestured at his rifle. "I've lived too long to let a pack of dogs drive me from my home."

Nassim hesitated. Wanted to argue, but there was no time. And he suspected that Aziz wouldn't listen anyway.

Instead, he clapped the older man on the shoulder. "My family thanks you," he said. "May Allah protect you."

Then he started after his family.

The orange grove seemed to stretch for miles, and every sound as loud as a bomb exploding. Nassim shepherded his family through the long rows of trees, expecting at every instant to be cut down by gunfire from behind, run down by the intruders in their pickup trucks, torn to shreds by their machine guns.

But nobody fired at them, and no truck engines roared. Nassim urged his children forward, held out an arm to steady his father. Thanked Allah that he'd married Freshta, found a wife who could hold her own on a night like tonight.

It was Freshta who led them to the edge of the orange grove. To the narrow dirt path beyond, to the ancient, battered Mitsubishi Pajero that sat waiting for them in the shadows. The SUV belonged to Aziz; he'd refused money for it. Had looked uncomfortable by Nassim's thanks, even.

"It will run if you need it," he'd told Nassim, avoiding his gaze. Glancing back to the courtyard, where he'd been regaling Bilal and Payam with stories of the old war, with glimpses of his crude prosthetic leg. "But let's hope that you don't."

Now, Nassim hoped the old man was right. He helped

Zarah and the boys into the rear of the truck as Freshta helped his father into the passenger seat. Opened the driver's-side door and climbed in behind the wheel, was just pulling the door closed when the first of the shots rang out in the distance, somewhere on the other side of the grove.

24

JALALABAD, AFGHANISTAN

ome now, father." Ghul smiled down at the old man, who lay bleeding on the floor before him, glaring up at the Taliban commander and the fighters who'd trained their AK-47s on him. "Surely you know something about the family next door."

The man spat. "What family?" he replied. "It is only the old man who lives there, Ramze. I've never seen anyone else."

Ghul pursed his lips. "We know that's not true," he told the old man. "We found evidence of more than one person when we searched the house just now. A meal cooked for a family. Children's clothes. We know that Ramze Nassim had guests."

The man's expression didn't change; he stared up at Ghul

with undisguised hate. "I am an old man," he said. "I mind my own business. You could perhaps learn a lesson from this."

Ghul laughed. Straightened, nodded to the fighter at his right, who leaned forward and brought the butt of his rifle down again, hard, into the man's stomach. Forcing the air out of the man's lungs, doubling him over, gasping, coughing. Cursing.

Inside, Ghul struggled to contain his frustration. Time was wasting. The house next door had been empty, but Ghul could see signs of a rapid escape—food still on the table, no luggage packed. The lights left on, but no one to be found, anywhere.

The house next door had seemed a logical place to begin the search. And though the old man who'd answered the door had come armed, it had not taken much effort to relieve him of the old rifle he carried, nor the prosthetic leg on which he stood. The man might have been a fighter in his youth; he still carried himself with that fierce determination. But he was no match for an army of young Taliban fighters out for blood.

Still, he wasn't talking. And the Nassim family was still out there somewhere, unfound. There were more houses to search in the compound. More neighbors to interrogate. This old man was beginning to get on Ghul's nerves.

"This family—" Ghul began. "They have betrayed our country. They are enemies of Afghanistan." He gestured to the old man's missing leg. "You've bled for this land, father. Why would you want to defend its traitors?"

The old man's face twisted. "Who is the traitor?" he asked.

"You, who murder your countrymen? Who've made yourself a dog to an American master? Who is the traitor among us?"

Ghul sighed. "You will die tonight," he told the man, drawing the knife from his belt. "It is your choice how much you suffer beforehand."

The old man spat again. This time, flecked with blood. "I have lived with honor. Do what you like."

"Suit yourself." Ghul shrugged. Knelt beside the man's intact leg, brought the knife to his Achilles' tendon. "This will be a long night for you, I'm afraid."

He leaned forward, about to make the cut, when one of the fighters rushed in from the rear of the house, the courtyard. "Sir," he said, breathless. "I found this."

He was holding a stuffed animal, a child's teddy bear.

"Near the rear gate," the fighter continued. "There's a grove beyond. They could have escaped into the trees before we saw them."

Shit.

Ghul turned to stand. Already directing his men to the grove, the old man on the floor already forgotten. He didn't sense the man lunging for him until he'd taken hold of the knife, wrenching it from his grip and propelling it down with surprising strength into the top of his boot.

Ghul screamed in pain and surprise as the knife sliced through the boot and into his flesh. The old man wasn't waiting to savor the victory; he tugged the knife out again, wrenched it free from Ghul's grip. Slashed, wildly, at Ghul, tearing the fabric of his jacket, before turning to swing the knife up toward another fighter nearby, who swore and scrambled back as the blade pierced his belly.

The room seemed to explode: gunshots at close range, a powerful flash, and a deafening roar. The old fighter fell backward and didn't move. The knife slipped out of his hand. The fighter who'd brought the teddy bear stood above him, the barrel of his rifle aimed at the man's chest.

Ghul's ears rang. Blood oozed from the top of his boot. The fighter who'd been stabbed gripped his stomach, groaning, beginning to turn pale. Ghul shook his head clear, fought off the pain.

"Find them!" he shouted, gesturing to the back door. His words were muffled in his ears, like he was underwater. "Find them, now."

25

EAGLE BASE
KABUL, AFGHANISTAN

The phone rang at last, a few minutes past nine in the evening, jolting Dominic Porter out of the haze he'd been comfortably wallowing in since popping the Tramadol sometime before sunset.

Rubbing his eyes, he rolled over in his bed. Reached for the phone on the night table, already anticipating the voice on the other end of the line. Already savoring the good news.

"This is Porter," he said. "Did it happen?"

He'd returned to Eagle Base after meeting Mohammed Ghul, found himself with nothing to do but wait. Wait, and watch the Agency pack up and prepare to abandon ship, the base already a ghost town and growing emptier by the hour.

Wait, and try not to think about the man he'd sacrificed to Ghul in order to guarantee what he'd done in Maidan Wardak would never make it Stateside.

He'd driven back to Eagle Base from the meeting alone, though that old Land Cruiser already felt full of ghosts. Though he could still feel Ikram's presence around him, smell the driver's sweat. Could still see the look of confusion, and then desperation, on his face when he'd realized that Porter wasn't going to save him. The terror as he'd stared down the barrel of Porter's gun.

Porter had closed his eyes when he'd pulled the trigger, but he'd known he would see Ikram's face anyway, seared into the backs of his eyelids. Hear the commando's screams echoing in his mind for the rest of his life.

The war would be over soon. Abdul Nassim would be dead, and Porter could go back to America clean. Go home and sleep for a month and forget everything, return to the person he'd been before he could even find Kabul on a map, but about a million dollars richer.

Except he couldn't sleep. Couldn't close his eyes without hearing those screams. Only the Tramadol helped, and just barely, sending him into a stupor that at least shut his mind down for a couple of hours. It was the best he could manage right now. But this phone call, Porter knew, was about to change everything.

On the other end of the line, Muhammed Ghul coughed. "We were not successful," he said.

Porter blinked. Tried to clear his head of the opioid haze.

Wondered if he was dreaming, if this was some kind of nightmare. "What do you mean?" he asked. "Nassim *had* to be there. The intelligence—"

"Was correct," Ghul interrupted. "But the family escaped us."

"E-escaped you." Now, Porter wanted to throw up. "Well, *find* them."

"We are trying. My men are patrolling the highways as we speak. We have interrogated every one of the neighbors and extracted very little useful information. Nobody seems able to tell us where they will go next."

"It's an old man and a couple of kids," Porter said. "I've paid a huge price for you to get this job done. Failure is not acceptable; do you understand?"

"You will get what you're paying for," Ghul replied. "I assure you; we are not finished looking. They cannot stay hidden forever."

"We said the same thing about bin Laden," Porter told him. "Turns out your country's more full of hidey-holes than we thought. Get to work."

He ended the call. Rolled over in bed, stared up at the ceiling. Listened to the whine of the old air-conditioning unit, wanting nothing more than to double his dose of the Tramadol, slip away again until Ghul really had finished the job.

But no. If you wanted something done right, as always, you had to do it yourself.

Porter forced himself out of bed. Pulled on his BDUs and

a wrinkled T-shirt from the floor. Downed the glass of water on his nightstand and clipped the Glock 19 to his belt. He laced up his boots and started for the door, wondering who was on duty tonight at the TOC, and if any of them owed him any favors.

26

NEW DELHI, INDIA

More rain. Endless, driving sheets of it, battering the city for weeks at a time. Months. And Apollo with a stomach flu.

Seth Brooks suspected it was the marinade on the steak Adam Hayes had given him that was doing it, rendering his Doberman's insides into a molten lava disaster zone. *One more reason to hate the guy,* he thought, hurriedly leashing the dog as he zipped up his raincoat, heading out again into the monsoon.

Of course, it wasn't Hayes's fault that Apollo wouldn't do his business in the yard, that the damn dog demanded a walk every time he needed to poop, but Brooks was almost grateful for the excuse to get out, truth be told. He'd had a thought running through his head since Peshawar, and it was time to do something about it.

The streets were nearly empty at this time of night, and Brooks pulled the hood of his raincoat over his head as he let Apollo lead him out through the front gate and into the storm. The dog hurried to a patch of scrub beneath the banana trees in the alley, and Brooks looked away to give him some privacy while he did what needed doing. With all business completed, Apollo turned out of the alley again, and began pulling Brooks back toward the front gate and the shelter of the house beyond, but tonight, Brooks had another idea.

"Come on, boy," he told the Doberman. "We could both use some exercise."

Though Brooks had moved out of the home he'd shared with Jolene and Daisy after the divorce, he hadn't moved far—only a few blocks, in fact, and still comfortably within a short drive of the city's diplomatic enclave, where both the U.S. Embassy and Daisy's American Embassy School were located. He'd wanted to stay close to Daisy, remain in her life—and he'd secretly hoped that maintaining proximity to Jolene would somehow convince her to take him back, though so far it hadn't quite worked out that way.

Still, it was only a few minutes' walk from Brooks's house to Jolene's, and once Apollo had accepted the fact that they weren't going back inside just yet, he allowed Brooks to lead him down the dark residential streets, probably already anticipating a snuggle with Daisy on the other end.

Jolene's house, like Brooks's, was protected by a security wall, with a camera and intercom system installed at the front entrance. Brooks led Apollo to the gate and pressed the button to call inside the house. Lowered his hood slightly so that the camera could see him, and waited as the intercom dialed.

A click. And then a voice, but it wasn't Jolene's. "Can I help you?" A man, a deep voice, guarded. American. The voice of a man who felt comfortable answering the door at 9:30 at night in a house where he didn't live.

Brooks tried to ignore the thoughts already racing through his mind. Cleared his throat and pushed back the hood a little further. "I'm here for Jolene," he told the voice. "I'm her husband."

Ex-husband, but the voice, whoever he was, didn't push it. "Just hold on."

The rain seemed to get harder. Soaking through Brooks's jeans, the soles of his shoes. He glanced up at the camera again, aware of how he must look—the disheveled, drowned-rat former lover, banging on the castle door in the middle of the night. He pulled his hood over his head again.

"Seth?" Jolene's voice, this time. "It's not your night with Daisy; what are you—"

"I need to talk to you," he replied. "Privately."

"*Seth*. It's nearly ten. Can't this wait?"

"I don't think so," Brooks said. "It's about Dominic Porter."

A pause. A long pause.

Then: "Give me a second."

Brooks expected his ex-wife to unlock the door, buzz him into the yard, the dry warmth of the house. Waited for the familiar click of the front gate unlocking, dreading the inevitable meeting with the owner of the voice, but hoping that Daisy might still be awake, at least.

But the gate didn't buzz open, and Brooks was about to call back to the house on the intercom when it swung open in front of him, instead, and Jolene slipped out to the street, fending off Apollo's nuzzles of greeting as she buttoned her rain jacket.

"We couldn't do this inside?" Brooks asked.

Jolene glanced back toward the house, perhaps unconsciously. "That's not a good idea," she said. "It's not a good time."

Brooks nodded. "Who is he?"

"Who—" Jolene flushed. Regained herself. "Seth. You had to know this would happen eventually."

Brooks said nothing. Debated with himself whether he should just turn around with Apollo and go home. He'd half hoped that this meeting would impress Jolene, would convince her there was maybe still some worth in trying to make things work. But clearly, that train had already left the station.

Jolene's face softened. "Look, I'm sorry. I didn't want you to find out this way. I was going to . . . tell you. Eventually."

"Eventually."

Jolene looked down the street. "You wanted to talk about Porter," she said.

He nodded. "I know what happened in Maidan Wardak. Do you?"

A pause. "I know there was an attack. A Taliban medical clinic, right?"

"Perpetrated by Dominic Porter," Brooks said. "An

unsanctioned hit, ostensibly on Taliban fighters inside the clinic. Except it was more than that, Jolene."

Jolene didn't reply. Watched him, her expression inscrutable.

"There's a witness," Brooks continued. "There's photographic proof that Porter was there. And according to a source in the Afghan National Army, he was there to meet with a Taliban money guy. He's been selling our weapons to the other side for cash."

He expected Jolene to scoff at the allegation. To immediately leap to discredit everything Brooks had told her. But she didn't.

"Why are you telling me this?" she asked.

"Did you know?" he replied. "Did you know Porter was running missions unsupervised? That he's been betraying our allies to the Taliban? Do you know about this, Jolene?"

"No, I didn't know." Her face darkened. She glanced up and down the street, as though somebody might be watching them. Listening. For all Brooks knew, they were. "You think I'd just sit on something like that, Seth? If I knew one of our guys was a *traitor*?"

Brooks wanted to believe her. She could sure make her case. But she was the psychologist, he reminded himself. Best to tread carefully.

"My eval of Dominic Porter was one of the scariest things I've ever seen," she continued. "That man is completely gone off the deep end—ethically, morally. He's a ticking time bomb, and he's probably on drugs. I recommended he be removed from duty immediately."

"So what happened?"

"Overruled." Jolene shook her head. "You have to understand, Seth, I don't just get *overruled*. Not in my position. Not unless someone way, *way* above my pay grade wants it done."

"Someone in Langley."

"Exactly. Whatever Porter's doing, he has good friends to insulate him. And that's what they're doing." She sighed. "So, you tell me he's gone rogue and sold out the Afghan Army for blood money, I'm not surprised. I just don't know what you expect me to do about it."

"Stop him."

"I *can't*. I don't have the power; not when Langley's involved," she said. "Listen, I'm sorry. I know you think I'm some CIA superspy, but I have bosses like everyone else. And sometimes they make really shitty decisions."

"So you're willing to let Porter go," Brooks replied. "Let him walk for what he's done over there. You're okay with that." He glanced up at the house. "You'd be okay if Daisy found out?"

"Oh, fuck you, Seth. Are you threatening me?"

"No," he said. "I'm not. I just want to know if you care."

"Of course I care. Porter gives me nightmares. I just can't *do* anything about it."

Brooks squared his shoulders. Looked her in the eye. "Okay," he said exhaling. "But what if you *could*?"

27

B rooks hadn't given Hayes much in the way of provisions to make it over Khyber Pass, and even less in the way of protection.

A beat-up old Corolla, the voice complained. *A few bottles of water. Not even an extra magazine for the Glock. Would it have killed him to at least give us some body armor?*

"Beggars can't be choosers," Hayes told it. "Just be glad we made it this far."

He'd been replaying the conversation with Colonel Tahir in his mind since leaving the guard hut high in the Khyber Pass, and even as he approached the medieval gates that would mark his entry into Afghanistan, Hayes still couldn't quite make sense of what the colonel had told him.

Someone within the CIA had paid Tahir to monitor Hayes—but not stop him. That meant the Agency cared enough about what he was doing to keep tabs, but not enough to intervene.

Or maybe they want to see where you lead them.

He figured it didn't matter, in the end. All that mattered was finding Abdul Nassim and getting him out of the country. The CIA could deal with the rest on its own.

The only problem was that Hayes had no idea how he was going to extract Nassim. Abdul hadn't made contact again since the night of the attack, and Hayes couldn't even be sure if his friend was still alive, much less where he'd disappeared to. Moreover, the Corolla wouldn't work as a rendition tool; it had barely made it over the Spīn Ghar mountains once, and jammed full of Nassim and his family, Hayes had no confidence it could survive a return trip.

You're going to need supplies, the voice said. *And you're going to need a plan.*

But first, Hayes knew he would need sleep. He'd been running on adrenaline since Nassim had called him at the Inter-Continental in Mumbai. Now, Hayes was running on fumes.

Just get somewhere quiet. Grab a few zees. Then figure out how to find Nassim.

He'd arrived at the border city of Torkham, the busiest port of entry between Afghanistan and Pakistan, and though it was well into the wee hours of the night, the medieval gates at the border were still crowded with people lined up on the

Afghanistan side, carrying their belongings on their backs or tied to the tops of their vehicles, an exodus of humanity fleeing for safer ground.

Unfortunately for the would-be evacuees, the Taliban had already taken control of the border checkpoint, and as Hayes drove closer to the gates, he could see dozens of the fundamentalist fighters standing guard, all of them armed with AK-47 rifles. Fortunately, most of the Taliban seemed to be occupied keeping their own citizens from crossing into Pakistan, and Hayes waited until an altercation broke out on the opposite side, drawing the attention of everyone Hayes could see holding a Kalashnikov.

As stealthily as one could in an ancient Corolla with apparent muffler issues, Hayes motored toward the gates and through, keeping his head down and in shadow, hoping nobody would make him for an American.

He could feel eyes on him from the crowd as he drove past, but no one seemed to care enough to stop him, and he continued into Afghanistan without being bothered.

Nobody cares if you come into this country, the voice observed. *But just see what they do when you try to leave.*

The city of Torkham had once been a strategy supply depot for American forces during the war. But if Hayes needed any reminder that times had changed in this part of the world, the turbaned fighters and black flags posted up outside of the old American base proved he was in Taliban country now.

The realization sent a sharp stab of anxiety down his spine, and Hayes knew he wouldn't get any rest until he'd put some distance between himself and this place. He followed

Asian Highway 1 north past a line of Humvees now bearing spray-painted Taliban insignia while still sporting American-made heavy machine guns. The evidence of America's hasty withdrawal was on full display: pallets of bottled water, pyramids of MRE rations, and industrial-sized tubs of cooking oil lined the side of the road. At one time, each item had fueled America's war effort, and now it was being used by the enemy to reverse twenty years of progress with alarming speed.

Never mind that. Just focus on staying alive.

Hayes drove away from the border crossing, grateful for the cover of darkness that would shield him from any prying Taliban eyes. The map emptied out for a ways as the highway wound deeper into Afghanistan, he knew; somewhere along the roadside there would be a place to hide out and recover.

But sleep wasn't in Hayes's future, not right away. As he followed the highway away from Torkham, his phone began to ring from the passenger seat. Frowning, Hayes reached over. Accepted the call without slowing the car. "Hayes."

"Still alive?"

Hayes recognized the voice. "Brooks," he replied. "I was just thinking about how grateful I am for this broken-down heap of a car. You're a real pal."

Brooks chuckled. "I can do you one better," he said. "How about a helicopter?"

"I'm listening."

"I have a spec-ops team and a chopper at your disposal," Brooks said. "Waiting for you in Jalalabad. All ready to help get your buddy out of Afghanistan."

Hayes pursed his lips. "And what's the catch?"

"The catch?" Brooks pretended to be surprised, but he was a hell of a bad actor. "No catch, Adam. You just have to agree to kill Dominic Porter."

Porter?

"I thought you didn't care about Porter. What changed?"

"Call it a crisis of conscience. Porter needs to be stopped, and you're the guy to do it."

Right, Hayes thought. "Who's supplying the helo?"

"The Taliban. From what I hear, they've got a hangar full of our birds at the old FOB. They just don't have anyone who can fly them."

"And the team? Who are they?"

"Contractors," Brooks said. "All ex-FAST guys. Don't worry; they're switched on."

Hayes frowned. The Drug Enforcement Agency's Foreign-Deployed Advisory and Support Teams *were* technically Special Ops members, he knew. They just weren't military.

Rangers would be better, the voice said. *Delta Force—hell, even a Navy SEAL.*

Beggars can't be choosers, Hayes told the voice again.

"Do we even know where Porter is?" he asked Brooks. "Is he still even in-country?"

"Eagle Base, last I heard. You won't be able to get to him there, but don't worry, I'm sure he won't sit still for long."

Hayes said nothing. Drove, the Corolla's dim headlights barely piercing the gloom. He fought a wave of exhaustion.

"I'm giving you men, equipment, and a helicopter," Brooks said. "How exactly were you planning to do this on your own?"

"I figured I'd think of something," Hayes replied.

"Yeah, well, now you don't have to. So what do you think?"

Hayes closed his eyes, the pull of sleep seductive. He forced himself awake. "Let me at least meet these guys," he said. "I want to make sure they can keep up."

28

I t was nearly dawn by the time Hayes coaxed the Corolla into the outskirts of Jalalabad, the ancient Toyota sounding as though it was only a few miles from death. Hayes had driven slowly from the border, both to conserve the car's laboring engine and to avoid drawing attention from any Taliban patrols.

Good thing there's a helicopter waiting, the voice said. *This heap won't make it another twenty miles.*

Jalalabad lay forty miles from the border with Pakistan, a center of trade and agriculture. It was Afghanistan's fifth largest city, with a population of around three hundred and fifty thousand. For many years during the war, its airport had housed American military units at Forward Operating Base

Fenty, including the 101st Airborne and the 1st Armored Division's Combat Aviation Brigade, whose "Heavy Cav" squadron flew AH-64D Apache helicopters and RQ-7 reconnaissance drones from the airfield.

But the 101st and 1st Armored were long gone now, and as Hayes approached the airport in the little Toyota, he could see no signs of life from beyond the barbed-wire fencing. No lights, no movement, and certainly no sign of a helicopter.

"They'll be waiting for you," Brooks had promised. "But they won't wait forever. It's open season on Americans, in case you haven't heard."

Again, Hayes was grateful for the cover of darkness as he surveyed the airfield. The airport served domestic flights as well as military purposes, but Hayes avoided the main terminal grounds and idled the Corolla toward the remains of FOB Fenty, a long, low complex of repurposed concrete hangars and temporary modular structures, crumbling and abandoned, tagged with graffiti and pockmarked with bullet holes from small-arms fire.

The Corolla's engine was in its death throes, the noise seeming to echo around the empty complex like thunder. Hayes pulled the car off of the road and killed the engine. Stepped out into the predawn stillness, drawing his Glock and peering into the shadows at the fence line that formed a perimeter around the airfield. It didn't take long before he found a break in the fence, a ragged hole someone had made with wire cutters, probably to loot the base. Nobody had bothered to fix it, and Hayes took advantage, ducking to slip through the fence and onto the airport tarmac.

Sticking to the shadows, he crept toward the long row of hangars, still studying the darkness for any sign of life. Wondering if the people he found here would be friends or foes. In the distance, somewhere among the hangars, a muffled cough. Hayes stilled. Searched the night, his eyes straining in the predawn gloom.

Then he saw movement. A shadow much darker than the others, posted outside the third hangar down. A man, Hayes could tell, though still too dark to see his face. Ducking low to stay out of sight, Hayes circled around the rear of the hangars. Hurried down the line to the third hangar and crept up the side toward where he'd seen the man standing. Made the front corner of the building and hesitated, listening, his Glock raised and ready.

A moment or two later, the man coughed again. Muttered: "*Shit.*" An American accent.

"Hell of a place to be fighting a cold," Hayes said, from around the corner. Tensed with the Glock, just in case.

For a moment, there was silence. Then: "You're Hayes?"

"You got it."

"Beetner," the man replied. "You going to stand there all night, or you want to check out the bird?"

The "bird" looked like it belonged in a museum, not a field of battle. And Brooks's team wasn't much better.

"Couldn't scrounge up a Black Hawk on such short notice," a man who'd introduced himself as Lauden told Hayes, noticing his expression as he surveyed the helicopter.

"Anyway, out of everything the Taliban have lying around, this bad boy is our best hope of getting airborne."

The machine was American, at least. A Bell UH-1 Huey of a design that dated back to the Vietnam War. The helo itself may have dated back to that era, Hayes figured, judging by the layer of dust on it. But according to Lauden, it wasn't *that* old.

"It's DEA, like the rest of us," he told Hayes. "Used it for counternarcotics ops, heroin raids. These birds saved our lives more than a couple of times in the poppy fields." He glanced across at the Huey. "It'll fly, boss."

"Sure, it'll fly." Another man—Malmon, according to Beetner—poked his head out from the other side of the helicopter, a wrench in his hand. "Mechanics look great. Only problem is we don't have a pilot."

Lauden shrugged, apologetic. "Our guy caught a Globemaster last night in Kabul and got the hell out of the country," he said. "We only found out when we were packing the truck."

Hayes looked from Lauden to the helicopter to the other two men. Wondering whose arm Brooks had twisted to get him *this* crew.

Lauden was obviously the leader. Hayes guessed he was in his mid-fifties, a Jerry Garcia type with a salt-and-pepper beard, hair to his shoulders, and a Hawaiian shirt. He'd offered a hit from the joint he was smoking to Hayes instead of offering his hand.

Beetner was younger, tall, and impossibly thin. He chain-smoked Marlboro Reds, filling the hangar with a mixture of tobacco smoke and Lauden's marijuana. Where the older man seemed strangely mellow, Beetner was clearly wound up, pacing the floor, his expression tight, only pausing to dig out another cigarette, or to cough again, loud and violent, his whole body bending with the force.

Malmon seemed decent and relatively normal, given the circumstances—if you discounted the fact that he barely looked old enough to vote.

Switched on, my ass, the voice said. *These guys are burnouts.*

He was about to reply to Lauden, make sure the men had brought *weapons,* at least, maybe get a sense of each man's abilities, when his phone began to vibrate in his pocket. Excusing himself, he walked to the far end of the hangar and answered. "Hayes."

"Adam, it's me." Nassim. The sound of the former ANA captain's voice brought a sudden relief that seemed to course through all of Hayes's body. "They are hunting us, like I told you. Not just Americans. We were lucky to escape with our lives tonight, but I don't think we can hide from them much longer."

"I'm on my way," Hayes replied. "Soon. Just tell me where to find you."

The line wasn't secure, but Hayes figured he had to take the risk. Had to believe that the Huey and the men in the hangar could help him defend Nassim, if anyone tried to intercept him.

"Do you remember that lovely little trail where we spent the afternoon so long ago?" Nassim asked. "It was where you and I first really got to know each other."

Hayes blinked. He remembered, all right. Remembered nearly dying in that Taliban ambush. Remembered Nassim dragging him to safety.

The Tangi Valley? the voice asked. *He can't be serious.*

"Yeah," Hayes replied. "I remember."

"There's a village nearby," Nassim said. "I always thought it looked beautiful at this time of year. Perhaps you should come visit."

Hayes didn't answer. Ran some quick mental calculations. The Tangi Valley lay approximately sixty miles to the southwest of Kabul, which put it about a hundred and fifty miles from Jalalabad. Hayes wasn't positive, but he figured the range of the Huey would max out at around two hundred miles—and probably less once they'd loaded all of Nassim's family on board—and that assumed the helo had a full tank of fuel. They would need to refuel somewhere, either before or after they picked up Nassim. Or just cross their fingers and hope the Huey could make it back to Kabul on fumes.

Nassim cleared his throat. "Adam?"

Going to have to hope we get lucky, Hayes thought. *There's not many gas stations left in this part of the world.*

"I'm coming for you," he told Nassim. "Just hold tight, Abdul."

He ended the call. Turned back to the helicopter, the men. Found Malmon tinkering away at the Huey's mechanicals, while Beetner was just lighting up another Marlboro Red. Lauden was cleaning his sidearm, a long-barreled revolver that looked like it dated from back in the Wild West. *Great.*

"How quick can we get this thing in the air?" Hayes asked.

Lauden scratched his head with the barrel of the gun. "Half hour or so," he said. "But who's going to fly it?"

"I am," Hayes replied. "Let's get to work."

29

EAGLE BASE

Inside the tactical operations center, Porter put down his headphones. "Who the hell's Adam?" he asked.

Beside him, the targeting officer shrugged. "Beats me. But he sounds American, don't he?"

He does, Porter thought. *And he sounds like he's determined to get in my way.*

He'd called in a favor with the targeting officer, a guy named Steck who Porter knew liked to gamble. Offered to cover his poker debts with the rest of the boys in the TOC if he'd run a trace on Ramze Nassim's cell phone. Abdul Nassim had apparently destroyed his old phone shortly after killing Akhtar Mansour in Maidan Wardak, but Porter knew the ANA officer would need to communicate eventually. He'd been sitting in the TOC with Steck for most of the night, listening to the geek outline the intricacies of no-limit Texas Hold'em, when at last the ANA officer broke his silence, using his father's phone.

The number Nassim had called was a dead end, Steck reported. Registered to a numbered company in Malaysia, no clue as to who lay behind it. "We could trace it," Steck told him. "But not from this desk. And it would take time."

More time than I have, Porter thought. Anyway, it didn't matter. Whoever "Adam" was, he was in for one hell of a surprise.

"Any idea where they were talking about?" Porter asked. "Some valley somewhere doesn't really narrow it down."

"No idea," Steck replied. "But it doesn't matter. Long as this guy leaves his phone on, we can trace it."

He typed in a few keystrokes on his computer. Brought up a GPS map, a flashing red dot roughly fifty miles to the southwest. A village in the mountains along a spur extending east from the Kabul-Ghazni highway. On the other side of Maidan Wardak Province from the medical clinic where this whole mess had begun.

"That's him," Steck said. He pointed at the screen. "And *that* is probably the valley they're talking about."

The Tangi Valley. The name meant nothing to Porter. He wondered what it meant to Nassim's friend, Adam.

"You going to intercept this guy?" Steck asked Porter. "If you can wrangle a chopper you could be there in thirty minutes."

Porter didn't answer immediately. An idea forming in his head.

"I need you to get me a Predator," he told Steck. "This job calls for Hellfires."

Steck laughed. Unsure if Porter was joking. "What, for *this* guy? You'll never get approval. We—"

"Not for him. For Muhammed Ghul."

Steck's smile disappeared. "The Taliban commander? *He's* there, too?"

"He will be."

"How do you know?"

"Because I'm going to put him there," Porter said, reaching for his phone.

30

KABUL

Muhammed Ghul groaned as he pulled off his ruined boot. Not even bothering to hide the pain anymore, or the frustration. His men had searched the outskirts of Jalalabad for Abdul Nassim through the night, with no luck. They'd roused the other families in the compound from their beds, interrogated them, too. None had any idea where Nassim and his family might have gone.

They'd suffered, anyway. At first to ensure they weren't lying, and then because Ghul was angry. The old cripple had severely wounded one of his men, wasted their time long enough for Nassim to escape. As far as Ghul could tell, they'd disappeared into the fields and orange groves that surrounded the compound, stolen away in the night. It was fruitless to try to find them in Jalalabad; Ghul didn't have the men or the patience for a house-to-house search in a city of more than three hundred thousand people. He would have to hope that the CIA man, Porter, had another way to find Nassim.

Ghul and his men had returned to Kabul, ninety miles to the west of Jalalabad, to regroup. They'd driven through the early hours and arrived in the city at dawn, though if they'd hoped to find peace there, they were bound for disappointment.

Kabul was chaos, and growing more so by the hour. Hamid Karzai International Airport was still open, and the Americans had set up a temporary embassy on the grounds, as their former embassy in the city took fire from the invading Taliban forces. This was victory, Ghul knew, the last gasp of the American occupation of his country. Within days, the so-called Islamic Republic of Afghanistan would be dead.

But in the meantime, there was panic. The streets clogged with westerners, foreign aid workers, military, and private citizens, queuing to escape on one of the massive planes that were landing and taking off from the airport's long runways. Joining them were thousands of Afghan citizens—traitors to Islam, Ghul knew, desperate to leave their homeland before the Taliban punished them for their sins.

The air in the city was filled with smoke, diesel exhaust, the blare of car horns, and the distant report of artillery guns and small-arms fire. The roar of jet airplanes overhead.

From the dim apartment where he and his men rested, Ghul felt an overwhelming urge to go outside and join in the battle, to be part of the final glorious push that drove the

Americans from the country, instead of lying inside, licking his wounds—wounds he'd suffered because of one of those Americans.

This is history, he thought. *And you are avoiding it.*

Still, he couldn't make himself forget about Abdul Nassim. Couldn't abandon the mission. Not only because he cared about the money Porter had promised, but because the old cripple in Jalalabad had nearly severed his toes. The old man had died, yes, for his actions—but he'd died painlessly. Ghul wanted someone to suffer.

Let Abdul Nassim suffer, Ghul thought, wincing as he pressed a damp cloth to his foot. *And let his family suffer, also.*

A knock at the bedroom door. One of Ghul's fighters, a promising young man named Jawid. Holding Ghul's satellite phone.

"The American," Jawid said.

Ghul took the phone. Nodded his thanks to the fighter and pressed the phone to his ear. "Have you found him?"

"There's a village near Qarya-I-Amir," Porter said, with typically awful American pronunciation. "Sixty miles south of Kabul. The Tangi Valley."

"You're sure he's there."

"He just made a phone call," Porter said. "We have him locked in. But he's going to move quick, so you'd better hurry."

"Send me the coordinates," Ghul told him. Reaching for his ruined boot. "We will find him."

31

TANGI VALLEY

The Huey motored west above the Tangi River, a darkening finger of black smoke trailing from its engine cowling, blotting out the morning sun. In the cockpit, Hayes eyed the oil-pressure gauge, the slow sink of the needle yet another reason to curse Seth Brooks.

As a pilot, Hayes knew that the odds of mechanical failure on a well-maintained helicopter were relatively low. But the key there was *well-maintained*, and neither Hayes nor the other three men aboard had any idea if the old Huey had enjoyed any maintenance at all since it had flown its last mission for the DEA.

It was a piece of shit, Hayes figured, but it was the best they could find in the boneyard at FOB Fenty, and with the rocky vastness of the Tangi Valley now surrounding them through the windshield, turning back was no longer an option. Especially with Nassim and his family waiting, somewhere up ahead.

A paved, two-lane road traced the north side of the valley, above the river and the narrow agricultural land that framed it on either side, a brilliant swath of green amid the featureless brown of the mountains. Hayes kept the Huey close to the rock face on the south side of the valley, using the ridgeline to mask the clatter of the rotors.

Beside him, in the copilot seat, Lauden studied the map clipped to his knee board, the frown he'd been wearing for the past ten minutes deepening to a scowl when he compared the map to the coordinates displayed on the helicopter's navigation system.

"You're sure this is the right valley?" he asked Hayes.

"I nearly died down there," Hayes replied. "This is the place."

"It's just this village you're talking about. There's nothing on the map at that spot."

"It's there. I promise."

"I hope you're right," Lauden said, nodding at the fuel gauge. "Because we're only getting one shot at this."

The Huey had come with a full tank of fuel, at least. That gave the men roughly two hundred miles to work with, and they'd covered nearly two-thirds of that just getting here. It was going to take some luck or divine intervention to get the bird all the way back up to Kabul, but Hayes wasn't thinking about that yet.

First, we find Nassim.

The village was exactly where Hayes remembered it, and as Hayes brought the Huey in low over the tilled farmland that surrounded it, he picked out a flat patch to land. While he held the helo in a hover, Beetner and Malmon peered through the haze of corn husks and dirt kicked up by the downdraft, Beetner on the Huey's M60 door gun, Malmon gripping one of the cut-down HK416 rifles the DEA men had brought with them.

Come on, the voice muttered. *Come on, Abdul. Where are you?*

The landing zone was empty, though a crowd was beginning to grow at the edge of the village.

"Movement," Malmon reported over the radio. *"I have five—no, six—people coming our way. Looks like three adults and three children."*

Hayes leaned forward in his seat. Craned his neck to see the group hurrying through the cornfield toward the helicopter. They were too far away to make out clearly, the downdraft from the rotors kicking up too much dust, but Hayes could see Malmon was right—an older man, two middle-aged. Three children.

Nassim's family. Though he'd only had Zarah when he'd saved Hayes's life.

Hayes set the Huey down gently on the dirt. Told Lauden to stay with the helo and grabbed his own HK416, and a frag grenade just in case. Opened the door and stepped out onto the landing zone as Malmon climbed down beside him, rifle at the ready, scanning the crowd in the distance for trouble.

Ducking to avoid the Huey's rotors, Hayes and Malmon hurried away from the helicopter. As they cleared the roiling tornado of dust that the rotors had kicked up, the faces of the family in the distance became clearer, and Hayes felt a sudden surge of relief as he recognized Abdul Nassim.

The former ANA captain had aged in the decade since Hayes had last seen him; there were more lines on his face, and his hair was beginning to gray. But he'd retained his powerful build and that same wry, ready smile; Hayes saw it cross Nassim's face as he, too, recognized an old friend.

The two men closed the last few yards between each other, and Hayes opened his arms, wrapping Nassim in a firm embrace. Felt Nassim's arms around him, too, holding on to him like a life ring, and Hayes could sense just how afraid his friend must have been.

They stepped back. Studied each other's faces. "It's good to see you," Hayes said. He gestured to the two boys who stood shyly beside their mother, watching him with wide eyes. "You've been busy since the last time we met."

Nassim winked. "Plenty of practice." Then his smile widened. "They are excited to meet the man whose life their father saved."

Hayes began to respond, but his words were interrupted by the clatter of gunfire in the distance. Over Nassim's shoulder, another cloud of dust had formed near the village. And from within it emerged a convoy of white pickup trucks, each with machine guns mounted in the bed. Technicals, coming in hot. And those machine guns were already firing.

"*Come on,*" Hayes told Nassim, pulling his friend

forward and then reaching for Freshta, for the children at her side. Zarah was already running, Malmon escorting her back to the helicopter as the older man—Nassim's father, Hayes figured—struggled gamely after them.

There was no time to waste. Gripping his rifle in one hand, Hayes scooped up the older of the two boys in the other. Carried him fireman-style across the empty field toward the helicopter, zagging out of Beetner's line of fire as the DEA man opened up with the M60 over their heads.

Rounds scattered the dirt around Hayes as he ran, and he turned back and fired wild with the HK416 as he carried the boy to the Huey. A few steps behind him, Freshta was carrying her youngest son pressed against her shoulder, seeming to barely notice his weight. In her other hand, Hayes saw, she was holding a pistol, a Beretta M9.

Hayes reached the helicopter, where Malmon and Zarah were already inside. He circled around to the Huey's far side, passed the boy in his arms to Abdul Nassim and helped Nassim's father up into the cargo bay. Gestured to Malmon to help Freshta and her boy, then hurried back around to his own door, pausing to take better aim at the convoy with his rifle, watching as Beetner found the lead pickup with a quick, savage burst.

But the convoy's gunners had found their range, too, and a long blast from a bed-mounted PKM came stitching across the side of the helo. Now close enough to see the effects of their rounds, the gunners adjusted, and the clang of bullets over Hayes's head told him they were targeting the turbine.

He climbed into the cockpit, deafened by the rotors and

the roar of Beetner's big gun. Felt the Huey shudder as the PKM's rounds found their mark. In the distance, a fighter climbed out of the disabled lead technical, and Hayes could see he was carrying a rocket-propelled grenade launcher.

In the copilot's seat, Lauden was yelling, and though Hayes couldn't hear him, the meaning was clear. He yanked back on the collective, black smoke pouring into the cockpit when the Huey lurched skyward. Hayes coughed and reached for the control panel, flicking the vent switch to clear his view of the gauges. Glanced outside in time to see Beetner cut down the Taliban fighter before he could launch the RPG.

The Huey was laboring now, and Hayes held his breath, spinning the helo around as the turbine struggled to create the power necessary to transition from vertical to forward flight. Finally, he had lift, and he shoved the nose forward, the landing skids barely ten feet off the ground as he raced back the way they'd come.

Suddenly, from behind the Huey—two massive explosions, the shock waves knocking the Huey off its trajectory. Lauden spun in the copilot seat as Hayes wrestled with the controls, thinking at first they'd taken RPG fire after all, but the shock wave passed and the helo kept flying, with no apparent permanent damage.

"What the hell was that?" Lauden shouted on the radio.

Hayes shook his head. "No idea. But let's not wait around to find out."

He eased the helicopter into a gentle climb, eager to leave the valley behind. Dimly aware that the streaks of tracer fire racing past the cockpit seemed to have stopped, but not

thinking much of it. Thinking only that somehow they'd
pulled it off, that Nassim was safe. That the only thing that
mattered now was getting back to Kabul.

But his moment of triumph was short-lived. Before he
could level the Huey off again, the helo's AN/APR-39 radar
detection system blinked to life, a triangular icon appearing
on the scope, followed by a monotone warning over the radio:
"Warning . . . missile lock . . . seven o'clock . . ."

Hayes stared at the screen in disbelief. "We're being
painted."

"No way," Lauden replied. "This piece of crap is probably
just malfunc—"

Before he could finish, the APR-39's warnings became
suddenly more urgent. *"Missile launch . . . missile launch . . .
seven o'clock . . ."*

32

nside the tactical operations center, Porter watched on a large LED screen as the drone operator maneuvered the MQ-9 Reaper above the killing field. Far below the drone, what remained of Muhammed Ghul's convoy lay scattered like children's toys, the three technicals shattered and twisted nearly unrecognizable, consumed by flame and smoke. Porter counted at least five bodies; there were undoubtedly more inside the trucks. But at least three men were still moving, and Porter wished he could instruct the operator to bring the MQ-9 around for another shot.

But the Reaper only carried four Hellfire missiles, and the operator had spent two on Ghul's convoy. That left two for Nassim, and whoever'd come swooping down in that helo to save the day. Porter knew shooting down a helicopter with a drone wasn't an exact science. He figured it was better to let Ghul's survivors walk—or crawl—away, rather than risk letting Nassim escape.

"Good work," he told the operator. "Now engage that helo."

From his control station, the operator glanced up at him. "Sir?"

"Do it," Porter said. "Finish the job."

He'd swung the Reaper by convincing the operator the attack met updated DoD protocol, that there would never be an easier chance to finish Muhammed Ghul if they didn't act quickly. Since Ghul was a top-level target, a Taliban commander, Porter knew the operator could at least cover his ass, if anyone from Langley came asking.

With Ghul neutralized, the operator probably figured he was finished. But Porter wasn't just here to kill Ghul.

"Take down that helicopter," he told the operator. "I have a high-value target aboard, and I need him eliminated."

The operator—a young guy, eyes red-rimmed from life in the TOC cave, jittery from the bottle of Mountain Dew on the desk in front of him—hesitated. Porter held his gaze, daring the man to disobey.

Finally, the operator shrugged. "Engaging the helo." As Porter watched, he swung the drone into position behind the helicopter, using the targeting laser to lock on.

No escape now, Porter thought. *See ya later.*

He touched the operator's shoulder. "Let 'er rip."

33

T he Hellfire left the rail at Mach 1.3, and before Adam Hayes could do anything about it, the missile exploded into the tail of the Huey. Mortally wounded, the helicopter began to break into pieces as it spun down toward the bottom of the valley, the centrifugal force shoving Hayes against the cockpit door, the radio full of screams from the passengers in the back as they struggled to hold on for their lives.

This is how it all started, the voice said. *A helicopter crash. And that's how it'll end.*

With the tail rotor severed, there was nothing Hayes could do to control the helo's sickening plunge, only hold on and brace for impact, praying to God for mercy.

"Hold on!" he shouted, as the ground approached through the windshield, skewed at an impossible angle, blurred almost unrecognizable. Then the Huey collided, plunging into a copse of trees along the riverbank, then spinning down into the shallows of the Tangi River, the impact jarring Hayes's head against the cockpit glass, nearly knocking his teeth from his mouth. The Huey plowing across the river, the water slowing its speed, before coming to rest on the opposite bank.

It was then that Hayes slipped into unconsciousness, and as his vision went black, he knew he wouldn't wake up again.

Except he did. No telling how much time had passed, though it couldn't have been more than a couple of minutes. The Huey lay on its side, Hayes still strapped into the pilot's seat, the tepid brown water of the Tangi River seeping into the cockpit around him.

Above him, in the copilot's seat, Lauden was dead. His face bloodied, his head tilted at an impossible angle. From behind Hayes, someone groaned. In the distance, a cow bayed.

The kids, Hayes thought. Thinking of his own family, of Annabelle and Jack and the child he might never meet. *Please let them be all right.*

Wincing, he tested his arms. His legs. Everything hurt, but still seemed to work right. He reached up and unstrapped his harness, fell sideways against the cockpit window, splashing into five or six inches of water. Collecting himself, he knelt against the window. Straightened and looked back into the Huey's cargo compartment to take stock of the damage.

Malmon was dead, too, or fatally wounded. He'd wrapped his arms around one of Nassim's boys, the younger, protecting him as best he could from the impact. Hayes studied the boy, praying for some movement. Praying that the deep gash on the boy's forehead was the worst of his injuries.

Hayes pushed himself to his feet. Kicked out the shattered front windshield of the Huey and climbed out onto the nose. Around him, the valley was silent, the only sound the trickle of the Tangi River, the cows in the distance, the wind.

And then another sound: a turboprop engine somewhere high in the sky. Faint, but just barely audible. Hayes wiped blood from his forehead, waited for his thoughts to catch up to this development. He'd imagined the Huey's fatal blow had come from a Taliban RPG. But there was something up there, something high in the air, obscured by the high midday sun. And Hayes had a terrible hunch he knew what it was.

In the TOC, Porter watched on-screen as the pilot climbed out of the helo's wreckage and looked around the valley. The man looked dazed, Porter thought, but otherwise not badly injured. His was the only movement in the wreckage that Porter could see.

Still, it was better to be safe than sorry. And there was one Hellfire left.

"Finish them off," he told the operator, who took a swig of Mountain Dew and reached for the controls. Instructing the Reaper to circle back into firing position, the command bouncing up from the TOC to a DoD satellite, then back down to the drone in the span of 1.2 seconds. On-screen, the drone began to turn, high above the valley walls.

Far below, the man on the wreckage hadn't moved.

It could have been the collision, or perhaps he was just tired, but Hayes felt like his whole body was moving in slow motion. His mind struggling to process information, his body lagging as his brain sent it commands.

That's a Reaper up there, the voice told him. *And it's circling back around to make sure we're dead.*

Hayes stared dumbly up at the sky, searching for the source of the noise. Wondering what he was supposed to do next.

Move, dumbass. Save those people.

"Get to work, Adam. It's not over yet."

This time it wasn't the voice he heard; it was Annabelle. Clear as day, like she was standing beside him. Reminding him that he'd promised to come home to her.

Shit.

Suddenly, the world switched from slow motion to fast-forward.

You have seconds. Maybe a minute. Get moving.

Quickly, Hayes turned and climbed from the nose of the Huey onto its side, now facing skyward as it rested in the water. Ignoring the pain in his legs and his ribs, he hurried to the open cargo bay door, where Abdul Nassim was the first person he found, strapped into the rear-facing bench seat, holding his daughter.

Zarah's eyes were open. She was sobbing.

"Come on," he told her in Pashto, reaching down to take hold of her hand, helping her unstrap her safety harness while he held her upright. When she was free, he pulled, dragging her out to the top of the Huey.

"Can you run?" he asked her. She nodded. "Good. Go."

She hesitated, but there wasn't time. Hayes nudged her toward the riverbank. "Go." Watched as she leapt for the grassy shore. Then turned back to the cargo bay.

Abdul was awake now. Groaning. Bleeding from somewhere.

"We have to move, Abdul," Hayes told him. "Hurry and let's get the kids out."

Abdul stared at him, not comprehending. His frustration mounting, Hayes reached for his friend's harness. But movement farther in the cabin caught his eye.

Freshta. Alive, but injured. Blood streamed down her face. Her left arm bent terribly, a bone piercing her skin. Still, she was moving. Fumbling with her harness, slipping it loose. Casting her eyes around the helo for her children.

Her youngest boy was still wrapped in Malmon's arms. But he was moving now, too. And Beetner, leaned up against the ruined M60 and partway submerged, had begun to stir also. Only the second boy, and Nassim's father, hadn't regained consciousness. But Hayes knew they'd all be dead within minutes if they didn't act quickly.

He reached into the cargo bay. Took hold of the youngest

boy, untangled him from Malmon's arms. The boy whimpered, but didn't struggle, and Hayes pulled him out of the Huey. Dimly aware that Abdul had unfastened his own harness and slid deeper into the cargo bay. By the time Hayes had the boy safely installed on the riverbank with his sister, Abdul and Freshta were passing up their eldest son, still unconscious and limp in their arms.

Hayes took the boy. Cradled him against his shoulder. Reached back in to help Freshta climb out of the helo. The drone was all he could hear now, roaring in his ear though Hayes knew it was impossible, knew it must still have been miles away. It wouldn't need to come close to destroy them, though. Any second now, the operator would input the fire command.

Perhaps he already had.

Abdul was still in the cargo bay, fumbling with his father's harness. As Hayes watched, Beetner nudged him out of the way.

"Go," the ex-DEA op told Nassim. "I'll get him loose."

Nassim tried to argue. But Hayes could see that his friend's hands were bloodied, that he was struggling with his motor function. Could see that Beetner had a better angle at the older man's harness anyway.

"Go," Beetner said again. Met Hayes's eyes at the top of the Huey. "Get them out of here," he said. "We're right behind."

Hayes nodded. He reached down to pull Nassim out of the helicopter. Had to drag him with both hands, levered against the sheet metal. Inside the cargo bay, Beetner had the elder

Nassim unbuckled, but the man still hadn't moved, hadn't woken up.

Hayes looked up. Looked around. Couldn't see the drone anywhere, but that didn't mean anything. He approached the cargo bay door again, ready to climb down and help Beetner haul the unconscious man up. But before he could drop in, he looked skyward and glimpsed the cotton-white contrail of the missile rocketing toward the Huey.

At maximum speed, a Hellfire missile could cover approximately one thousand miles per hour, or just under fifteen hundred feet per second. There was no time to save Beetner. No time for Nassim's father. Hayes turned on instinct, dove onto the grassy riverbank. Landed on top of Zarah and her youngest brother and shielded them from the blast.

An instant later, the Hellfire collided with the downed Huey, obliterating the helicopter. The shock wave tore at Hayes, trying to launch him skyward, a searing heat and molten shards of metal filling the air above him. He held on to the children as the force of the explosion caught him like a riptide, clutching them to his chest. Within a second or two, it was over.

"Everyone okay?" he called out in Pashto, choking through the black smoke that billowed up from the wreck.

There was no answer.

34

EAGLE BASE/TANGI VALLEY

Porter watched the screen as the operator circled the Reaper above what remained of the helicopter, now nothing more than tangled steel and smoke.

"Looked like a Huey," the operator said. "How'd the hell they learn to fly one of our birds?"

Porter was wondering the same thing. Wondering who "Adam" was, and how he'd become mixed up in the whole mess. He'd nearly gotten Nassim out of there, and would have succeeded if Porter had relied solely on Ghul and his men.

Thank God for good old American firepower, he thought, studying the wreckage. *Whoever Adam was, he's not a factor anymore.*

Except that might not be entirely true, Porter realized.

Because as the smoke cleared around the downed Huey, Porter could see movement on the riverbank. Survivors, crawling slowly away from the helo.

"Shit," the operator said. "I'm out of Hellfires, sir. And I'm nearly out of gas."

Porter stared at the screen. Counted at least four people moving. Maybe five.

Suddenly, there didn't seem to be enough Tramadol in the world.

Goddamn it, Nassim, he thought. *Why can't you just die?*

Freshta Nassim's arm was broken. She'd suffered a head injury, her face pockmarked by tiny cuts from the Huey's shattered glass. Abdul Nassim had probably suffered a major concussion, and his hands were in bad shape, mangled and bloody. Zarah and her youngest brother—Bilal, Hayes learned—seemed to have escaped with only cuts and bruises. But their brother, Payam, had taken a wicked piece of shrapnel to his chest. He was still unconscious, his breathing shallow, blood seeping out from the jagged wound.

He needs medical help immediately, the voice said. *They all do.*

For his part, Hayes figured he might have a couple of broken ribs. Definitely a concussion. His whole body ached, but he could still move. Still react. Still try to save Nassim's life.

As for the others who'd been aboard the helo, there was no hope. Lauden and Malmon had died in the initial crash. Chances were, the impact had taken Ramze Nassim's life, too. And there was no way that Beetner could have survived the second missile, not a direct hit.

Whoever those DEA men were, Hayes thought, *wherever Brooks found them, they gave their lives for this family.*

There was no time to dwell on that now. Not with that Reaper still somewhere high above them. Not with the CIA *and* the Taliban wanting them dead.

Hayes brushed dirt from his clothes. Joined the Nassim family where they'd gathered around Payam beneath a cluster of ash trees. Abdul held Bilal; both looked shaken, dazed. Freshta wiped tears from her face with her good hand, but she still seemed to have it together. She'd salvaged the Beretta, Hayes saw, as she'd escaped the helicopter. Beside her, Zarah stood, numb, staring out at the smoke still rising out of the Huey.

"We have to move," Hayes told them. "The people who shot down the helicopter aren't going to be satisfied until they know we're all dead."

Quickly, he removed his T-shirt. Used it to fashion a sling for Freshta Nassim. Tore strips from Abdul's tunic and wrapped his friend's hands with them. Did what he could to pack dirt around the wound in Payam's chest, bind it with whatever spare cloth he could find, but the boy needed a hospital or he wouldn't survive.

No weapons but a pistol. Hostile territory. Children. You really know how to have a good time.

Hayes called up the map of the Tangi Valley in his memory. The river flowed west, he remembered, back toward the village. Beyond that, both the road and the river wound down the valley to Highway 1, which led north to Kabul.

There was another route east, Hayes knew, but it was longer, climbed higher into the valley before meeting up with another road to Kabul. There were fewer villages. Normally, Hayes would have chosen that option, tried to steer clear of any towns. Tried to slip out of the valley undetected.

But that would take time, and with Payam's injury, Hayes knew they would need to risk the faster option. He just wished he'd kept his hands on a rifle.

"We'll go west," he told the family. Gesturing down valley the way they had come. "Stick to the river and try to stay hidden. Hopefully I can find us a car."

Within a couple of hours they'd made it back to the outskirts of the village. Thin tendrils of smoke still rose from the ruined technicals that had belonged to the Taliban attacking force, the wreckage strewn across the empty field that had served as Hayes's landing zone.

Hayes was still trying to wrap his head around the entire situation. According to Abdul, it had been those Taliban trucks that had come for him and his family in Jalalabad—*not* Dominic Porter. But Porter must have okayed the drone strike, Hayes knew, which meant there were two opposing forces both trying to kill Nassim.

And they're trying to kill each other, too, the voice said. *Porter had that Reaper destroy the technicals before he came after us.*

In the short term, it didn't matter. The more pressing issue was that the village now appeared to be crawling with Taliban.

Nassim said he had relatives in the village, who could shelter them temporarily. He had a vehicle, too, that could carry them to Kabul, where Hayes hoped he could talk his way into the airport with the family, and from there get medical attention for their injuries from the Marines who were still holding the area. If that didn't work, Hayes figured he could find a doctor in Kabul willing to accept a bribe.

But Kabul was still sixty miles away. And the going was slow already, with Payam still unconscious, Hayes and the boy's father taking turns carrying him, gingerly, through the fields that lined the river. Hayes could see that Freshta was in serious pain herself, though she tried not to show it. There was no way the family could walk much farther. They would need a vehicle. But the village—and Nassim's Mitsubishi— was now closely guarded by more than a dozen heavily armed Taliban. They would have to find another ride.

Hayes left the Nassim family to take shelter in a stand of trees along the Tangi River as he crept closer to the village. Left them Freshta's Beretta, also, opting for stealth over firepower. Hayes stayed low, trying to keep out of sight of the Taliban sentries who now patrolled the outskirts of the town, AK-47s at the ready. Timing his dash when he was sure nobody was looking, Hayes sprinted across the twenty yards of open space between the trees along the river and the first row of mud-brick houses. He pressed himself flat against the wall and drew the ceramic blade from his belt.

First order of business: Find a gun.

Hayes edged along the wall of the building until it reached a corner. Slowly, he peered around the wall into the laneway beyond, bracing for shouts of recognition, or gunfire. Ten yards away, a Taliban fighter with a black turban paced, looking bored, his rifle hanging from the sling on his shoulder. Not far beyond him sat a dusty Land Cruiser.

As stealthy as he could, Hayes crept up behind the man. Brought the knife to his throat and his free hand across the man's mouth, muffling the man's shouts as the blade cut into his flesh. Hayes dragged him backward down the laneway and back around the corner again. Lay him on the ground as he bled out, slipping the rifle from his shoulders.

When Hayes was sure the man was dead, he checked the rifle over. Patted the man down through his *perahan tunban* and found a Soviet Makarov semiautomatic pistol hidden in the folds of his tunic. Hayes pocketed the pistol, then he rounded the corner again and hurried up the laneway to where the Land Cruiser waited, ready to open up with the AK on anyone who discovered him. Glancing inside the SUV, he could see the keys were in the ignition.

Perfect.

Hayes returned to the edge of the village, then sprinted back across the twenty yards of exposed space to the stand of trees where the Nassims were hiding.

"I found a truck," he told Abdul. "Can you help me get the kids to it without anyone seeing?"

Abdul nodded. He appeared to have recovered somewhat from his concussion, though he was still moving slow, and his hands were obviously causing him pain. Hayes wondered if his friend would be physically able to fire a weapon, if the need arose. He gave Abdul the Makarov anyway, then loaded the unconscious Payam into Abdul's arms. Briefed Freshta and Zarah on the location of the Land Cruiser. On the need to be fast and silent. Then he took Bilal's hand and swung the AK-47 ready with his free hand. Looked out across the expanse of empty space, and muttered a prayer.

Here we go.

Pulling Bilal up into the crook of his arm, Hayes gestured to Freshta and Abdul to start running. He hung back a few paces to cover them with the rifle if they needed it, but no voices rang out as they sprinted across the dirt. No gunfire. Nobody had noticed them.

Quickly, Hayes followed. Caught up to the Nassims at the wall of the first mud-brick home and joined them hurrying up the laneway to the Land Cruiser. The doors were unlocked, and Hayes pulled them open, helping Freshta and Abdul load their children into the SUV. Laying Payam carefully across his mother and siblings' laps in the backseat, then circling around to the driver's-side door.

Climbing behind the wheel, Hayes wedged the AK-47 between the seat and the driver's door, hoping he wouldn't have to fire while he drove, but not seeing any other choice given the state of Abdul's hands, and Freshta's broken arm. He turned the key in the ignition and was relieved to hear the truck rumble to life. Shifting quickly into gear in case anyone had heard, he stepped on the gas pedal and guided the Land

Cruiser out of the laneway. Cut the wheel over and aimed for the main road, just barely visible along the riverside at the far end of the village.

"Get your heads down," he told Abdul and his family. "If anyone sees us, this is going to get ugly."

35

Muhammed Ghul studied his fresh wounds and wondered why he'd been so foolish as to ever make a deal with the CIA. Why he'd believed Porter could be trusted, when the operative had willingly betrayed his own country, and then his own driver, to gain Ghul's trust.

An American snake. Like the rest of them.

Porter had not warned Ghul that an American helicopter would be waiting for his men in the Tangi Valley when they arrived to collect Abdul Nassim. He'd neglected to mention that there would be men with machine guns and assault rifles prepared to defend the target and his family—American men. And Porter had certainly not mentioned that he intended to obliterate Ghul and his men with an air strike; he'd conveniently omitted that part.

Betrayal. A trap. So typically American.

The missiles that had destroyed Ghul's technicals and nearly all of his men had blinded the Taliban commander in his left eye and filled his body with shrapnel. He'd crawled away from the burning wreck certain he was dying, cursing Porter and the CIA and America with his last breaths. From the ground where he lay, half-dazed, he'd watched the American helicopter explode in the distance. Watched it crash down into the Tangi River with a sense of grim satisfaction. If he was dying, at least Abdul Nassim was surely dead, too.

Though Ghul didn't really care about Nassim anymore. And after his surviving men had discovered him still alive, they pulled him upright and carried him back to the village, where more Taliban fighters were arriving from farther down the valley, Ghul had all but forgotten about the corrupt CIA operative's target.

If he lived through that crash, then may God bless him, Ghul thought. *I have more important enemies to punish.*

He could tell from the faces of his men that his injuries were bad. That his face, in particular, must have suffered horrifically. He supposed he would never see again out of his left eye, knew he should find a doctor for the rest of his wounds. But at that point, Muhammed Ghul didn't care anymore.

Never let them see you bleed, he thought. *And if they do, show them it takes more than blood to kill you.*

Porter would suffer. Ghul would see to it. But assassinating a CIA operative would be a lot more difficult than killing a citizen of Afghanistan—and Ghul knew the clock was ticking. Sooner or later, Kabul would fall completely, and Porter would go back to America.

No, Ghul thought. *We will have to act fast. But how?*

He didn't have any answers, as he lay half-blind and bloody on his back on some terrified villager's rug. He lay there, ruminating, raging against Porter and the CIA and America, for some time—hours, perhaps. Wondering if he would die here in this dirty hovel, impotently planning his vengeance.

And then one of his men entered the room. "Sir," he said, breathless. "They've murdered Tariq. They are stealing his truck."

Ghul pushed himself up to an elbow. "*Who* is doing this?"

The man hesitated. "The targets, I believe," he said. "The Nassim family and an American man. Nasir witnessed them as they drove away."

Ghul muttered a curse. Another American who couldn't mind his business.

"We've sent two technicals after them," the fighter continued. "They won't get far. I've ordered them brought back to you, sir. Alive, if possible."

"No," Ghul said.

The man frowned. "I beg your pardon, sir?"

"Let them go. Do not intercept them. They're of no use to us here."

The man stared at Ghul, confused. "Sir—"

"They will go to Kabul," Ghul told him. "To the airport, no doubt. It's the only way out of this country for them. Call our friends in the city; tell them to watch the highway. Instead of playing chase, we will lie in wait for them."

The fighter smiled as realization dawned. "I will tell the men in Kabul to look out for the vehicle. Should I tell our men to capture them there?"

"No," Ghul said. "They're not of any consequence anymore. But we'll use them as bait. Because wherever they go, we can be sure that the man who did this"—he gestured to his useless eye, his mangled face—"will be nearby."

36

TANGI VALLEY

The technicals had been gaining in the rearview mirror for the last several minutes, as Hayes piloted the Land Cruiser toward Highway 1, causing a tight knot of anxiety to wind around his stomach. Two Toyota Hiluxes, distorted by distance and the heat of the pavement, but clear enough that Hayes could see the machine guns mounted in their beds.

Those things will tear us apart, the voice said. *They won't even have to get close.*

The Land Cruiser's engine wheezed as Hayes pushed it harder, the needle on the gas gauge somewhere around an eighth of a tank and falling. *Even if we can outrun them,* Hayes thought. *We might not make it to Kabul anyway.*

He watched the rearview as the highway wound down through the valley, trying to conjure some kind of plan.

An AK-47 and a couple of 9-millimeter pistols against two PKM machine guns. Fat chance.

The odds were stacked. Short of stumbling over the world's greatest hiding place, Hayes couldn't think of any options that wouldn't get them all killed. And even hiding would waste time, time that Payam Nassim desperately needed.

Hayes glanced at the pickup trucks in the rearview mirror again. Knew it wouldn't be long until they were in firing range.

And then . . . the trucks seemed to slow down. Hayes thought it was a mirage at first, his eyes playing tricks, but then the lead truck pulled over to the side of the road, and the second truck pulled off alongside it. And gradually, Hayes watched the distance between them and the Land Cruiser start to increase again.

What are they doing?

Hayes had no idea. They seemed to be giving up. He watched the rearview mirror until the trucks had disappeared, and even then, he still didn't trust what he'd seen.

After a few more miles, the road out of the valley came to a T-junction, the Kabul-Ghazni highway stretching to the north and south, marking the terminus of the valley. From here, Hayes figured it was about forty-five miles on a relatively straight shot up to Kabul, though he wasn't foolish enough to think the road north would be easy, not through a country in the throes of collapse.

It's midafternoon, he thought. *If we can make the airport by dusk, I'll be happy.*

Assuming the kid has that long, the voice replied.

Turning the wheel to guide the Land Cruiser onto the highway, Hayes twisted around to look into the backseat, where Freshta, Zarah, and Bilal all cradled Payam, the shrapnel still embedded in his chest, the fabric around the wound fully soaked in blood.

"How is he doing?" Hayes asked Freshta, who forced a weak smile.

"Breathing, still," she said. "Not well, but he is breathing. I am trying to have faith."

"We'll get him some help as fast as we can," Hayes assured her. Hoping he could keep that promise. Hoping there weren't any surprises waiting on the road ahead.

He turned back to the wheel, to the long, flat, featureless road north. On either side of the highway, in the distance, lay low desert mountains, but the paved route was quite flat. Flat did not equal *safe,* though; the three hundred miles of National Highway 1 that stretched from Kabul to Kandahar were notorious for Taliban ambushes, kidnappings, and other misfortunes. Five years ago, Hayes remembered, seventy-three people had died on the highway when two buses collided with an oil tanker. The drivers had apparently been speeding, desperate to make it through Taliban country as quickly as they could.

Forty-five miles, the voice said. *Just get them there.*

Hayes settled in for the drive. In the passenger seat, Nassim turned from the window, studied his hands, the bloody strips of fabric that Hayes had fastened into bandages. He said nothing for some time. Then he sighed.

"We are even, Adam," he said.

Hayes glanced at him. "What?"

"No matter what happens, from here on. There is no more debt to be paid."

"Sure there is," Hayes replied. "I haven't got you out yet."

"But you've saved my life, and my family's, already, once. I don't expect you to save us again."

"What are you talking about, Abdul?"

Nassim glanced at him. "It will be easier for you to get out of Kabul without us," he said. "If you can get my boy to a hospital, and my wife, we will find our own ways to survive."

Hayes said nothing. Just drove, pushing the Land Cruiser, watching the fuel gauge dip lower.

"It's not safe in this country for you anymore," Hayes said, finally. "And especially not for your kids. We're getting you out."

In the passenger seat, Nassim didn't reply. Hayes could tell his old friend didn't believe him.

They drove in silence for some time. The only sound the wind outside and the tires on the pavement underneath, the rumble of the Land Cruiser's engine. Now and then, someone shifted in the backseat, and Hayes turned, hoping that it was Payam who'd woken up, finally. Hoping for good news.

But it was Bilal, inevitably, yawning, his eyes drooping as

the adrenaline of the day wore off and fatigue began to over-power him. Or it was Freshta, maintaining her brave face though every bump in the road must have been causing her unspeakable pain.

Only Zarah still looked focused, wide awake, and atten-tive. She stared out from the middle seat between the center console to the windshield beyond, watching the highway un-fold. Hayes met her gaze in the rearview mirror, gave her a wink. Watched her smile and look shyly away.

His thoughts turned to Annabelle again. To Jack and the child he'd thought, at one point today, he would never meet.

Another son? he wondered. *Or a daughter? And what would I do to defend them?*

Anything was the answer. It had always been. And Hayes knew Nassim felt the same.

He glanced across the SUV at his friend. "So we've got Taliban chasing you," he said. "And the CIA trying to blow us out of the sky with Hellfire missiles. How'd you get so many enemies, Abdul?"

Nassim shook his head. "I wish that I knew. I was afraid enough when it was only the American I had to worry about. I don't know how the Taliban became involved, too."

"You know you can talk to me, right?" Hayes said. "Whatever you're mixed up in, I promise I won't judge. I just want to help."

"I swear to you, I don't know," Nassim replied. "I had imagined the American had enlisted his Taliban friends to kill me. But now he's trying to kill them, too, and that has noth-ing to do with me." He reached into his pocket, pulled out a tiny thumb drive and showed it to Hayes. "Whatever is on here must have incredible value."

Hayes looked at Nassim again. At the thumb drive in his hand.

He's not lying, the voice said. *For the number of bodies that little thing has racked up, there had better be a goddamn treasure map inside.*

The Land Cruiser rolled on. Twenty miles out of Kabul now, traffic on the highway thickening, slowing progress to a crawl. Trucks, buses, cars packed full with people, riding low on their springs—everyone desperate to reach the airport before the last of the planes left, everyone hoping to get out.

If the Taliban wanted to kill us, the voice said, *we'd be easy targets here.*

The voice was right, but there was nothing Hayes could do. He pressed on, scanning the traffic around him for potential threats. But there were so many vehicles, so many faces. His mind didn't register as the Land Cruiser overtook a battered Suzuki Jimny, the driver hardly glancing across at the Land Cruiser, barely seeming to notice the people inside as he pulled in behind Hayes and the Nassims and continued the slow pilgrimage to the city.

37

EAGLE BASE

I t was getting harder and harder to get any work done in this country, Dominic Porter thought. Every day—hell, every *hour*—saw more resources pulled from his disposal, loaded on board transport planes and flown back home, or to some other ass-backward nation and some other war. Porter couldn't figure out how he was supposed to accomplish anything at all in Afghanistan, at this point; Eagle Base looked like one of those abandoned Western movie sets, all false fronts and tumbleweeds, barely a soul in sight.

And to top it off, the Tramadol was nearly gone.

The short answer was he *wasn't* supposed to be accomplishing anything. Not anymore. Orders from Langley had come in just now—a C-37 jet waiting at Hamid Karzai

International Airport, departing midnight for Ramstein Air Base in Germany. From there, back to Langley. Back in from the cold.

The Mi-17 helicopter Porter had planned to use to hunt down Abdul Nassim had been conscripted instead to shuttle personnel from Eagle Base to KBL, three miles away. Most of the operatives he'd hoped to use were among those on the helo, except for a handful of his most loyal men, and a few stragglers who'd stayed behind to plant demolition charges around the compound, to prevent the Taliban—or anyone else—from discovering the base's secrets.

Last one out, light the fuse, Porter thought.

Even the drone he'd used to kill Muhammed Ghul was gone, the operator and his station packed up and destined for a C-17 Globemaster III departing tomorrow, the drone already safely out of Afghan airspace. If Langley had its way, any trace of Eagle Base would be erased within days, and anything useful—Porter included—reassigned to other duties.

But Porter had no intention of boarding that jet out of country. Not yet. Not while Abdul Nassim and his family could still be alive. There was still enough manpower to assemble a small team, finish what needed to be done, and still catch a flight before the whole country imploded. Assuming everything went well, which it hadn't so far.

You'll be lucky if you don't get court-martialed after this, he thought. *Much less keep your job.*

Yeah, well. If Abdul Nassim's story got out to the world, Porter knew a court-martial would be the least of his worries.

Knew he'd likely spend the rest of his life behind bars. Or face a firing squad.

Nassim must not be allowed to escape from Afghanistan. That was the bottom line.

Porter's phone rang. An unfamiliar number, though there weren't many people who knew how to reach him here. He answered. "Yes?"

"Abdul Nassim is in Kabul," said the voice on the other end, heavily accented, in English. "Heading to the airport with his family, and the American man. If you wish to stop them, you'll have to hurry."

"Who is this?" Porter asked. "How did you get this number?"

"They are in a white Land Cruiser." The voice read a license plate. "National Highway 1. They have just passed the Kabul Zoo now."

Porter stood from his desk. The zoo was six miles from the airport. Roughly ten miles from Eagle Base. He pulled on his jacket and hurried out of his barracks, the phone still to his ear.

"Who are you?" he asked. "How do you know this?"

But the line was already dead.

38

AMERICAN EMBASSY SCHOOL, NEW DELHI

This time, Jolene didn't even let Brooks get out of the Audi before she confronted him.

Another one of Daisy's soccer matches. This time, Brooks had made sure to leave the embassy on time, though whether it was his daughter he was more eager to see, or his ex-wife, the State Department official couldn't be sure. But when he pulled into the parking lot of Daisy's school and found Jolene waiting for him, Brooks knew by the expression on her face that he'd probably be better off just turning the Audi around.

Daisy was already heading to the pitch, Brooks saw, looking past his wife. Watching his daughter laughing with a couple of friends and feeling his heart stir. But Jolene quickly pulled him back to the foreground.

"Walk with me," she whispered, fierce, taking his arm as he stepped out of the car. Brooks saw little option but to obey; there was no sense in resisting Jolene when she was like this.

His wife hurried him across the parking lot to a far, empty corner. Released his arm and turned to glare at him, her hands on her hips.

"I just got a phone call from Langley," she said. "This morning someone requisitioned a Reaper drone and a couple of Hellfire missiles to take down a Huey helicopter sixty miles south of Kabul. Said there was a 'high-value target' aboard."

Brooks said nothing. Felt suddenly sick.

"I did some asking," Jolene continued. "You know who pulled the trigger and blew up that bird, Seth?"

Brooks knew. He hoped Jolene wouldn't make him say it.

But she was waiting for an answer.

"Porter," he said.

"That's right," Jolene snapped. "And whose Huey did he shoot down?"

Brooks cleared his throat. Couldn't meet her eyes. "Ours."

"No, Seth. Not *ours*. *Mine*. Along with three ex–Special Ops contractors who I cashed in all my Agency favors to get you, and who I assume are now dead. Because you told me you could get Dominic Porter."

All that rain last night, Brooks thought. *And this goddamned soccer match couldn't get rained out for once?*

"I put my *ass* on the line for this, Seth," Jolene continued. "Because *you* told me *your man* was good. Do you know what happens when Porter finds out about this? When his friends at the Agency figure out what we did?"

She raised her eyebrows. Brooks realized she was, again, waiting for his response.

"Uh—" he said.

"If Porter finds out, he kills us," Jolene said. "Me. You. Us. Daisy. Maybe even your stupid dog. You don't think he has the contacts to make that happen? You think I'm being dramatic?"

She was pacing now, and behind her anger, Brooks could see real fear. Could see that Dominic Porter—and whoever his friends were at the Agency—*terrified* her.

He'd never seen his wife so scared before. And frankly, *that* scared him more than anything.

"I know you're not being dramatic," he said.

"You *told* me your guy was good. You swore he'd never let Porter get out of Afghanistan. And Porter just—" She snapped her fingers. "Swatted him out of the sky. Fucking us all, Seth." She looked at him. "We're fucked."

Brooks's shoulders slumped. "I'm sorry."

"*Sorry.*" Jolene shook her head. "*Sorry* might cut it for the State Department, Seth. But we're playing big boy games here."

Again, he said nothing.

Jolene glared at him. "There's an Indian Air Force transport flight leaving Palam AFB for Kabul in ninety minutes. I called in my last favor and got you a seat."

Brooks stared at her. "*Kabul?*"

"You got it, my friend. Play stupid games and win stupid prizes. You're going to Afghanistan."

39

KABUL

This must be what Saigon felt like, the voice muttered, as Hayes guided the Land Cruiser slowly through the throngs of people—young and old, men and women, families, their belongings stuffed into suitcases or wrapped in blankets atop their heads—who crowded the road, choking the flow of traffic to a near standstill.

It would be faster to do this on foot, Hayes thought. Around the vehicle, the crowd was indeed moving faster, and Hayes knew that if he were alone, he would have abandoned the SUV a mile or so back. But the Nassim family, even healthy, would have a hard time keeping their young children close at hand in the mob, and there was no question at all of trying to carry

Payam, or asking Freshta to navigate the crush of humanity outside with a badly broken arm.

Every now and then, eyes from outside would glance into the Land Cruiser, take in the sight of Abdul's bloody hands, Freshta's sling. Payam lying unconscious across his mother's lap. But rarely did the sight of the trauma register on any faces. The folks outside on the street were carrying their own trauma, as sure as they were carrying suitcases. Their faces spoke to fear, desperation. And in some, resignation.

The crowd only intensified, the closer they came to the gates of the airport. Hayes wasn't exactly sure, but he figured they still had a quarter of a mile or so to cover, and looking outside, he wasn't confident in their chances. This was no longer a parade around them; it was a mosh pit. Even the pedestrians had stopped moving forward.

It was late afternoon. Shadows growing long, the sound of jet engines screaming to life audible overhead, the incessant *thump* of artillery fire from somewhere outside of the city. Hayes couldn't imagine what the scene must be like at the gates, the pressure as the mob pushed forward against the barrier, the Marines behind trying their best to sort through the crowd, to allow the Americans through and those locals with a valid claim to a plane ticket out of here, and filter out the rest.

This wasn't working. It would take hours to get to the front gate, even from here, and there was no way they'd get Payam through the crowd, not without risking even more serious injury. Hayes pulled out his phone, switched off the kill switch that masked his location. He dialed Seth Brooks.

Brooks didn't answer right away, and when he did, he sounded harried. Traffic noise behind him. "Brooks."

"I need an escape plan," Adam told him. "Out of Kabul, party of six. The airport's a no-go."

On the other end of the line, the State Department man snorted. "Is that all you need, Adam? How about another Huey?"

"Whatever works," Hayes replied. "I just need it quick, Brooks. I have a kid—"

"What happened to Porter, Adam?"

Hayes blinked. "What?"

"Porter." Brooks bit the name off. "We had a deal, Adam."

"And I'm working on your end. But I need you to help me get these folks out of here. This kid's going to die if he doesn't see a doctor tonight."

Beside him, Nassim stiffened. Hayes glanced in the rearview, hoped Freshta didn't hear him, was actually asleep and not just pretending.

"Helicopter, jet, army tank, I don't care," Hayes said. "These people just need to get out."

Brooks didn't answer immediately. "I'm sorry, Adam," he said finally. "That's just not my problem."

"Brooks—"

"This isn't a one-way street. We had a deal. You hold up your end and I'll hold up mine."

"There's no *time*." Hayes slammed down on the steering wheel. "What aren't you hearing, you—"

"Porter's booked on a transport out of Kabul at midnight.

If he gets on that flight, I promise, I'll make sure his first stop is New Mexico."

Annabelle.

"Say that again," Hayes replied. "Next time I shoot you off a building, I'll make sure you're dead when you land."

"Just do your job," Brooks said. "Please."

Then he ended the call.

In the passenger seat, Nassim looked his way. Gestured out the window. "This is hopeless," he said. "You should go."

"I'm not leaving you," Hayes said. "But you're right. This isn't going to work."

He shifted the Land Cruiser into reverse. Leaned on the horn and twisted around in his seat to guide the SUV out of the crowd. But before they'd reversed more than a couple of feet, Hayes heard screams from outside and then the sure sound of gunfire, as a line of 5.56 NATO rounds stitched across the front of the Toyota.

40

KABUL

There was no time for caution. Hayes stepped on the gas pedal and the Land Cruiser launched backward, pedestrians in the rearview mirror leaping out of the way, scattering, panic overtaking the mob. More gunfire from somewhere in front of the SUV; Hayes fumbled with the AK-47 between the seat as he drove, searching the crowd for the gunmen. Knew he couldn't fire into the mass of people blindly anyway, knew he'd do more harm than good with the rifle if he tried. Best bet was to get the hell out of here, minimize damage to the innocents both inside and outside the vehicle.

Twin white Mitsubishi SUVs somehow materialized behind the Land Cruiser. Appearing out of nowhere as the crowd around them dispersed. Hayes wrenched at the wheel as more gunmen piled out of the SUVs, swerving around the first and colliding hard with the front bumper of the second, sending a jolt through the Land Cruiser but barely slowing it down.

More gunfire spiderwebbed the windshield. Bullets pinged off the Toyota's bodywork.

"Duck down," Hayes told the family behind him. "Keep your heads low."

Beside him, Nassim had the window down. The Makarov aimed at the nearest Mitsubishi. The 9-millimeter rounds wouldn't do much damage to the vehicles, Hayes knew, and probably not to their occupants, either. Still, it might make them think twice about poking their heads out from cover.

The gunmen wore masks, Hayes noticed, as he wrestled with the Land Cruiser in reverse. Wore black—western clothes, not the *perahan tunban* of the locals. They weren't firing Kalashnikov rifles but, it looked like, HK416s.

They don't fight like the Taliban, either.

Hayes twisted in his seat again. Arm against the headrest, watching out the rear window as he drove. Figured they might have a chance at this, might get away, the bullet-riddled Land Cruiser still chugging, the gunmen still taking cover from Abdul's pistol rounds—when the little girl wandered out into the middle of the roadway, oblivious, directly into the Land Cruiser's path.

There was no time to think, just react. Hayes wrenched the wheel over and the Toyota jerked sideways, tires screaming, just narrowly missing the child. The Land Cruiser swung clear, but there was no time to celebrate. Directly in Hayes's path now was a lamppost he just couldn't dodge.

The Toyota slammed into the lamppost at speed, stopping the truck instantly, jolting Hayes hard in his seat, his head slamming into the headrest. Behind the truck, the lamppost toppled to the ground with a shower of sparks. Hayes slammed the Land Cruiser back into gear, as another round from the gunmen down the street peppered the Toyota's front grille.

The engine made a coughing sound and then died, smoke or steam rising from the bullet holes across the hood. Hayes didn't waste time.

"Go," he told Abdul and his family. "Find cover somewhere. I'll catch up."

He shoved open the driver's-side door. Raised the AK-47 from between the seats and took aim at the gunmen as they advanced toward him.

His first burst sent them diving for cover, knocked one of them flat on his ass, but there were too many, and they regrouped quickly. A bullet sparked off of the doorframe, inches from Hayes's head, sending him ducking and scrambling across to the passenger side of the SUV just as Freshta pulled Bilal to the street, Abdul already running, carrying Payam in his arms. Hayes couldn't see Zarah.

Handle these guys. Then pray she's all right.

But the team was too good. They'd spread out wide, spanning across the street, advancing slowly but steady, gradually closing in.

You have to get out of here. Fall back.

Ducking as low as he could, Hayes rolled out to the pavement. Landed hard, his ribs screaming with a pain he didn't allow himself to feel for long. He raised the rifle again, took aim at the closest gunman. Pulled the trigger and—

Boom! Behind the gunman, one of the Mitsubishi SUVs exploded. More small-arms fire erupted from somewhere behind Hayes, and ahead of him, the gunmen scattered. Flattened to the pavement. Began returning fire at an attacking force that Hayes couldn't see.

Behind them, someone slipped out of the second Mitsubishi and started running, but Hayes barely paid attention. He was suddenly in the middle of a firefight he didn't understand, and the smartest course of action now was to get the hell out.

So he did.

Crouched into a half-crawl, half-run, he hurried after Abdul and his family, found cover behind a concrete building that had apparently once housed a beauty salon. Down the block, the Nassims were still trying to escape, Abdul limping, his strength clearly flagging with his son in his arms. Freshta and—thank God—Zarah pulling Bilal along with them.

Hayes swung his rifle back to cover their exit. Backed down the side street ready to fire at whoever showed their face at the intersection, but nobody did. On the main road, the gunfire continued, unabated. Staccato pops that echoed in all directions. And then the *whoosh* of a rocket-propelled grenade, the thunder when it found its target.

Up the block, Abdul had dropped to his knees. Freshta beside him, urging him up. Hayes caught up, glanced over his friend's shoulder. Saw Payam in his arms, fresh blood gushing out from the wound in his chest.

Shit.

"It came loose," Abdul said. He was sobbing. "The bandages—they fell off."

The shrapnel had been jarred, Hayes could see. Opening the wound wider, causing more damage. There was no hope that more battlefield dressing would save the boy. He needed a doctor right now.

"There is a hospital—two blocks," Freshta told Hayes. Pointed ahead to an intersection. Around the corner. North, toward the airport. Toward where the gunmen had come from.

The streets were emptier now, though people still lingered. Staring wide-eyed at Hayes, at the boy in Abdul's arms. *Just another day in paradise.*

Hayes pulled Abdul to his feet. "Come on," he told his friend. Scooped up Bilal in his arms and pushed Abdul gently forward, urging him onward as Freshta and Zarah led the way.

41

KABUL

You *trap me, I trap you,* Muhammed Ghul thought, watching with grim satisfaction through his good eye as the RPG obliterated Porter's SUV. At least three of the CIA traitor's operatives were down already, the ambush catching them completely out in the open, off-guard, too focused on killing Nassim and his American friend to maintain situational awareness.

So far, he couldn't see Dominic Porter, but Ghul suspected his target had probably lingered in one of the vehicles, content to let his men do the dirty work while he avoided any serious danger.

The kind of man who murders by drone, Ghul thought. *From thousands of miles away. A coward.*

Porter hadn't expected the RPG, Ghul knew. Hadn't expected much resistance at all. He'd come here to kill a family. This was a fairer fight.

It had not taken Ghul and his men long to catch up to Nassim and his friend, not with the entire city nearly choked to a crawl. Ghul knew Kabul like few others, knew back roads and secret passages that enabled him and his fighters to move like ghosts through the capital. With Nassim mired in the suffocating current of humanity heading to the airport, Ghul had been able to overtake on their flank, relying on his spies in the crowd, on foot, and on motorbike, to relay the Land Cruiser's updated position.

As expected, Porter had taken the bait, the man so desperate to save his skin that he'd walked right into an obvious trap. And now his men were paying for his lack of foresight, pinned down by ten Taliban gunmen, their blood mixing with the blood of the Afghan civilians they'd murdered already in their attempt to kill Abdul Nassim.

Outside of Ghul's technical, the Americans were falling back. Searching for cover, attempting to retreat.

"Press forward," Ghul instructed his men. "No mercy."

But the roar of a helicopter drowned out his words. More Americans, this time in the air, roused from the airfield by the sounds of the firefight. They'd come to save American lives, Ghul knew. The game was over.

He picked up his radio. "Fall back." Then he turned to his driver. "Get us out of here. We've done all we can."

The driver nodded. Reversed the pickup as Ghul's fighters climbed into the truck's bed. On the street outside, the rest of

Ghul's men loaded into the other two trucks as the fighters already aboard provided covering fire.

The helicopter would still need to be dealt with. Ghul pressed the talk button on the radio again. "Omar."

"I will handle it," Omar replied. As the lead technical sped away with Ghul in it, he watched in the sideview mirror as the fighter stood in the bed of the second pickup, holding a rocket-propelled grenade launcher on his shoulder.

Omar took aim at the American helicopter, a UH-60 Black Hawk that had begun to trail the convoy of technicals as they attempted to escape. As Omar fired the rocket, the pilot in the helicopter took evasive action, dodging the RPG by mere inches and no doubt putting the fear of God into everyone aboard.

The rocket had missed, but Ghul didn't mind. His men knew the streets of Kabul better than any American invader. In the thirty seconds it took for the pilot of the Black Hawk to recover, Ghul and the rest of the convoy had disappeared, melding into the backdrop of the ancient city and leaving their pursuers high above hopeless to follow.

42

KABUL

can make him stable," the doctor told Hayes and Abdul Nassim. "But the boy will need surgery, and a blood transfusion. And we are not able to do such things anymore."

Looking around the clinic, Hayes could see the man's point. The hospital had been nearly empty when they'd hurried through the doors, two of the windows smashed and the ceiling lights flickering, nearly everything of value in the lobby already taken by looters, and the rest of it strewn across the floors.

There'd been no one in sight and Hayes had felt his heart drop, knowing the doctors and nurses who worked here had probably already fled. Praying that at least there would be fresh bandages here, something to sterilize Payam Nassim's wound. Stop the bleeding and pack everything tight and then try again to get the boy to the gates of the airport.

Hayes had been searching the nurses' stations when he ran into the doctor. A short, slender man who looked terrified to see him, raised his hands and froze, instantly, his eyes fixed on Hayes's rifle.

"Please," he said in English. "Take what you want. It's okay."

"I'm not here to rob you," Hayes replied. "I have people who need help."

He'd gestured to the doctor to follow him back to the lobby. The doctor obeyed, reluctantly, like he thought Hayes was leading him into a trap. Like whatever was happening, it was just another headache he didn't need.

Well, he's right about that, the voice said. *But that's too bad for him.*

Abdul had laid Payam down on a bench in the lobby, then returned to stand guard by the front door with the Makarov. Freshta knelt by her son, tending to him as best as she could, Hayes's crude sling barely stabilizing her arm anymore. The other two children sat idly nearby, Zarah reading to her younger brother from a magazine she'd found on the floor.

The doctor's eyes went wide.

"He'll die without you," Hayes told him. "Please. Help us."

The doctor looked skyward. Hayes could tell he was calculating the risks. Could tell that the man wanted to say no. Turn them away. Could tell that this was an imposition that the doctor didn't need.

But Payam was dying; that much was obvious. And ultimately, the doctor's humanity won out.

"Bring him with me," he told Hayes. "The woman, too, with the arm. The others stay here for now."

Hayes gave Abdul the AK-47 and hoisted Payam gently into his arms. He and Freshta followed the doctor to a rickety, death-trap elevator that somehow managed to climb to the hospital's fourth floor. And when the door slid open, Hayes was amazed at what he saw.

Patients in hospital beds, at least a dozen of them. Elderly, mostly, and all of them obviously very ill. They were hooked up to heart monitors and breathing machines, and most barely moved. Only a few heads turned to watch as Hayes and Freshta followed the doctor off the elevator.

Here and there, other doctors hurried between the beds, tending to their patients, checking their monitors. The doctors were all male, Hayes observed.

"We sent the women away," the doctor told him. "Nurses and doctors. It is not safe to be an educated woman in Afghanistan anymore."

It's not safe to be any *woman in Afghanistan anymore,* said the voice. *Hell, it's not even that safe to be a man.*

"These are the patients we're unable to evacuate," the doctor said, leading Hayes and Freshta to an empty bed in the corner of the room. "They are fragile from advanced cancers, or other serious illness. They would not survive if we moved them."

Hayes set Payam down on the bed. He stood back as the doctor immediately went to work, calling out to his colleagues for assistance, supplies. As two more doctors began to help Payam, a third took Freshta by her good arm, and ushered her to a chair. He began examining her broken arm.

"We can buy this boy time," the doctor told Hayes. "Hours, at least. Days, if he's lucky. But he will need proper care, care that we can no longer provide."

"Just do your best," Hayes replied. "Let me handle the rest."

He stepped away from the bed. Left Payam in the hands of the doctors. Tried to formulate a plan, some way to get the Nassims through the gates of the airport without having to battle through the mob.

He looked around the clinic. The beds full of the sick and dying, and the doctors who'd stayed behind, at great risk, to treat them.

Brooks wouldn't help. That much had already been established. Not until Porter was dead, anyway, and Payam Nassim didn't have that kind of time. Hayes considered leaving the Nassims here, fighting his way through the crowd to the airport gates himself. The Marines would let him in, he knew, with his American passport. Maybe inside he could plead the family's case to somebody in charge, wrangle a convoy to come out and retrieve Abdul and his family under guard.

Fat chance. They'd more likely try and get you into a transport plane and fly you the hell out of here. Nobody's going outside the gates to save a random Afghan family, not now.

Shit. Hayes knew that really left only one option, and that was a long shot. He didn't relish even trying, but there was no other choice.

He pulled out his phone. Dialed the number. Typed in his account number, ended the call, and waited.

A few minutes later, the phone rang.

"I need an extraction," Hayes said. "Downtown Kabul; I'll give you the coordinates. Me and five civilians. And I'll need a good medic."

A long silence. Then Levi Shaw chuckled. "Is that all?"

"I'm out of options, Levi," Hayes told him. "I have an eight-year-old boy who's going to die if he doesn't get proper care for the shrapnel wound in his chest. And the rest of his family's not in much better shape. Can you help me? Because if not, I have to hang up and find someone who will."

He imagined Shaw back in the Treadstone offices in Georgetown. It was early in DC, Hayes knew, around seven in the morning, but his boss had always been an early riser. He was probably lounging on that big expensive Chesterfield he was so proud of, savoring this moment.

"I can probably pull a few strings," Shaw replied, after a long beat. "But Adam—are you sure you want to owe me a favor like this? You know I'll collect on it someday."

"I know you will. And I hate having to ask. But I don't really have any other choice, Levi."

"Just so long as you know my help doesn't come free. Send

me your coordinates. And for God's sake, stay put. I'll see what I can do."

The line went dead.

Well, there you go, the voice told Hayes. *You've just made a deal with the devil. Wonder what it'll cost you.*

43

KABUL

Hayes left Payam Nassim and his mother in the care of the doctors. Avoiding the elevator, he took the stairs back down to the hospital's main floor, where Abdul Nassim still stood at the smashed windows, the AK-47 in his hands and ready.

In the lobby, Zarah paged through a magazine, while Bilal slept curled up in a chair. It was dusk now, daylight all but slipped away, and more than half of the lobby lights seemed to be in their death throes. The night crept in from outside, bringing shadows and the relief of cooler air. Hayes felt suddenly very tired; his stomach growled. He couldn't remember the last time he'd eaten or slept.

He went searching, found a cafeteria down a long hall

from the lobby. Grabbed a few candy bars and a couple of cans of soda, a bottle of water. Nearly everything else had been already taken.

Bringing the impromptu dinner back to the lobby, he split one candy bar in half for Zarah. Set the other half beside Bilal and gave another full bar to Nassim, along with one of the sodas. Kept one bar and one soda for himself.

The sugar rush was immediate, and instantly gratifying. Hayes hadn't realized how hungry he was, but now that he was eating, he had to make himself slow down, savor it. There wasn't much else in the cafeteria, and God only knew when they'd eat again.

As Hayes ate, he walked to the window to stand with Abdul. The two men gazed out into the street. In the distance, they could still hear the sound of the crowd outside of the airport. Hear the planes taking off and landing. Hear the guns.

Hayes's phone buzzed. A message. From Levi Shaw.

Extraction team will be at your coordinates 1000 tomorrow. You owe me.

Hayes felt a sudden surge of relief.

"I made a call," he told Abdul. "It's going to cost me, but I got us a way out of here tomorrow morning. We just have to make it through the night."

"Whatever the cost," Abdul said. "I will pay."

Hayes smiled, wry, at his friend. "It's not that kind of cost."

Abdul glanced at him. Chewed his candy bar and said nothing. When he'd finished, he cracked open the soda and took a swig. Swallowed.

"I was thinking about my father," he said quietly. "I have been so worried all day about my children, my wife—I haven't had any time yet to mourn."

"There will be time," Hayes said. "He would want you to focus on keeping your family safe."

Abdul took another sip from the soda can. "He told me to leave him behind," he said. "In Jalalabad. He was afraid he would only slow us down." He paused. "He would have died to protect us."

"As you would die for your children. And me for mine."

Abdul nodded.

"He would be proud of you," Hayes said. "He would be happy to know you've kept your family safe."

"We are not out of danger yet. Payam, especially. If he . . ." Abdul didn't finish the thought. Hayes could see his friend's eyes were glistening.

"He won't. He's in good hands up there. And we're going to get him out of here."

Abdul said nothing. Stared out through the broken window into the street, and in the dim light, Hayes could see his friend's jaw set firm, his mouth a thin line, determined not to break.

His hunger pangs sufficiently quelled for now, Hayes's exhausted body began to scream for sleep. He found a couple of chairs close enough that he could lean back and put his feet up, and felt his eyes start to close the minute he'd sat down. Hayes blinked, pushed himself awake.

You need an extra-large coffee, the voice said. *Or a Red Bull.*

"Sleep," Abdul told him, from the windows. "I will watch out for trouble. You surely need rest."

Hayes's every instinct protested; it was a bad idea to fall asleep on the job, and this hospital wasn't anywhere near secure. But Hayes figured the last time he'd slept was on the flight to Peshawar the morning before, a brief and unsatisfying few hours in his seat aboard the State Department's C-37, any hope of rest dashed by nightmares and turbulence.

You've gone nearly a day and a half without closing your eyes. Sooner or later, it's going to affect your ability to perform when it counts.

Fine, Hayes thought. *But not yet.*

"Let me have a look at that thumb drive first," he told Nassim, who dug it out from his pocket and handed it over. The drive was a compact one-terabyte model, Hayes saw, reinforced with a rugged shock-proof casing that had hopefully done the trick since it had come into Abdul Nassim's possession. Hayes wasn't sure what kind of real-world testing portable flash drives were subjected to, but he suspected that being shot out of the sky by a Hellfire missile had probably pushed this one's protection to the limit.

Retracing his steps through the hospital, he returned to the hallway that led to the cafeteria. About halfway down, he'd noticed a small office. Inside, he thought he'd glimpsed a laptop.

He had. A battered old Acer lay abandoned on the desk, and Hayes pulled a chair over and flipped the laptop open, hoping it would boot up. By some miracle, it was still operational, and Hayes signed in with a guest account, plugged the drive into the USB port, and opened the icon when it appeared.

He wasn't sure at first what he was looking at. Nearly all of the drive's terabyte of storage had been filled, though mostly with spreadsheets and text files that seemed to be in some kind of code. There was video, too, though, and when Hayes clicked the first .mp4 file, he realized he was watching what had driven Dominic Porter to kill.

It was a clip of Porter and two other Americans standing at the rear of an olive-green Ford F-250 Super Duty pickup equipped with a matching canopy. Surrounding them were a handful of men in tunics and turbans, carrying AK-47s. The clip had obviously been shot in secret; the picture blurred and jostled, ducked away whenever Porter or his men glanced over. But it stayed focused long enough to catch Porter's men opening the rear hatch of the canopy, and the camera operator got close enough to the action to register the F-250's cargo.

Inside the truck bed were at least seven FGM-148 Javelin anti-tank missile systems, including shoulder-mounted launch tube assembly, the Command Launch Unit targeting component, and the missiles themselves. From what Hayes remembered about the Javelin system, each individual setup was said to cost somewhere north of two hundred thousand dollars—which made this around a $1.5 million truckload.

The Taliban fighters didn't hand Dominic Porter a million and a half dollars in cash, but they did seem to come to some visible understanding. As the camera rolled, Porter's men handed over the keys to the F-250 to one of the fighters. The camera operator panned as the Americans walked away to a Humvee and sped off across the desert. Then the picture went black.

There were more videos. There were plenty of coded spreadsheets. But Hayes figured he'd seen about enough to know that Abdul Nassim had been right. Dominic Porter was a traitor, to America and to her Afghan allies, and if the contents of this flash drive were to make it into the hands of his superiors, Porter would hang.

We can help with that, the voice said.

The battered Acer wasn't connected to any internet source, so Hayes used the Librem 5 to set up a mobile hotspot. Then he opened a web browser and logged in to his encrypted cloud storage account, and began the long task of uploading the contents of the thumb drive. With nearly a terabyte of data to upload, and the Librem's satellite connection spotty at best, the transfer would take hours, Hayes knew. He left the laptop and the phone in the office and returned to the hospital lobby, where Nassim stood guard.

"You were right," Hayes told his friend. "About Porter. All of it."

Nassim only nodded wearily, lacking the energy or the enthusiasm for any kind of celebration. It wouldn't matter now, Hayes knew, if they couldn't get out of Kabul. If Payam didn't survive the night.

Nassim must have noticed the expression on Hayes's face. He smiled, weakly. "I am happy. Really, Adam," he said. "I just . . ." He gestured around the lobby. Upstairs, to where Payam and Freshta had gone.

Hayes nodded. He knew he couldn't blame his friend.

"Get some sleep," Nassim said. "Morning will come soon enough."

Hayes stifled a yawn. His eyes were drifting closed again. This time, he didn't bother to stop them.

He dreamed. Of Hellfire missiles and downed helicopters, the blood spurting out of a Taliban fighter's throat. The blood oozing out of the wound in Payam Nassim's chest. He dreamed of Annabelle, and Jack. Of Haiti.

He dreamed until everything ran together, until he was standing atop the wreckage of the downed Huey back in the Tangi Valley, but instead of Abdul Nassim's family trapped inside, it was his own, the Hellfire screaming toward them as he leapt for safety. Watching them die, hearing their screams as the Huey burned.

He slept restlessly, shifting against the hard plastic chairs, his ribs screaming with every movement, his back and neck sore. He slept until the pain grew too much to ignore, and then, blinking and groggy, he opened his eyes.

And found himself staring down the barrel of a rifle.

HAMID KARZAI INTERNATIONAL AIRPORT

Seth Brooks unbuckled himself from the jump seat inside the Indian Air Force C-17 Globemaster III's cavernous cargo hold as the plane taxied off of the runway. The big transport jet was nearly empty around him, aside from a few cargo pallets loaded with food and water, but Brooks knew that on the plane's return trip it would be packed full of human beings desperate to flee Kabul before the final curtain dropped and the Taliban took over.

And where will you be when that happens?

Of all the places in the world Seth Brooks could find himself, Afghanistan was, without a doubt, the worst-case scenario. Brooks still wasn't quite sure how he'd wound up here, what bizarre confluence of events had led to him catching this flight.

But on second thought, scratch that; he knew. It was Jolene. It was always Jolene.

He'd only meant to impress her, convincing Hayes to kill Dominic Porter. Solve a problem that was clearly bothering her, get rid of a thorn in her side. He'd failed, obviously. Spectacularly. Not only had Hayes *not* killed Porter, he'd tipped his hand by letting Porter see that Abdul Nassim—whoever he was—had American friends.

Sooner or later, Jolene figured Porter would trace Adam Hayes and that wrecked Huey helicopter back to her. And given Porter's tendency to violence, Brooks figured his ex-wife had a right to feel scared.

So here Brooks was. The Collapse of Saigon—encore performance. Kabul in its dying days. Even the IAF aircrew thought he was insane for being here.

The Globemaster came to a halt somewhere on the vastness of Kabul's international airport. The last holdout of American influence on the region. Brooks waited as the rear cargo door lowered, then stepped out into the night air, the smell of jet fuel almost overpowering. At least it wasn't raining.

The Kabul airport had been built by the Soviets in the sixties, bombed by the Americans after 9/11, rebuilt and expanded by American and coalition forces during the mid 2000s to handle international flights, and then expanded yet again to house the headquarters of the Afghan Air Force. In a few days, it would become property of the Taliban again.

For now, it was the last stronghold of American and NATO forces in Afghanistan.

The airfield was vast, with a single runway stretching more than two miles southeast to northwest, and the grounds around it encompassing the AAF base as well as the original, Soviet domestic terminal, and the newer international facility. Stepping out onto the tarmac, Brooks wondered if the airport had ever been as busy as it was at that moment—and if it would ever be as busy again.

Aircraft of all descriptions lined the aprons on both sides of the runway, military and civilian alike, from C-130 Hercules turboprops and C-17 Globemasters belonging to American and coalition forces, to commercial Boeing 737s and Airbuses repurposed for the evacuation, to chartered Gulfstreams and everything in between. Helicopters buzzed steadily overhead as planes queued to take off; everywhere, military vehicles threaded between them, as civilian trucks and buses slowed just within the airport gates to add to the mass of humanity waiting for their ticket out of here.

The scene was overwhelming, an assault on every one of Brooks's senses. *My God,* he thought. *I heard it was bad, but this . . .*

There were no words. In the distance, the chatter of small-arms fire and the thunder of artillery shells detonating only added to the sense that the world was ending, and made Brooks want to do nothing more than climb back on that Indian jet and get the hell back home.

Instead, he squared his shoulders and waded into the chaos.

It took the better part of an hour before Brooks found anyone who even knew who Dominic Porter was, and by that point, the State Department man was drenched in sweat and woozy from the jet fuel fumes that hung heavily in the air.

He'd been shuttled by a fresh-faced U.S. Marine corporal to a gunnery sergeant, who'd paused in directing a long line of terrified-looking civilian contractors to gesture Brooks across the runway to a hangar about a half-mile away.

"Spooks are all on that side of the circus," the Marine told Brooks, hollering to be heard over the whine of jet engines. "Just don't tell them *I* told you that."

Brooks hiked across the airfield, dodging more taxiing jets, tanker trucks, and Humvees in the dark, expecting to be gunned down at any moment by an overzealous Marine. The dash across the runway itself was truly terrifying—the pavement hopelessly wide and seeming to stretch endlessly in both directions, the lights of distant jets impossible to track as they hurtled through the night.

Brooks ducked low on the fringe of the runway as a massive German Air Force A400M Atlas transport plane thundered past and climbed into the night, the roar of the Airbus's four turboprops nearly deafening and the wind in the plane's slipstream almost blowing him back onto his ass. Once he'd picked himself up, he'd looked hard down the runway to make sure no plane was following in the Atlas's wake, closed his eyes, and, muttering a prayer, ran for it.

He'd never been so thankful to feel grass under his shoes as when he reached the other side of the runway, though he still had at least another quarter mile to cover before he reached the CIA hangar.

A Gulfstream G550 jet sat parked in front of the hangar, similar to the C-37s that Brooks was used to flying in as a member of the State Department, but this plane appeared to be under civil registration.

Typical for the Agency, Brooks thought. *Probably leased from some impenetrable wall of shell companies, just so nobody sees the CIA's fingerprints here.*

Two well-armed Marines stood guard at the plane's airstairs. They stiffened as Brooks appeared out of the shadows, their M16A4 rifles at the ready. Slowly, Brooks withdrew his State Department identification. Showed it to them in the light.

"Who's in charge around here?"

The Marines glanced at each other. Then motioned up into the plane. "There's a man named Gardner calling the shots, sir," one Marine told Brooks. "But it sounds like he's about ready to forget about this place."

"You mind if I talk to him a second?" Brooks asked.

The Marines swapped glances again. Shrugged. While one of the soldiers hung back with Brooks, his partner climbed the stairs into the Gulfstream to find Gardner.

Gardner turned out to be a lean, dark-haired, middle-aged man with a strong jaw and the air of someone who'd just discovered his steak has been cooked well-done, not medium rare. "Who are you?" he called down from the Gulfstream's open door. "Can't you see we're trying to get out of here?"

"Seth Brooks, State Department," Brooks replied. "I'm hoping you can help me find Dominic Porter."

The mention of Porter's name brought a deep crease to Gardner's brow. "If I could find Dominic Porter, I'd be halfway to Ramstein by now," he said, coming down the airstairs to the tarmac. "He's supposed to be on this flight, but he's flown the fucking coop again. What does the State Department want with him, anyway?"

Brooks hesitated. Not sure how much to tell Gardner, not sure on whose side the CIA man's allegiances lay.

Gardner studied him, waiting. Examining Brooks in that way the Agency people always seemed to do, that creepy, expressionless gaze that left you thinking they knew your thoughts before you could even think them.

"My wife is Dr. Jolene Andrews," Brooks said, finally. Taking a chance. "I'm here on her behalf. She asked me to make sure Porter made it out of Kabul as soon as possible."

At the mention of Jolene's name, Gardner's face softened by a degree. "Thought your name sounded familiar," he said. "Always wondered how the doc wound up hitched to one of you State guys. Almost like sleeping with the enemy, isn't it?"

"We'd like to think we're not quite the Taliban," Brooks said.

Gardner looked at him again. Like he wasn't sure if Brooks was joking. Finally, he sighed. "Porter's supposed to be here. Has orders. He caught the bird out of Eagle Base just like everyone else, but somewhere along the way he wandered off again. Last I heard, he was outside the wire chasing ghosts."

"You have anyone looking for him?"

"Looking for him, hell." Gardner spat. "I've got thirty of my staff crammed into this little jet that's supposed to only hold twenty. Far as I'm concerned, if Porter misses this bus, he can hop a C-17 like everyone else. We're not waiting."

He gave Brooks an apologetic shrug. "Sorry I couldn't be more help. But hey—give my best to the doc, would you? I always did enjoy when she'd come around and see us."

He slapped Brooks on the shoulder, turned and walked back to the jet, and climbed up the airstairs. Brooks saw him duck into the cockpit, say something to the pilot, before turning right and disappearing into the plane. A moment or two later, a uniformed flight attendant appeared in the doorway and the airstairs began to ascend. As Brooks watched, the stairs locked away and the cabin doors closed. The Marines moved clear as the jet began to taxi away from the hangar. Within minutes, it was just another handful of blinking lights against the dark Kabul sky.

45

Muhammed Ghul grinned down at the American man. Prodded him with the barrel of the Kalashnikov.

"Sorry to disturb you," he told the man in Pashto. "But we didn't want to leave you behind."

The American blinked. Looked around the lobby of the hospital, his eyes going dark when he registered what he was seeing. Ghul's men, six of them. One for each child, two for Abdul Nassim. Two beside Ghul, ready to act if the American tried anything foolish.

As far as Americans went, Ghul would have preferred to be aiming his rifle at Dominic Porter right now. But if everything proceeded according to plan, that would come soon enough.

Ghul had been alerted to Abdul Nassim's presence in the hospital by one of his spies, of which there were many in Kabul right now. A family hiding out in the lobby of the clinic, a man with an AK-47 standing guard at the doorway. An American man accompanying them.

One did not have to be a genius to make the connection. Ghul did not know what Abdul Nassim's plan was, nor did he care. He'd thanked the spy for the information. And then he'd assembled his team and gone to find Porter's target.

Truthfully, Muhammed Ghul was exhausted. His body ached; he was tempted to cut his foot off to lessen the discomfort caused by the old man's knife the night before. He'd bandaged his blind eye and now felt dizzy, unused to the lack of perspective, off-kilter. Part of him would have been grateful, somewhat, if Dominic Porter had just left the country with the rest of the Americans—denying him his chance at revenge.

But Ghul knew that if he allowed Porter to leave, he would spend the rest of his life wishing he'd claimed his vengeance when it was offered to him.

And this—Abdul Nassim—was vengeance being offered.

Beneath Ghul, the American wet his lips. "Who are you?" he asked in Pashto. His accent passable—better than Dominic Porter's, anyway.

"My name is Muhammed Ghul," Ghul told him. "We met yesterday, in the Tangi Valley."

"You tried to destroy my helicopter."

Ghul nodded. "Yes, and Dominic Porter tried to destroy both of us." The American frowned at the mention of Porter's name. Ghul smiled. Gestured to the men behind him to lift the American to his feet.

"Come with me," he said. "We will have plenty of time to talk on the way."

Hayes let the Taliban men pull him upright. Let them bind his wrists, roughly, behind his back, and push him forward toward the hospital doors. Stifling a groan as the men bumped against his chest, his ribs. Fighting to keep the pain off of his face.

The men had Abdul bound, too, Hayes saw. He watched as another one of the fighters lifted Zarah Nassim, struggling, into his arms, while a fourth of Ghul's men hoisted Bilal. Hayes met Abdul's eyes as the men muscled them out to the street. Knew his friend was thinking the same as he was.

Freshta. And Payam.

Neither Abdul's wife nor his eldest boy were here. Nor were they waiting outside in any of the three white Toyota Hiluxes parked at the curb. Was Ghul not aware of the other Nassims? Did he not care?

Hayes wasn't about to ask. He knew Abdul wouldn't, either.

Keep your mouth shut. Hope Ghul leaves them behind.

It was still dark outside. Nowhere near mid-morning yet. Whatever Levi Shaw had cooking for the extraction, it was a long ways away.

Ghul hadn't asked about the thumb drive, and Hayes hadn't told him anything. The drive was still back in the small office room in the hospital, plugged into the laptop. Hayes realized the Librem 5 was still back there, too. He'd left it behind to upload the drive's data.

There goes your GPS, Hayes thought. *Hope this guy doesn't plan to take you far.*

He let Ghul's men shove him into the back of the technical. Turned in his seat to watch the other Taliban men install Abdul in the second truck, his children in the last. In front of Hayes, Ghul climbed in the passenger seat, while one of his men took the seat beside Hayes, the barrel of his AK-47 pressed tight against Hayes's broken ribs.

The driver climbed behind the wheel and turned the key in the ignition. The truck rumbled to life. From the passenger seat, Ghul turned back to grin at Hayes.

"My apologies," he said. And then Hayes's vision went dark, as the man beside him pulled a black canvas bag securely over his head.

By Hayes's reckoning, they drove for nearly an hour, though it was impossible to know for sure. In the city, at first, lots of stopping and starting, the driver leaning on his horn and shouting out into traffic. But after maybe fifteen minutes of that, the ride became smoother as the truck picked up speed, the timbre of the engine increasing and the sound of the wind outside louder.

They stayed on pavement for a long time. Relatively, mercifully smooth, not many bumps to jostle the rifle barrel still pressed into Hayes's side. Then the truck slowed, and made a sharp turn, and from then on, the ride was pure torture.

Hayes couldn't see the landscape, but he imagined the technical was driving over a boulder field, the truck's shocks apparently sold off or given away long before this journey. Nobody else in the vehicle seemed to care about the rough ride, and the driver certainly wasn't being shy with the gas pedal, but for Hayes, the dark fabric that blinded him suddenly became a fireworks show, every bump in the road bringing fresh, excruciating pain, taking everything he had not to cry out.

It might have been ten minutes, or ten hours. Finally, the truck slowed and the driver cut the engine. Hayes's blindfold was pulled off his face, and he looked out through the passenger window at the dark of the desert beyond.

It was impossible to see much. They were out of the city and the night was pure dark around them, just the barest hint of dawn beginning to show in the east. Giving form to the low hills in the distance.

Guess the blindfold was probably overkill, the voice said.

The wash of the second technical's headlights illuminated a small building as the truck pulled in beside the first. A mudbrick structure, one floor. Hayes couldn't imagine what it was doing out here.

Wherever here *is.*

Ghul stepped out of the truck, and Hayes let his guards pull him out behind. Let them nudge him toward the doorway of the building. Heard the rumble of a generator coming to life as he followed Ghul inside, and then there was light.

It might have been a house, at some point—Hayes could see what remained of a cooking area, a living space. There was a desk and a chair, a rug on the floor, and some cushions for resting. But it was the other room of the building, barely visible through a narrow doorway, that caught his attention the most.

Bloodstains on the walls and the floor. Shackles. A Taliban flag and a camcorder mounted on a tripod. This was a killing place, Hayes knew.

This was where men came to die.

46

SOMEWHERE EAST OF 'OMAR KALAY, AFGHANISTAN

Behind Hayes, the Taliban fighters muscled Abdul into the killing house, and then Zarah and Bilal. Zarah had stopped struggling, though Bilal was crying. Hayes could see the muscles in Abdul's neck grow taut as he struggled against his bonds, wanting to comfort his children. But his guards held him in place, firm.

Ghul waited until they were all inside the building, then he addressed Hayes. "I'm afraid we don't have much time," he said. "Every minute in Afghanistan is the same as an American year. Everything changes, and one must be quick to capitalize."

Hayes said nothing. He was studying the room. The guards. His mind probing for weak spots. For the bored guard.

The tired guard. The guard who would let his attention wander just long enough that Hayes could do something.

Six guards, all with assault rifles. You make one bad play and they'll cut you all to shreds.

"As I say, time is precious," Ghul continued. "But I must know—who are you to this man?" He nodded to Nassim. "Why have you chosen to die for his family?"

Hayes said nothing. Ghul smiled.

"You realize that I'm asking politely," he said. "Making pleasant conversation. I'm not always so courteous."

Hayes figured he knew that. He'd heard stories about Muhammed Ghul. The bloodthirsty Taliban commander. It was said that when he wanted information out of you, he had his men cut something off your body before he'd even asked the question, just so you knew he was serious.

"You are American," Ghul said. "You speak Pashto better than most of your people. Clearly, you've been to Afghanistan before. Which means you were military, but you're not anymore."

"This man saved my life," Hayes told him. "Fighting your people. A long time ago."

Ghul nodded thoughtfully. "And you owe him your debt," he said. "It's a pity you will fail at repaying him."

"Maybe. Maybe not."

Ghul grinned at him. That carnival funhouse leer. "Not many men have your confidence. Not by the time they are here."

He turned away from Hayes, apparently satisfied. Pulled a phone from his pocket. Aimed it at Abdul Nassim and pressed a button. From what happened next, Hayes could tell he must be recording.

"State your name," Ghul told Abdul.

Abdul coughed. Stared at the phone, dull-eyed. But he spoke his name. Ghul moved the phone to face Zarah and Bilal. "And these are your children, are they not?"

"They are."

"Their names?"

Abdul closed his eyes. "Zarah Nassim." His voice came out strangled. "And Bilal Nassim."

"Thank you," Ghul said. He pointed the phone at Abdul again. Being careful, Hayes noticed, to keep him out of the screen.

He knows he's in deep shit if word gets out he has an American hostage. That means he's probably sending this to Porter.

"So you see, they are alive," Ghul said. "As am I, despite your best efforts. And I assure you, Dominic Porter, that if you don't come to retrieve them from me by dawn, I will drive them out of Afghanistan myself and see to it they survive until they're in American custody. Until they can tell the world whatever secrets you're hiding."

He pointed the camera out the doorway. "You know where to find me," he said. "Don't make me wait too long."

He pressed a button to stop recording. Fiddled with the phone—probably sending the video to Porter, Hayes thought—and then tucked it away.

Then he looked at his guards.

"I am done with them," he said, nodding at the captives. "Do with them what you like."

HAMID KARZAI INTERNATIONAL AIRPORT

Seth Brooks sat on the rear bumper of an Afghan National Army Navistar 7000-MV four-and-a-half-ton cargo truck, watching the endless procession of planes taking off and wondering how he was supposed to track down Dominic Porter now.

Outside the wire, Gardner said. *Chasing ghosts.*

Brooks was pretty sure he knew which ghosts Porter was chasing. And he was just as sure he didn't want to go out there to find him.

The CIA Gulfstream was long gone; it had disappeared into the night sky hours ago. Brooks had wandered this side of the airfield, ducking into each of the long line of hangars, asking anyone who looked like they spoke English if they'd seen Dominic Porter. But the whole thing was useless, and only served to make Brooks sweatier and more tired. There were six thousand American troops on the ground at the airfield. Hundreds of thousands of civilians. Millions more outside the gates. Trying to find the CIA man now would be practically impossible even if he were still on the grounds of the airport. Venturing outside the gates to look for him, alone, would be suicidal.

Brooks had found his way to the parked Navistar, the big six-wheeler sitting apparently abandoned alongside the CIA's hangar. America had supplied nearly ten thousand of the versatile heavy-lift trucks to the ANA and Iraqi Ministry of Defense, and Brooks wondered what would become of the vehicles in Afghanistan now that the United States was withdrawing.

He suspected the Taliban was about to land itself a whole shitload of new trucks.

Beyond the outskirts of the airport, to the east, Brooks could see black of the night sky had turned a deep blue while he rested. Could sense dawn was coming, a nearly imperceptible shift in the light that marked the inevitable beginning of another new day.

He was tired. Wanted to be home in New Delhi, with Apollo. Wanted more to be back in America, home for good, with Jolene and Daisy.

Brooks was letting his eyes drift closed, thinking about the old house in Alexandria, the big oak in the front yard. The way the sun dappled the living room floor in the afternoons, how Daisy used to like to sit there and play with her dollhouse while he and Jolene read. If he concentrated hard enough, he could forget the sound of the planes and the smell of their jet fuel, hear the birds in that oak tree instead, the smell of the barbecue on a summer afternoon . . .

Then someone was shaking him back awake again. "Sir."

Brooks opened his eyes to find himself back in Afghanistan. *Shit.* One of the Marines who'd been guarding the CIA Gulfstream had come back, he discovered. Behind him was a young Afghan man wearing camouflage fatigues and Afghan National Army insignias. The Marine stepped back. Gestured to the ANA man.

"You're the guy who was asking about Porter, right?" the Marine asked.

Groggy, Brooks nodded.

"This guy says he can help you."

The young soldier told Brooks his name was Mehdi. He moved closer to Brooks as the Marine disappeared again, his work here apparently done.

Mehdi's English was accented, but very good. His brother had worked with Dominic Porter, he said. A commando with the ANA, Mehdi's brother had gone on missions with Porter. "Very secretive," Mehdi said. "All I know is that many Taliban were being killed."

Brooks tried to stifle his impatience. To the east, the sky continued to grow lighter. Somewhere out there was Dominic Porter.

"Two days ago—" Mehdi said. He swallowed. Looked down. "Two days ago, my brother Ikram was murdered by the Taliban. Dominic Porter was with him."

He paused a moment to gather himself. Then continued. "It was Muhammed Ghul who did this. The Taliban Blood Unit. Porter told us he was lucky to escape with his life."

"Where is Porter now?" Brooks asked. "Is he close?"

"He was in Kabul yesterday. Not far from here. There was a gunfight between his men and Ghul's, on the streets outside of the airport. Many people died—Afghans, Taliban. American."

"What about Porter?"

"He escaped, thank God," Mehdi said. "And I have just heard from one of my brother's friends that he has gone out into the desert to find Ghul. It's known the Blood Unit has a hiding place outside of Kabul."

Perfect. Send Porter into this Ghul guy's headquarters and let them kill each other. You don't even have to get your hands dirty.

But he knew that wouldn't cut it. Not for Jolene.

Did you see *the body, Seth?* he could imagine her asking. *How do you know he's dead for sure?*

Anyway, what if this Muhammed Ghul person wasn't at his hidey hole? What if Porter went all the way out there and nobody killed him? And then what if he decided to hop on a plane and go home, after all?

"You said everyone knows this Ghul guy has a hideout in the desert," he said. "How come nobody just bombs the shit out of it?"

Mehdi shrugged. "They try. He just finds a new place to hide."

"Send the army, then. Take him out."

"Too many Taliban. Not enough men. We are trying to defend the capital city."

"But you know Porter's going out there. To find Ghul."

Mehdi nodded. "This is what I've heard. But with only a few men. Not nearly enough to overpower the Blood Unit."

Don't say it, Brooks thought. *Please don't you say it.*

"If we hurry, we can catch him," Mehdi said. "I have men—relatives of the commandos the Blood Unit has murdered. We can join Dominic Porter and have our revenge on the Taliban dogs. And then you can speak to Dominic about whatever is your business."

"We can't just go out there," Brooks said. "You said it yourself—too many Taliban."

"I am afraid there is no way Dominic will survive without us," Mehdi said.

Doesn't sound so bad to me, Brooks thought. But then again, what if Porter *did* survive? Damn it, where was Adam Hayes when you needed him?

Brooks muttered a curse word. Mehdi leaned in. "I'm sorry?"

"I said, how many men do you have?" Brooks asked him. "And how soon can you be ready to go?"

48

KABUL

I n the passenger seat of the Humvee, Dominic Porter
watched the video on his phone one more time.

*If you don't come to retrieve them from me by dawn, I
will drive them out of Afghanistan myself . . . You know
where to find me.*

Ahead of the SUV, to the east, daylight was beginning to
show over the distant mountains, and though the sun hadn't
quite risen above the peaks yet, Porter urged his driver to step
on the gas pedal, praying they would make it to Ghul's hideout in time.

It had been a hell of a night. Porter had lost three men—
good men—in the shootout in Kabul. Two more were in a
medical tent at KBL, clinging to their lives. Ghul's forces had

come out of nowhere, ruining the operation just when Porter had Adam Hayes dead to rights, just when Abdul Nassim and his family had nearly run out of options.

He'd allowed himself to savor the victory. Knew his men had Nassim's American helper surrounded, knew it wouldn't take more than a minute before *that* nuisance was dealt with. Before his men had the Nassim family bundled into the backs of the two SUVs, destined back to the now-empty Eagle Base and a long, unpleasant debrief.

And then—*boom*—one of the Mitsubishis was a fireball and the whole street was a killing field. Porter knew he'd been lucky to get out with his life, knew if the Black Hawk hadn't showed up overhead he might have died in the crowd somewhere outside of the airport gates, whether shot dead by Ghul's men or dragged away to be tortured like those poor bastards in Somalia.

He'd let the Marines who'd suddenly appeared on the street hustle him and his men back to friendly territory inside the airport gates. Had disappeared into the chaos before anyone with too many bars on their uniform found him to ask what the hell he'd been doing. He'd gathered his men, found a quiet corner of the old Soviet terminal. There, they'd licked their wounds and cursed their luck.

Porter had done a little bit of research in those predawn hours. Wanting to know more about the American who continued to stymie his efforts to kill Nassim. As best as Porter could tell, the man was Adam Hayes, a first lieutenant who'd fought in Afghanistan alongside Nassim a decade before. Nassim had been given a Bronze Star by the United States

Armed Forces for saving Hayes's life in the Tangi Valley, and Hayes had apparently come back to return the favor.

Though how a former ground pounder like Hayes could seemingly infiltrate the country unchecked—with a goddamn *Huey*—was still beyond Porter's understanding. There were some blank spaces in Hayes's military records that even Porter couldn't access—and that, Porter knew, meant this guy was for real.

Whoever he was, Hayes had successfully kept Abdul Nassim and his family alive for much longer than Porter figured was reasonable. Except now, in Ghul's video . . . there was no sign of the American. Porter dared to believe this meant the man was finally dead.

The video had pinged Porter's phone at a little after five in the morning. Launched him out of his seat and sent him scrambling for the door, forgetting for an instant that he wasn't at Eagle Base anymore, that Steck and the rest of the geeks in the TOC were long gone. That there were no more Reapers and Hellfire missiles to play with, when now, more than anything, the situation demanded an air strike.

He told you where he is. He showed you he has Nassim. You drop a Hellfire in there and all of your problems are solved.

There were no Hellfires. No more CIA presence in Afghanistan, not officially. In truth, there was no more war in Afghanistan, not for America. Not even to deal with the likes of Muhammed Ghul.

Porter knew he had no time to waste. Dawn was in an hour or so, tops. He roused his men. O'Malley, Spinarski. A couple of others. Told them to gather what ammunition they could. Told them prepare to ride out in five.

The Humvee was old Afghan National Army stock. Provided by America, of course, but abandoned at the airport as the ANA crumbled. The Marine at the gate gave Porter and his men a double take as the Humvee rolled toward the exit.

"Sir, you don't want to go out there. It's a madhouse."

"Appreciate the heads-up," Porter told him. "But I think we can manage."

"Orders are, you go out there, you're on your own. Just so you know. We don't have the manpower to do any more rescue missions."

"Understood," Porter told him. "We'll find our own way back."

He instructed O'Malley to pilot the Humvee out of the airport and into the crowded streets outside. Two of his men in the backseats were armed with HK416s, Spinarski up top in the machine gunner's turret, manning the belt-fed M240. O'Malley leaned on the horn, and Porter picked up the headset and spoke through the Humvee's external loudspeaker, calling out in Pashto to the pedestrians around the vehicle to get the hell out of the way.

Whether it was the speaker or the machine gun mounted above, the crowd dutifully cleared a path, though nobody seemed happy about it. Porter had O'Malley take them a couple of blocks away from the gate and then pull over in an alley. There, producing a can of black spray paint that he'd swiped at the airfield, he stepped out of the Humvee and sprayed over the ANA markings, replacing them with crude approximations of Taliban symbols. Porter knew his artwork wouldn't stand up to close scrutiny, but from a distance, the Humvee would look like just another abandoned American vehicle repurposed by the Taliban.

If you're heading into Indian country, he thought, *you might as well look the part.*

Now the Humvee sped east out of Kabul and into the desert, racing the sun as it slowly began to peek over the mountains ahead. Porter gripped his HK and replayed the video again, studying Abdul Nassim's exhausted face, hearing the fear in his voice.

Muhammed Ghul would be waiting, Porter knew. This was a trap. But Porter realized he welcomed the challenge. Welcomed even the prospect of death.

One way or another, he thought, *this ends now.*

49

Do *with them what you like.*

"It's nothing personal, you understand," Muhammed Ghul told Hayes. "But you are not my objective; Dominic Porter is. And I must now make sure that we are ready for his arrival."

Outside, Hayes could hear more truck engines, the crunch of tires on the rocky desert. He knew that Ghul must have called in reinforcements, must not want to take any chances with Porter this time.

Hayes watched the Taliban commander shoulder an AK-47 and walk out of the little mud-brick building. From the light outside, Hayes could tell dawn was breaking. Knew that Ghul expected Porter would waste no time coming out here.

Not so long until Levi's evac team hits the hospital, the voice said. *You need to hop to it if you're going to make it back in time.*

One thing at a time, Hayes thought. *I don't even know how we're going to get out of this mess.*

Ghul had taken three of his fighters outside with him. That left three in the building with Hayes, Nassim, and the children. All three of the fighters held AK-47s. One man stood at a distance from Nassim and Hayes, covering them both with his rifle. The other two held the children.

"Stand together," one of the fighters instructed. Gestured with his rifle toward the wall of the building. His partners shoved the kids over to stand with Hayes and Nassim; they huddled close to their father, both of them crying now.

Hayes's hands were bound in front of him. He brought them to rest above his belt, searching for an opening to draw the ceramic blade hidden in the buckle. If he could just cut the rope, he might have a chance.

But the men were too far away to attack and disarm, even if he did get free. And even if he could neutralize one of the fighters, the other two would cut them all to pieces.

This is a numbers game. And the numbers suck.

The Taliban men studied them. Hayes noticed one of them leering at Zarah. He felt sick to his stomach, knowing that death might be preferable to whatever the man had in mind for her.

Maybe that's it. Make your move. At least you'll all die quick.

The lead fighter raised his rifle. Gestured into the killing room adjacent to the main room. "Which of you wishes to die first?"

"Me," Hayes replied, before Nassim could say anything. "I'll go first."

For an instant he was afraid that the fighter would pull the trigger right there, kill him where he stood. But the man only smiled. "Good," he said, and motioned to the room again. "Go."

Hayes let the man prod him toward the killing room. As soon as his back was to the rifle, he raised his hands to his belt buckle again and began to slide the blade out of its sheath. When the blade was free, he maneuvered it in his hand until it was lying against the rope that knotted his hands together, and began to saw, stealthily, at the cord.

The room smelled of sweat and fear and desperation. The air was hot and suffocating; there were bloodstains on the floor and bullet holes in the walls. An empty window frame on the side wall allowed bleak, colorless light to illuminate the space.

Hayes slowed his walk as he sliced into the rope, letting the Taliban fighter close the distance between them. In the other room, he could hear Zarah crying louder now. Heard Abdul swearing, struggling, as those cries turned to screams.

This is falling apart. You have to act now.

Then a gunshot rang out from the main room, and there was no time to think, just react.

Hayes spun at the Taliban man, his wrists still partially bound by the rope. As he turned, he twisted the blade of his knife outward so that it stabbed through the man's clothing as Hayes bodychecked him to the floor. The man's rifle went clattering into the corner as the men collided with the camcorder and tripod, sending it tumbling after the gun. Hayes rolled on top of the man. Plunged the blade into his sternum, over and over, until the man ceased to struggle beneath him and his blood covered both of their clothes.

Then Hayes turned the blade back against the rope and cut through the last of it. His hands now free, Hayes crossed the room to pick up the fighter's rifle and then hurried back to the door. Not knowing what to expect when he reached the main room again, praying the children, at least, were all right.

He was not prepared for what he saw.

Zarah had a gun. A pistol, Hayes saw, the 9-millimeter Beretta that Freshta had been carrying when he'd picked them up in the helicopter in the Tangi Valley. Hayes had no idea where the girl had found the gun, but it seemed she'd smuggled it here in the folds of her dress—and she'd apparently shot one of their captors in the leg.

The man who'd leered at Zarah lay howling on the floor now, clutching at the gunshot wound high on his thigh while Zarah sobbed on her knees a few feet away, the pistol dangling from her grip. Hayes couldn't see Bilal, but Abdul was in the fight of his life, wrestling with the third Taliban fighter, his bound hands gripping the barrel of the man's AK-47, holding it skyward as the fighter struggled to bring it level.

Hayes raised the rifle he'd stolen, but before he could assist Abdul, the door to the little building flew open and another fighter rushed in. Hayes cut him down in the doorway before the man could get off a shot. The sound of the rifle momentarily distracted Abdul's opponent, who glanced at Hayes long enough for Abdul to wrench the rifle from his hands and send him sprawling backward to the floor.

Hayes unloaded his rifle into the man's chest. Saved a couple of shots to finish off Zarah's captor. Then he hurried to Abdul and used the blade to free his friend, who hurried to Zarah and took the pistol, gently, from her hands, before wrapping her in a hug.

Across the room, Hayes could see Bilal now, hiding under the desk, apparently unharmed. Hayes crossed to the boy and knelt at the desk, extended his hand, and pulled him out from underneath. Called across to Abdul as he stood again.

"There's a window in back. Take them there."

Abdul nodded and straightened. Grabbed his daughter's arm with one hand as he held the Taliban fighter's AK-47 in the other.

Hayes nudged Bilal. "Go with your father."

The boy clung to Hayes, crying, but allowed Hayes to guide him gently toward Abdul, who called to him softly and finally coaxed him over. Hayes hurried to the bodies of the dead Taliban men, scrounging for extra ammunition for the rifle. Came up with three extra magazines, and the Makarov pistol he'd stolen from the fighter in the village. Just as he was pocketing the pistol, the door to the building flew open again. Hayes braced on the trigger, but no fighter appeared.

This time, it was a frag grenade.

50

Hayes dove backward as the grenade rolled into the room. He scrambled into the killing room, expecting the world to blow to pieces behind him any instant.

But whoever had thrown the grenade hadn't let it cook off first, and those extra seconds saved Hayes's life. He made the window and was pulling himself up and through when the grenade finally detonated with such force that Hayes thought the whole building might collapse on him. But the walls held, and he slid through the empty window frame and tumbled down to the rocks below, landing hard on his broken ribs and feeling the air *whoosh* from his lungs as starbursts of pain appeared before his eyes.

He picked up the AK-47 and rolled clear of the building, scanning his surroundings for Abdul and the children, for any more threats.

The rear of the building backed onto a steep, rocky hillside rising right to left. To Hayes's right, as the hill descended, was a narrow gap in the terrain before another long rise began. Hayes figured Abdul had led his children in that direction, hoping to find cover somewhere. But before Hayes could think about following, more shots rang out around him— from above him this time.

Ghul's men were everywhere. They'd set up a defensive position to guard against Dominic Porter's arrival, but the high ground they'd staked out would do just as well for cutting down Hayes and the Nassims. Hayes couldn't be sure, but he thought he'd suddenly come under fire from at least three different positions.

Let Abdul worry about the kids for a minute. If you can't silence a couple of these guns, none of you are going to make it out of here alive.

Flattening himself against the wall, Hayes edged to the corner of the building and peered around. Caught sight of a target moving quickly along a long slope opposite where the trucks had been parked out front, about sixty yards distant. The man had his head down, too focused on changing position and pinning Hayes down to notice Hayes taking aim. Leading the target, Hayes squeezed one shot and caught the man center mass, knocking him to the ground. Immediately, a volley of returning fire rained down on his position.

Hayes ducked back behind the rear of the building but heard shots strike the wall above him and scatter the gravel at his feet. Moving quickly, he ran toward the gap in the rocks, scanning the rises above him for the shooter and zig-zagging to prevent being sniped.

There was a large boulder just ahead, and Hayes dove behind it, feeling 7.62mm rounds crease the air above his head. Once safely behind, he raised the barrel of the AK over the top of the boulder and fired off six or seven rounds blind, then twisted back and searched the hillside above for the sniper again. Caught movement in his peripheral vision about forty yards away, a blur of dark against the pale rock. Fired toward the blur as bullets ricocheted off the rocks around him, on the move before he could tell if he'd hit anything.

Then he was in the narrow gulch between the two rocky hillsides, the terrain beginning to remind him of his ranch in New Mexico, the back acres where he'd hoped to take Jack hiking and maybe shooting someday. He was seized by a sudden, intense longing for his family, a wish to see Jack and hold Annabelle at least one more time before he died. The thought tempered by the knowledge that he probably would never meet his unborn child, not unless the odds changed here real fast.

His thoughts were erased by the sound of an engine behind him, and his mind had just processed the implications when he caught sight of Abdul and the children up ahead, diving for cover as the first rounds from a PKM machine gun tore the world to shreds around them.

A technical. Hayes found what cover he could amid the rocky walls of the gulch. Turned just in time to see the pickup roar past, the gunner swiveling the PKM in his direction but the driver clearly focused on Nassim and the children. Hayes took aim at the gunner and emptied his magazine. Watched sparks shower the technical and the rear window shatter. Watched the gunner plummet over the bed to the ground as at least one of the bullets from Hayes's AK-47 found its mark.

The driver didn't seem to realize he'd lost the PKM, but Nassim did. Hayes watched him break cover, raising his rifle at the onrushing truck. Watched him paint the windshield with a quick burst of fire, watched the pickup jerk sideways and careen into the rocks, the engine still revving high but the truck completely stuck.

Nassim hurried around to the driver's side of the truck. Wrenched open the door and pulled the driver out. The man fell limp to the rocks, dead, and with his foot off of the gas pedal, the engine calmed down.

Swinging his rifle back down to cover the entrance to the gulch, Hayes made his way across to the technical. "Can you back this thing out of here?" he asked Nassim. There was nowhere for the truck to turn around.

Nassim nodded. "I can."

"Good. Get the kids in and keep them low. I'll man the gun."

He pulled himself up into the bed of the truck, glancing down at the dead gunner at the far side of the vehicle before swinging the PKM back around to face back down the gulch the way the truck had come. On the floor of the bed beside the machine gun's mount were a handful of boxes of ammunition; as Nassim hurried Zarah and Bilal into the cab of the truck, Hayes fed another belt of 7.62x54mm rounds into the feed tray, slammed closed the cover, and cocked the PKM.

No sooner did he have the gun loaded than a pair of Ghul's men appeared from behind the rocks at the head of the gulch. Hayes squared the first man up and pulled the trigger, cutting him down with a rapid-fire burst before swinging the PKM's sights to his partner. In the span of two seconds, both men were on the ground, not moving.

In the cab of the pickup, Nassim shifted into reverse. The floor of the gulch was narrow and his visibility restricted by Hayes and the PKM in the bed, but he hit the gas pedal hard nonetheless, nearly jolting Hayes over the side as the truck jostled backward over the uneven terrain.

Hayes gripped tight to the PKM as the truck careened toward a stout boulder before swerving to narrowly avoid it. The path out of the gulch looked dubious, and Nassim was giving the truck more speed than Hayes might have, but he forced himself to trust his friend behind the wheel. Surfing unsteadily in the bed of the truck, Hayes focused on the PKM, scanning the rocky walls of the gulch for more bad guys.

Another gunman appeared on the slope above, to Hayes's right. Hayes swiveled the PKM to track him and squeeze off another burst, sending the gunman ducking for cover behind the nearest rock. As Nassim kept the technical moving, Hayes swung the PKM to hold aim at the rock, waiting for the gunman to appear again.

At the first sign of movement, he pulled the trigger again, kicking up a flurry of dust and gravel around the gunman's cover. Not sure if he'd neutralized the man, Hayes prepared to fire again, but the rapid-fire *crack* of bullets into the body of the pickup tore his attention away.

Doesn't matter if you kill them all. Just clear a path out of here.

Ahead of the technical's rear bumper, the gulch opened up to the desert again, and Ghul's hideout stood maybe forty yards away. The little building was surrounded by Taliban fighters now, all of them armed and taking aim at the pickup.

Ducking their fire as best he could in the nonexistent cover of the technical's open bed, Hayes opened up with the PKM, dropping some of the gunmen and scattering others, trying to predict where Nassim would aim the truck. More bullets slammed into the side of the pickup from all sides, but Nassim didn't slow down; free of the confines of the gulch, the Toyota's 2.4 liter turbodiesel roared as Nassim made for the far side of Ghul's building.

There, partially protected by the walls of the Taliban hideout, Nassim took the opportunity to swing the truck around to face forward. He slammed the truck into gear and stood on the gas pedal as Hayes once again gripped the PKM for his life, swinging it around to the rear of the truck to provide covering fire for their escape, and then turning back forward again as the technical sped out from behind the hideout.

Used up a full belt already. Shit.

He'd fired one hundred rounds at Ghul's men, and from what Hayes could tell, he'd barely put a dent in their numbers. Scrabbling around the roiling bed of the pickup, he grabbed another box of ammunition and loaded it into the PKM—as the gunmen took advantage of his momentary distraction to unleash another volley down toward the truck. Through the shattered back window, Hayes could see the front windshield had a couple of fresh holes. Could see smoke or steam beginning to rise from underneath the truck's hood.

Nassim was still driving, though, crouched low in his seat and working the steering wheel like a Formula 1 driver, racing the truck out away from Ghul's hideout and up a barely visible trail through the rocks.

With the PKM reloaded, Hayes set to work clearing their way again. Ghul's men had been set up to ambush Porter coming toward the hideout; they'd had to hastily change positions to take aim at their escaping captives, and their cover positions weren't as sound, their formation disorganized. Hayes took advantage of the confusion, peppering every square inch of desert that might have held an insurgent with 7.62 fire, not caring at this point whether he hit anyone, just buying time for Nassim to get them out of there.

The pickup came up over a low saddle, and in the distance Hayes could see the desert dropping steadily to a narrow strip of black two-lane asphalt.

The highway.

Nassim saw it, too, gunning the engine. Both he and Hayes were tasting freedom now, escape. Hayes swung the PKM back to cover their exfil, scanning the rocky hillside for more movement. Caught a glint out of the corner of his right eye, and unloaded the PKM into it. Then swung back around just in time to see Muhammed Ghul stand up from behind a low outcrop, holding a shoulder-mounted RPG launcher.

Quickly, Hayes fired again, but his rounds missed wide

and low, and Ghul didn't flinch. As Hayes adjusted his aim, Ghul pulled the trigger, and the rocket-propelled grenade exploded out of the launcher in a cloud of gray-blue smoke, snaking down toward the technical.

"*RPG!*" Hayes shouted, but Nassim didn't need to be told twice. With the RPG bearing down at them at nearly three hundred meters per second, he jerked the wheel of the pickup hard over, the rocket passing so close to the back of the truck that Hayes could feel the heat from its exhaust as it narrowly missed its target.

Nassim's evasive maneuver had set the technical off of the path, though, and onto more rugged, uneven terrain. At the speed it was going, the effect was immediate. The truck pitched and yawed like a rowboat in a Category 5 storm, Nassim fighting like hell to keep the truck under control, keep it from tipping over or running aground amid the sudden minefield of jagged rock and sand.

But Hayes didn't see most of that. As the technical swerved violently, inertia threw him from the truck bed and out into the desert, his whole body screaming out in electric-hot pain as he collided with a pile of sharp, unforgiving rock.

In the driver's seat, Nassim didn't seem to notice, and Hayes turned his head to watch the pickup drive off, a cloud of dust on a Hail Mary dash for the highway.

Good, the voice said. *Get the kids out of here. Get them safe. We'll be fine.*

Hayes figured the voice was just trying to cheer him up, knew it was inarguable he was in deep shit now. But as long as Nassim and his children got out, he figured he could accept whatever came next.

But as he lay in the rocks, fighting to stay conscious, barely able to twist his neck to watch Nassim get away, Hayes heard the technical's engine cough and then suddenly stall. Watched the cloud of dust start to settle over the now stationary Toyota, still a good fifty yards from pavement.

51

Maybe the American wasn't invincible after all, Muhammed Ghul thought, staring down from the rocks to where he'd last seen Abdul Nassim's guardian angel, lying motionless amid a pile of rocks after being thrown from the back of the technical. It was impossible to gauge how much damage the man had done this morning, how many of Ghul's men he'd killed. And though Ghul knew, now, that he'd won—the American still hadn't moved, and the stolen technical had just died, farther down the long slope to the highway—he cursed the man nonetheless, with equal parts frustration and admiration. Whatever else could be said about Adbul Nassim, the former ANA captain knew how to choose his friends.

Ghul heard the sound of an engine coming up to the saddle behind him. He turned to find Omar speeding up the rise in one of the Blood Unit's old Nissan D22 pickups. Behind Omar, down by the hideout, Ghul could see signs of the violence that had erupted: the bodies of his men where the American had cut them down, fresh cracks in the wall of the mud-brick building, scorching in the doorway from the frag grenade.

No matter. There would always be more Taliban than Americans here. Nassim and his friend had no hope of survival. Nor would Dominic Porter, when he finally arrived.

Ghul flagged down Omar, who slowed the pickup to a stop beside him. Stowing the RPG launcher in the bed of the truck, Ghul climbed into the passenger seat, wincing from the pain that still overwhelmed his body, even through the adrenaline rush of the fight. He'd lost track of his injuries at this point; the gunshot wound he'd suffered weeks ago might as well have happened to someone else, given all of the abuse he'd suffered since.

Still, he was on his feet. He was moving. And he would be victorious.

Soon, Porter will be here. And then you can end this madness forever.

Aboard the pickup, Ghul took a radio from Omar. Called a message to his men. "The captives have been eliminated. We regroup and hold our positions until Dominic Porter arrives."

One by one, his surviving fighters acknowledged the instruction. Satisfied, Ghul directed Omar down the slope of the rise to where he'd seen the American thrown from the bed of the technical. *We'll do a little housekeeping while we wait for Porter.*

. At the stretch of the trail where Ghul remembered the technical swerving, he instructed Omar to park the Nissan. Both men pulled rifles from behind the seats of the truck and stepped out to find the American. To confirm he was, in fact, dead.

But at some time during the drive down from the saddle to here, Ghul had lost sight of the American momentarily. And now, as he approached the patch of rocks where the American had been thrown, Ghul was surprised to find the rocks empty. No sign of the American except for a small patch of blood staining the dust.

Ghul looked around. Met Omar's eyes, who shrugged. The American was gone.

Except . . .

As Ghul turned back to survey the rocky slope, the gradual declination of the land back down to the highway, he heard movement behind him. And then Omar screamed. Ghul spun back around just in time to see his fighter collapse onto the rocks, the American dragging him backward against the jagged terrain, fighting to get hold of the rifle in Omar's hands.

Hayes had had barely enough strength left to hide as he heard the Taliban truck coming down from the saddle. His whole body protested as he rolled across the pile of rocks to a shallow gully out of sight of the trail, just wide enough to give him some semblance of cover.

Not that it would matter. His rifle was gone and the Taliban were everywhere. Hayes wasn't even sure he had enough energy to stand at this point, much less fight anyone off. Much less cover the distance down to join Nassim and the children at the stalled-out technical, to try and figure out some heroic last stand.

If the Taliban pickup had continued down the hill, Hayes knew he would have tried. Would have pulled himself to his feet and forced himself after them, died fighting to save his friend's life. But the pickup stopped a short distance from Hayes, and Hayes heard the doors open and slam closed again. Heard voices, the words muffled by the wind, by the rocks he'd hidden underneath.

If they came close enough, they would see him. There weren't many places to hide in this kind of terrain. But Hayes pressed himself tighter against the rocks anyway. Removed the ceramic blade from his belt once again.

And soon enough, he'd found his one chance at survival.

He'd recognized Muhammed Ghul's voice. The other man, Hayes didn't know. But it was the other man who stood closest to Hayes, his back to the gully where Hayes lay, motionless, gripping the blade. Hayes waited until he could hear the man breathing. Until his every move and footstep seemed right on top of the gully, seemed like it would bring the rocks crashing down on top of him. Then, gambling that Ghul would be looking off in some other direction, he pushed himself out of the gully and up, slashing at the other man's Achilles' tendon and bringing him crashing down to the dirt.

Hayes dragged the man backward into the gully, wrenching at the sling of the AK-47 in his grip. The Taliban fighter fought against him, reached back, clawed at Hayes's face, his hair, his eyes. He was younger than Hayes, and stronger, and probably not as wounded. Hayes knew that as soon as he lost the advantage of surprise, he'd be done. He needed to work fast.

But Ghul had seen what was happening. The Blood Unit commander spun and let off a burst with his AK-47, filling his fighter's body with hot lead. The fighter went limp in Hayes's arms and he pulled the man's rifle free as Ghul continued to fire, rolling away from the spray of bullets and dropping down into the narrow gully again.

Ghul's bullets followed him down. It was too soon to tell if any found their target. Hayes's adrenaline was pumping too strong. He aimed the rifle over the top of the rocks and fired blind. Then kept moving, more pain now, almost blinding. Expecting more bullets to follow.

None did.

Hayes pushed himself to his elbows. Peered out over the rocks. Saw Ghul's boots pointed toward him, the Blood Unit commander lying flat on his back. Not moving. Hayes studied him for a moment. Glanced beyond Ghul back up to the saddle and searched for movement up there. Couldn't see much, the view hidden by a large pile of rock. From the lack of activity, Hayes surmised that the Taliban fighters couldn't see their boss, either.

Sooner or later they'll come down here to see for themselves, the voice said. *You don't want to be here when that happens.*

Slowly, he forced himself to his feet. Bracing himself against the rocks, feeling suddenly light-headed. Now aware of a burning pain in his chest, he looked down and saw blood soaking his T-shirt from a ragged furrow carved out of his flesh by a bullet.

Shit.

Voices up at the saddle now. Men yelling to each other. No movement up there that Hayes could see, but they'd be coming down soon. This was just getting worse.

Hayes stood. Blinking away the pain and the black spots behind his eyes. Using the rifle as a crutch and focused only on getting up to the Nissan still parked on the trail. On getting back down to Nassim and the kids.

Ghul hadn't moved. Not since Hayes had poked his head up from the gully. But as Hayes struggled past him, the Taliban commander suddenly shot out his leg, kicking the rifle out of Hayes's grip and knocking him back down to the rocks beside him.

In an instant, Ghul had rolled on top of Hayes. Fending off Hayes's blows, Ghul brought his hands to Hayes's neck, squeezing hard in a death grip, and began to choke the life out of him.

52

hul's hands squeezed tighter, bringing more black to the edges of Hayes's vision. Reducing his world to the Taliban commander's twisted face, the blood-soaked bandage over his eye, the bruises and scars, his yellowed teeth, and foul breath as he leered down above Hayes.

Hayes could feel his strength waning. Could feel his body begging to give up, surrender to the darkness and just fall asleep. Just let go.

But the voice wouldn't let him.

You're better than this, it said. *This is not why the government spent all of that money creating you, not so you could die like this. Not while Nassim and his family still need you.*

This is not why you came back to this country.

Ghul sensed victory now. His smile grew wider, inches

above Hayes's face. "Go to sleep," he whispered in English. "And remember who is truly Afghanistan's master."

Hayes forced himself to relax. Stopped fighting, let Ghul believe he had won. Felt the Taliban commander's grip relax, almost imperceptibly, as Hayes closed his eyes.

As soon as he felt it, Hayes exploded upward into Ghul. Drawing on every ounce of strength he could muster to drive his opponent off him, creating just enough space that he could wriggle out from underneath. Ghul landed back down on him, heavy, reaching for his throat, but Hayes turned his head away, ducked his chin, fought off the attack with his left hand while scrabbling around with his right for a weapon.

He'd been hoping to find his knife, or maybe Ghul's rifle. His fingers came back with a rock instead.

No matter.

Hayes swung the rock hard into Ghul's temple. Heard the dull thud as it connected, the sound of Ghul's breath escaping his body. The blow knocked Ghul sideways, and Hayes scrambled after him. Pressing his knees down on the Taliban commander's chest and striking him again with the rock, and again, as Ghul tried in vain to fight back.

Treadstone hadn't trained Hayes to show mercy, and he didn't. Not until he was sure that Muhammed Ghul was dead.

Then, and only then, did he set down the bloody rock. Push himself to his knees above the Taliban commander's body. Cast about for the rifle again, and, using it to hold himself upright, resumed his painful walk to the truck.

More action from the top of the saddle. The Taliban men entrenched in their ambush positions up there could see Hayes clearly now, walking toward the Nissan from behind the rock pile that had concealed him. Hayes knew they were realizing that he must have killed their commander.

As he trudged toward the Nissan, he could hear their voices calling out to each other, could hear the crack of their rifles and the *whiz* of the bullets striking the ground around him.

By the time Hayes reached the Nissan, a truck had appeared at the top of the rise. Then another. They slowed there, briefly, to allow more men to jump into the pickup beds, and then they resumed their journey, speeding down the desert trail toward him.

Hayes climbed behind the wheel of the Nissan and shifted into gear. Made himself ignore how good it felt to sit down, to rest. Forget how much he wanted to just close his eyes. Instead, he released the brake pedal and stepped on the gas, guided the little truck as quickly as he dared down the slope of the hillside to Nassim's stalled technical.

Be alive, he thought, as he approached the ruined truck. Seeing how the bodywork was torn apart by bullet holes, one of the tires flat, and the engine still smoking. *Be alive, and be ready for me.*

He didn't let up on the gas until he was nearly on top of the technical. Then he slammed on the brakes and brought the Nissan to a stop, hoping the cloud of dust behind him would provide some cover from the Taliban giving chase.

Opening the door to the Nissan, he called out to the technical. "Abdul!"

There was no response. Hayes stared at the dead pickup, searching through the dust for movement, for any sign of life. Praying.

"Abdul!"

Still no answer. And then, from the far side of the technical, Zarah Nassim poked her head into Hayes's view.

"Zarah!" Hayes called to her. Watched her eyes go wide with recognition, saw her glance back behind the technical, then quickly back to Hayes.

Hayes shifted the Nissan into gear. Idled it around to the front of the technical. There, amid the dust and the smoke from the Toyota's engine, he saw Abdul Nassim lying motionless on the ground, his daughter and youngest son at his side.

Fuck.

In the distance, the sound of the approaching Taliban vehicles grew louder. Hayes forced himself out of the truck. Staggered across to Nassim, steadying himself against the hood of the Toyota. Nassim still wasn't moving. He was bleeding from at least two wounds in his torso. There was no time to check for signs of life.

And Hayes sure as hell wasn't leaving him behind.

He dragged Nassim the short distance to the back of the Nissan. Dropped the tailgate and bent down to hoist his friend into the bed. Nassim was more solidly built than Hayes, a good twenty pounds heavier. As Hayes struggled to lift Nassim, Zarah Nassim joined him. Her eyes clenched closed with effort as she tried to lift her father's legs.

Hayes managed to get Nassim halfway into the bed of the truck. Let him down on the tailgate and climbed in after him, placed his hands under Nassim's arms and hauled him the rest of the way. Crawled back out of the truck and nearly dropped to the desert floor, managed to pull himself back around to the driver's seat, hand over hand, propped against the Nissan's body.

"Get in," he told Zarah and Bilal. Zarah bustled her brother into the passenger seat and climbed in behind. The dust was settling around the Nissan, and Hayes could see the Taliban vehicles in the distance. He slammed the driver's door closed and hit the gas.

53

The highway was empty this far out of Kabul. Every now and then Porter and his men would pass a bus or an overloaded pickup truck headed in the opposite direction, back toward the city, but for the most part, the road was clear, traffic nonexistent.

Everyone's already in Kabul, Porter thought. *Trying to bargain their way out of this godforsaken place.*

He noticed how other drivers would stare at the Humvee, curious, as it approached. How their eyes would register the Taliban markings he'd spray-painted on the truck's body and how quickly they would look away. Could practically see their sphincters tighten as they registered, no, this wasn't the good guy Americans come to save the day again. No, that day was done.

He'd come to Afghanistan hoping to do good. Believing in the mission, the cause. Believing that there was plenty that America could bring to this ass-backward land, that given enough time and faith, they could fix things.

He knew now there was no fixing this place. Had figured it out driving through Kabul, past the boarded-up restaurants and nightclubs and gyms, the bombed-out ANA M1117 Armored Security Vehicles and the shells of the buildings destroyed by artillery fire. A new day was dawning on Afghanistan, but as far as Porter was concerned, it was the same as it ever was here, same as when the Soviets had tried their luck and seen their tanks and aircraft destroyed, their people killed.

Some people just didn't want to be helped.

He'd tried his damndest. He'd come here to disrupt the Taliban, and, damn it, he'd fulfilled that mission. If a few innocent lives had had to be sacrificed along the way, well, that was just the price of progress. He would do it all again the same way, if he could.

Except he would have killed Abdul Nassim in that alley. Before he could escape with that photograph and Akhtar Mansour's thumb drive of evidence.

Anyway, it didn't matter now. None of it did. In an hour or so, Nassim would be dead. Porter would make sure of it, and he would retrieve the thumb drive. And then he and his men would drive back to KBL and catch the first flight out anywhere but here.

The end.

"Another couple klicks," Porter told O'Malley, studying the desert as it unfolded ahead of them. Replaying the drive out here the first time, with Ikram. Remembering how terrified he'd been when they'd pulled up on the Taliban roadblock just around this next bend.

Beside him, O'Malley nodded. In the backseat, Porter's two men checked their HK416s again. Porter leaned back, called up to Spinarski in the machine gunner's turret.

"Look alive up there," he said. "We're a long way from Kansas right now."

The road eased through a long curve and then straightened out again, a ruler line of black pavement against undulating rock, stretching out toward low mountains in the distance. Far ahead, Porter caught the glint of a windshield, squinted his eyes through the heat haze rising up from the blacktop. Another vehicle oncoming, he saw. A little white pickup truck.

"Could be Taliban," Porter told his team. "Let's be ready."

He watched the truck approach. Fixed his eyes on the windshield until he could make out the face of the man behind the wheel.

Adam Hayes.

And beside him, if Porter wasn't mistaken, two children.

Before the pickup could speed past, Porter leaned across the Humvee. Grabbed the steering wheel and wrenched it into the oncoming lane.

"*What the fuck?*" O'Malley shouted, slamming on the

brakes and struggling to maintain control of the vehicle. Outside, the driver of the white pickup did the same.

The two vehicles narrowly missed each other, and came to a stop fifteen yards away.

"Reverse," Porter told O'Malley. *"Now."*

Shaking his head, the driver did as instructed. In his rearview mirror, Porter could see the brake lights of the pickup go out. Watched the rear end of the truck fishtail just slightly as Hayes gave it more gas.

"Those are our guys," Porter told the turret gunner. "Stop them."

Spinarski spun the turret back toward the rear of the Humvee. Let off a burst with his M240 across the bed of the pickup. Porter watched both rear tires burst, the bed of the truck slamming down suddenly and sparks kicking up as rubber shredded on steel rims.

"Get in front of them," Porter told O'Malley, as the pickup slowed. The driver obliged, sending the Humvee surging alongside the pickup until it had passed them. "Good. Block them off."

The driver turned the Humvee sideways across the highway as Spinarski maneuvered his turret to keep the pickup in his sights. In the passenger seat, Porter reached for the handset for the Humvee's external loudspeaker.

"It's over, Hayes," he said. "I just want Nassim and the thumb drive. Then you can go."

In the driver's seat of the Nissan, Adam Hayes did nothing. Porter met his eyes and the two men stared at each other across the blacktop.

Beside Hayes, Porter could see the tops of two heads just barely poking out over the dash. Then Hayes said something, and the heads disappeared.

That won't help you, Porter thought. *Not against that M240.*

He twisted back and craned his neck up toward the turret. "Keep that locked on them," he told the gunner. "If anyone tries anything, you cut them to pieces."

54

JALALABAD HIGHWAY, KABUL

*W*ell, *shit,* the voice said. *How on God's green earth are you going to get out of this one?*

The Humvee staring Hayes in the face had once belonged to the good guys, though any American or ANA markings had been deleted courtesy of someone's hasty work with a can of black spray paint. Now, the vehicle looked like any other piece of military equipment the Taliban had captured. But the men inside, and manning the machine gun turret, were all American.

Including Dominic Porter.

Hayes had only seen photographs of the CIA paramilitary operative, images that Seth Brooks had pulled from Porter's file. Admittedly, with the sun in his face and Porter hidden behind the Humvee's dusty windshield, Hayes couldn't have sworn on a stack of Bibles he had a positive identification. But he knew, anyway.

The man in that Humvee had sold American weapons to the Taliban. He'd tried to murder Abdul Nassim and his entire family. Forged an alliance with Muhammed Ghul and the Taliban's Blood Unit to get his dirty work done.

He'd sold out the lives of his allies in the Afghan Army.

And then he'd tried to kill Hayes. Had succeeded in killing Ramze Nassim and three American contractors with a Reaper drone and a couple of Hellfire missiles. Who knew how many people his men had killed and injured when they'd ambushed Hayes and the Nassims in the streets of Kabul. They'd opened up in the middle of a crowd of desperate civilians, firing indiscriminately. Hayes knew that casualties must have been numerous.

And now here he was, in a stolen Humvee with a truckload of mercenaries and a big M240 aimed square at Hayes's head. Blocking the highway in the middle of nowhere, the last obstacle between the Nassim family and safety.

And Abdul Nassim bleeding out in the bed of the pickup, his life draining away more with every wasted minute.

Hayes tried to tamp down his frustration. Anger made him want to pull out the Kalashnikov from behind his seat and empty the magazine into Dominic Porter and his friends, to hell with the consequences. Even if he knew it was a death wish. Abdul didn't have time for this. Shaw's Hail Mary evac wouldn't wait forever.

The turret gunner with the M240 could have opened up

already, but he hadn't. There was no benefit to Porter to keeping anyone in the pickup alive. For a moment, Hayes couldn't figure out why the CIA operative hadn't instructed his men to get the job done already. But the voice put the pieces together.

Porter didn't see Abdul in the back of the truck. He doesn't know Abdul's with you.

An instant later, Porter confirmed the voice's suspicions.

"Where is Abdul Nassim, Adam?" he called out through the Humvee's loudspeaker. "Tell me where he is, and we can all go home."

Hayes leaned out through the window. "And the kids?"

"Them, too. I just want Nassim and what he took from Mansour."

Lies. There was no way Porter could afford to let anyone but his own men survive this standoff. Hayes's mind raced, searching for a way out.

Until he finds Nassim, he won't kill you.

Yeah. But the Taliban who just saw me kill Ghul probably will.

"We left him behind," Hayes called to Porter. "At Ghul's hideout. He's already dead."

A pause. "And Ghul?"

"Also dead. You're welcome. I think he still has the drive, though. I was too busy trying to save these kids' lives to ask."

Porter didn't respond. Hayes watched him confer with the other men in the Humvee. Prayed the CIA operative would fall for it.

Let him go back to Ghul's hideout to see for himself. Let him and the Taliban take care of each other.

It would be a long drive back to Kabul on two busted tires, but at least they wouldn't be staring down the barrel of that 240 anymore.

Finally, Porter picked up the handset again. "I'm going to need you to take us to the body."

Hayes shook his head. "Can't do it. These kids need medical attention. ASAP."

"Not a request, Adam. Get those kids unbuckled. You can all ride back to Ghul's place with us."

The rear side doors of the Humvee both opened, and two of Porter's men stepped out, carrying HK416 assault rifles aimed at the truck. Hayes watched as they began to advance, cautiously, down the highway toward him. He still couldn't figure a way out of this. If anything, the situation was getting worse.

Soon as those men reach this truck, the voice said, *they'll see Abdul bleeding out in the bed. And then it's curtains for all of you.*

In the passenger footwell, Zarah and Bilal Nassim huddled together, Bilal crying quietly. Zarah looked up, met Hayes's gaze. Hayes could see her fear, those wide eyes begging him to do *something.*

Not sure there's anything we can do, kiddo. Just keep our heads down and hope it ends fast.

He could probably take out one of Porter's gunmen before the 240 tore him apart. If he spun the truck sideways and took the brunt of the assault, maybe the kids could escape out the other side of the vehicle.

And then what? Run for their lives across the empty des-
ert until that machine gunner cuts them down?

Even if they did escape, the Taliban would find them. Or
they would die of thirst, alone in the desert.

Maybe it's mercy, Hayes thought. *Maybe the only thing*
now is to hope they die clean.

He was still trying to wrap his head around the idea when
he heard the reverberation of a diesel engine in the distance.

55

JALALABAD HIGHWAY, KABUL

Seth Brooks wasn't planning to crash into the Humvee. Would have liked to have avoided it, all things being equal. But the Navistar weighed four and a half tons, not counting the seven or eight Afghan National Army soldiers in the back, and Brooks had the truck pushing seventy miles an hour as he rounded that sweeping curve. By the time his brain had registered the spray-painted Humvee parked crossways in the middle of the highway, there wasn't a braking system in the world that could slow the truck down in time.

"Shit!" Brooks tried anyway, stomping down on the left pedal and wrestling with the wheel as the truck threatened to slide out of control. *"Hold on!"*

In the passenger seat beside him, Mehdi reached for the *oh shit* bar above his head, muttering a quick fervent prayer to Allah. The Navistar plowed into the rear quarter of the Humvee with the force of a freight train, punting the smaller vehicle into a 270-degree spin and nearly obliterating the back end.

The Navistar steamrolled past, Brooks still standing on the brake pedal, willing the big truck to a stop as his mind tried to comprehend the tableau in front of him.

The Humvee parked in the middle of the highway. The white pickup with ruined rear tires twenty yards away. The man picking himself up, dazed and bloody, behind the turret gun of the Humvee looked American. He wasn't Taliban, anyway. Two of his friends had apparently been advancing on the pickup, though they now stood, mouths agape, watching the carnage. They held assault rifles and wore Operational Camouflage patterned–fatigues—American gear.

What the hell is going on here?

Brooks turned his attention to the pickup, and then it all started to make sense. The man behind the wheel looked a hell of a lot like Adam Hayes. No sign of Abdul Nassim or his family, from what Brooks could see. But he had no doubt it was Hayes. And that meant the men in the Humvee were with Porter.

"Get ready," Brooks told Mehdi. "We just found your guy."

Mehdi leaned forward to look past Brooks out the Navistar's driver's-side window. "Where?"

"In there." Brooks gestured to the Humvee, which had come to a rest facing the opposite direction as the bigger truck. From his vantage point, Brooks could only see the driver, who didn't look like any picture he'd ever seen of Dominic Porter.

On the other side of the Humvee, the passenger door swung open. And out stepped Dominic Porter to the blacktop.

Brooks rolled down the window of the Navistar. Watched as Porter surveyed the big ANA diesel over the hood of the Humvee. Porter looked lean. Gaunt. Like whatever he'd done in Afghanistan had eaten most of his body away. He rubbed his neck, wincing.

"Guess that'll teach us to block the highway," he called across to Brooks. "Where the heck are you headed so fast, anyway?"

Below the window, out of Porter's line of sight, Brooks reached for the Beretta M9 he'd "borrowed" from the ANA arsenal back in Kabul. He inched it slowly higher, thumbing off the safety. Trying to think of a lie to tell Porter, trying to look nonchalant. Wishing that Hayes would wake up and do something.

You're the fucking spy, Hayes. Don't just sit there.

He hadn't had time to think of a story for Porter before Mehdi blew the cover. And fucked them all.

"We are looking for you," the young ANA soldier called out of the cab. "You are Dominic Porter, correct? We are coming to help you kill Muhammed Ghul."

Porter's lips drew tight in a vague semblance of a smile. He swapped a glance with the turret gunner. "I'm Porter," he said. "Who are you?"

"We are ANA. Nine of us." Mehdi pointed to Brooks.

"And he is American. He was looking for you, back in Kabul."

Shit, Brooks thought. *Just shut up, would you?*

Across the Humvee, Porter studied him. "Well, I'd say you found me, whoever you are. But as much as I'd love to get acquainted with you all, I'm afraid I'm in a bit of a hurry."

He glanced up at the turret gunner, and Brooks watched the turret swivel until the machine gun atop it was pointed directly at him.

"I'm sorry you came all this way for nothing," Porter said. "We'll try to make this fast."

Brooks stared at the barrel of the machine gun. Suddenly paralyzed. The black hole in the center seemed to expand in his vision until it had swallowed him up.

Jolene, he thought. *I'm so sorry.*

Hayes watched the turret gunner swing the M240 around toward Brooks in the Navistar. Had no idea where his old State Department friend had come from, or where he'd gotten his hands on that massive truck, but none of that mattered right this instant. Brooks had just wandered into a minefield.

He reached around behind the driver's seat to the AK-47 stashed back there and pulled it out. *"Brooks, get down!"* he called out the window of the ruined Nissan, just as the machine gun on top of the Humvee roared to life, launching 7.62s at 2,800 feet per second into the side of the Navistar.

There was no time to worry about Brooks or whoever else

he'd brought with him. Hayes brought up the Kalashnikov and swung it out the window toward where the nearest of Porter's men was advancing on the Nissan. Before the other man could react, Hayes had cut him down with a quick burst, then set to quieting the machine gun.

But there was no good angle at the 240 from inside the Nissan, the truck's A-pillar and windshield blocking his aim.

"Stay down," Hayes told Zarah and Bilal in Pashto. "Don't look up until I say so."

He pushed the driver's-side door open and exited the pickup. Found Porter's second gunman taking aim in his direction with his HK416. Hayes dropped low behind the Nissan's engine block as the gunman opened fire, the impact of the pavement underneath him sending starbursts of pain across his vision again.

Quickly, Hayes crawled to the front of the Nissan. Stayed low and aimed his rifle across the pavement toward the other man's boots. Opened fire and watched the gunman drop to his knees and then sideways, clutching his feet. Hayes used the truck's bumper to push himself up. Put three more rounds in the gunman, center mass, and then turned his attention back to the 240.

The machine gun was chewing apart the Navistar, but on the opposite side from the gunfire, Hayes could see that at least a couple of the truck's occupants had made it out alive. They looked like ANA soldiers, from what Hayes could tell, but that still gave him no idea why or how Seth Brooks had just appeared out here.

The State Department man might have just saved his life,

though. Hayes ducked down behind the front of the Nissan, taking as much cover as he could as he took aim at the gunner in the Humvee's turret. Centered his sights and fired, missed by inches, the round sparking off of the turret's titanium shield.

The shot did catch the gunner's attention, though, and as Hayes watched in horror, the turret swung back around toward the Nissan, the M240 spitting more fire, raking the front of the pickup truck as Hayes scrambled for cover and hoped the engine block would protect him.

On the far side of the Navistar, Brooks's ANA men were regrouping, and Hayes was vaguely aware that a couple of the soldiers had taken advantage of the machine gunner's distraction to circle around the rear of their truck, out of his line of sight.

Below the turret gunner, the Humvee's driver had entered the fray, stepping out onto the pavement with his H&K raised to fire, meeting the two ANA soldiers just as they came around the back of the Navistar, dropping one before the second put him onto the ground.

Hayes kept his head down. Made himself as small as possible as the 240 continued to unload on the Nissan. He prayed that Zarah and Bilal had their heads down in the footwell. Wished, desperately, for the machine gun to stop firing. In a corner of his vision, he saw the surviving ANA soldier at the rear of the Navistar exchanging fire with Dominic Porter. Watched another ANA soldier drop out of the cab of the truck, landing on the passenger side and slowly inching his way around the front grille. The soldier met Hayes's eyes, and Hayes saw he was holding a frag grenade.

There's no way he'll get it off, the voice said. *Not unless you occupy the gunner.*

Shit.

Hayes usually liked being the guy throwing the frag, as opposed to the bait guy drawing fire. But beggars couldn't be choosers in a situation like this. He stretched across the pavement to the body of the dead gunman nearby. Closed his fingers on the strap of the man's HK416 and raised it as high as he dared over the hood of the Nissan, firing wild at the turret gunner's position. Silently imploring the ANA soldier to chuck the grenade, throw a strike, bring peace back to the valley.

The play worked as designed, bringing another rain of hellfire from the machine gun down on top of the Nissan, nearly blowing off Hayes's shooting hand in the process. He ducked low as the machine gunner kept firing. Saw the ANA soldier step out from behind the Navistar just long enough to size up the throw. Pull the pin and chuck the frag high in the air, arcing down toward the Humvee.

From Hayes's perspective hiding from the machine gun, he never saw the grenade land. Just ducked his head low and waited for the *boom.*

56

Porter didn't see the grenade land, either. And the way his ears were ringing from the constant hammer of gunfire, he wasn't hearing much, but if his ears had been working correctly, he would have heard Spinarski swear, loud, as the grenade arced overhead and dropped perfectly through the turret into the cab of the Humvee.

Porter was vaguely aware that the 240 had stopped firing, as the gunner first frantically felt around for the frag grenade underneath him and then tried even more desperately to get clear of the blast. He was busy, though, crouched behind the open passenger door of the Humvee as he engaged with one of the Afghan National Army soldiers who'd appeared out of nowhere in that big fucking truck, more or less ruining his day.

As it was, the 240 was only silent for a couple of seconds, hardly long enough for Porter to register the change. And then he was flying. Launched sideways by the force of the blast, the whole world turned to fire and confusion and pain. He landed hard on something rough and unforgiving, bounced, and then slid, his body tearing apart. Caught sight of the Humvee behind him, engulfed in flame and black smoke, Spinarski's body draped over his turret, not moving.

The whole world was silent except the ringing in Porter's ears. He couldn't be sure, but he imagined that the gunfire had finally stopped.

Hayes heard the grenade blast the Humvee apart. Felt the Nissan shudder from the force of the blast. Looked out from around the Nissan's bumper and saw the young ANA soldier who'd thrown the grenade advancing out from the cover of the Navistar. Saw his partner at the rear of the transport truck stepping cautiously out into the open as well.

With what little strength he could muster, Hayes gripped what remained of the Nissan's A-pillar and pulled himself upright. Across the highway, the Humvee burned. Hayes could see the gunner's body in the flames, but he couldn't see Porter.

He glanced into the cab of the Nissan. Found Zarah and Bilal crouching where he'd left them. Zarah holding her hands tight over her brother's ears. She relaxed, a little bit, when she saw him. But not much.

"It's okay," Hayes told her. "Wait here."

Using the dead gunman's rifle for support, he started across the pavement toward the remains of the Humvee. Circled around slowly to the far side where he'd last seen Porter. Found the CIA operative flat on his back on the highway shoulder, bleeding from multiple wounds and breathing shallow, his eyes open and staring up at the sky.

One of the ANA soldiers, the young guy who'd thrown the grenade, joined Hayes above Porter. He looked grimly down at the operative. Then toward Hayes.

"I don't understand," he said, in accented English. "This is Dominic Porter, yes?"

Hayes nodded.

"American. Just like you. He was going to kill Muhammed Ghul."

On the ground, Porter watched them. Hayes held the rifle on him, but Porter didn't move.

"He was working with Ghul," Hayes told the soldier. "To kill Afghans."

"Impossible. My brother fought with him as did many others. Dominic Porter was going to find Ghul to avenge them."

Hayes shook his head. "Porter was going to kill those two kids in my truck. And my friend Abdul Nassim, a former captain in the Afghan Army."

The soldier narrowed his eyes. "Why should I believe you?"

"Because I killed Muhammed Ghul. And Dominic Porter just killed a lot of your friends."

The soldier looked from Hayes to Porter. Porter watched them, his breathing getting shallower. He still hadn't said anything.

"Is this true?" the soldier asked Porter. "What he says? Why did you shoot at us?"

Porter closed his eyes. When he opened them again, there was a trace of a smile on his lips. It was Hayes's eyes he found, not the soldier's.

"*Fuck you,*" he whispered. His words flecked with blood. "*And fuck this country.*"

In the distance, down the highway, Hayes was suddenly aware of engines approaching. He glanced to his right and caught the glint of the sun against one windshield, then another. Then another. Technicals.

"Time's up," he told the soldier. "We've got to move, unless you want to interview the Taliban about what happened to your brother."

The soldier followed Hayes's eyes down the road. Pursed his lips. He studied the approaching technicals for a beat. Then turned back to Porter, drawing a Beretta from a holster at his hip and aiming it down at Porter's forehead.

"Fuck you, too," he told the CIA operative. Then he pulled the trigger.

57

H ayes drove. Pushed the Navistar's DT 530 diesel as hard as he dared, though for most of the occupants of the truck, there was no longer any hurry.

Seth Brooks was dead. Hayes suspected he would never know just how the State Department man had come to show up in the middle of the Afghanistan desert in the nick of time, but however he'd done it, he'd saved Hayes's life. And he'd saved Zarah and Bilal Nassim, as well.

Most of the Afghan Army soldiers he'd brought with him were dead, too. Cut to pieces by Porter's machine gunner in that initial burst of fire, mostly. Though at least a couple had managed to escape the truck and return fire before Porter's men shot them down.

"Their relatives fought with the Americans," the soldier called Mehdi had told Hayes. "Alongside my brother. We were told that Muhammed Ghul murdered them. And that Dominic Porter had come out here for revenge. But now—" He shrugged. "I don't know."

Hayes had given him the executive summary, as they'd hurried to load Abdul Nassim and his family into the rear of the Navistar. What little he could tell him, anyway, as the Taliban technicals sped closer.

He'd told Mehdi, at least, about what he'd seen on the thumb drive. About Abdul's photograph and what Abdul had heard from Akhtar Mansour. Hayes could tell by the young soldier's expression that he wasn't quite sure how much to believe, but in the end, he supposed it didn't matter.

Dominic Porter was dead. As were his men.

And Abdul was, for the moment, alive.

"This man will not survive," Mehdi had told Porter as they lifted him gingerly into the back of the Navistar. "Chances are he will die before we make it back to Kabul." He'd looked Hayes over. "You are in need of medical attention, too."

"Luckily, we're going to a hospital," Hayes had told him. Starting for the front of the Navistar, the driver's seat. "You and your buddy ride in back. Try and keep my friends alive, and if those technicals get close, scare them off."

Mehdi had smiled a humorless smile. Gestured to the frag grenades clipped to his vest. "I can be scary," he said.

Now Hayes pushed the Navistar to its limit, watching his mirrors as the smaller and lighter technicals closed the distance. Ahead, the city rose out of the desert, though with it, Hayes knew, would come traffic. Civilians. Innocent lives to keep out of the crossfire.

The face of his watch was cracked, but it looked to Hayes like it was still keeping time.

Hope that minute hand's wrong, the voice said. *You've got twenty minutes.*

Behind the Navistar, the chatter of small-arms fire. Hayes kept the truck rolling, trusting that Mehdi and his friend would find some way to fend off the Taliban. The firing continued for another three or four seconds. Then the whole truck shook and the image in the mirror turned to flame and flying dirt, and Hayes knew the boys in the back were throwing their grenades. He watched one of the technicals swerve out of the way of the blast. Nearly lose control. No sign of the other two, but the highway was curving into the city now, and Hayes had other things to worry about.

Like traffic.

Leaning on the horn and easing up on the gas pedal just slightly, Hayes slalomed the big cargo truck off the highway and into the streets of Kabul. Aiming for the hospital but taking the long way around, avoiding the airport as much as he could, hoping the streets would be less crowded with desperate would-be evacuees.

Horn blaring and lights flashing, the truck raced through Kabul, drawing looks of astonishment from civilians on the sidewalks, and probably worse from drivers who watched the truck loom in their rearview mirrors. There was no time for courtesy; Hayes used the Navistar's bumper to nudge cars out of the way, scraping the side of the truck against buses and other trucks, squeezing through narrow openings to the squeal of metal on metal.

The gunfire behind the Navistar had stopped, from what Hayes could tell. Though the whole city was a nest of Taliban at this point, and Hayes wasn't foolish enough to expect that this cannonball run through the streets of Kabul would remain a secret for long.

He scanned the skies as he drove, looking for any sign of Levi Shaw's evacuation team. Knowing they would come by air, a quick extraction force in at least one helicopter. Knowing the skies above Kabul weren't exactly the most welcoming place for American aircraft these days, and that Shaw's pilots wouldn't want to stick around for very long.

Hayes navigated the transport around a sharp corner, the truck wanting to rise up on its three left-side wheels or maybe even tip over, but somehow staying upright. Ahead, Hayes could see the hospital in the distance. He could also see a Mercedes-Benz SUV double parked dead ahead, its four-way hazard lights flashing.

There was nothing to do but drive through it. Hayes braced himself as the Navistar collided with the rear of the Mercedes. Called an apology out the window as he used the big diesel to bulldoze the smaller vehicle down the narrow street. A glance in his side mirror told him the technicals were back, rounding that same corner that had nearly tipped him over, and Hayes urged the Navistar faster, shoving the Mercedes ahead of him until the street opened up wider and the SUV on his bumper was pushed out of the way.

Above the truck now, a helicopter nearby. Getting closer. Maybe more than one. Hayes searched the sky again but still couldn't see anything. Prayed the helos belonged to Levi Shaw.

He made the front of the hospital. Glanced in the rearview and saw that one of the technicals had collided, hard, with the rear end the Mercedes-Benz. That left only one pickup, and it was still coming, steering around the wreckage and speeding after the Navistar. Quickly, Hayes steered the Navistar to a stop outside the hospital doors and the shattered front windows. Threw himself out of the truck to the pavement, ignoring the pain as he hurried around to the rear, where Mehdi was already helping Zarah and Bilal to the street.

"Go inside," Hayes told them. "To the elevator. Wait for me there."

He reached into the rear of the truck to help Mehdi and the other soldier carry out Abdul Nassim's unconscious body, but Mehdi waved him off. Gestured to the technical now rapidly closing the distance between them, at least two AK-47s aimed out of the windows and spraying wild swaths of 7.62 rounds across the front of the hospital.

"You will only slow him down," he told Hayes. "We will carry him. Just protect us."

Hayes made to argue, loath to give up his friend. But he realized the young soldier was right; there was no way he could carry Nassim. And the shooters in that technical were quickly refining their aim.

Taking a frag grenade from Mehdi's vest, Hayes pulled the

pin and, gauging the distance to the onrushing technical, let the explosive cook for about a second before rolling it out into the middle of the street. The grenade bounced toward the pickup, the driver never seeing the danger until it was too late. The grenade exploded just as it rolled underneath the Toyota's front bumper, launching the pickup's front end skyward with a noise like the apocalypse. Hayes didn't wait to check on the results of the blast. He reached into the back of the Navistar and found a blood-spattered M16, pulled back the charging hammer and flipped the selector to full auto. Then, bracing himself against the pain, he forced himself to shuffle toward the hospital doors.

Abdul and the children were already inside, waiting at the elevator door. Abdul hung limp in the arms of the two young soldiers, seemingly bleeding from everywhere, while Zarah held Bilal tight against her and stared back toward Hayes. Hayes thought he saw her relax, just a little, when he walked through the empty hospital door. But just as quick, she turned back to the elevator, the bank of lights above the silver steel door indicating that the car was descending, but it was sure coming slow.

Come on! the voice shouted. *Where the hell is this elevator?*

Behind Hayes, a spray of gunfire burst across the lobby, shattering what intact glass was left. Zarah screamed and Hayes turned with the M16 to see two of the Taliban fighters from the technical advancing, their Kalashnikovs spitting flame. Hayes returned fire through the hospital doorway without bothering to aim, saw one of the Taliban fighters leap for cover while the other stumbled and fell. Now Hayes steadied his aim, dispatched the man on the ground, and waited for his partner to show his face.

With a *ding*, the elevator door finally opened. Hayes glanced over his shoulder to see Zarah bustle Bilal inside, the soldiers following with Abdul. He backed up as best as he could, the M16 still on his shoulder, aimed out to the street beyond. Heard Zarah call out for him. Then Mehdi.

Go, he thought. *Don't wait for me.*

But it was suicide staying down here, Hayes knew. Sooner or later, the carnage outside would attract more Taliban fighters. The elevator was clearly slow as shit, and there was no way that Hayes could manage the stairs.

He backed to the elevator door. Caught a glimpse of movement from the corner of his eye, swung around to see the last Taliban fighter poke the barrel of his AK-47 through an empty window pane to his right. Hayes took aim. Waited until the fighter crept forward just enough to show his face. Then he pulled the trigger, and the fighter disappeared.

Happy? the voice asked. *Now get on the damn elevator.*

Scanning the lobby one more time, Hayes backed into the car. Pressed the button for the top floor and watched the door slowly slide shut.

The elevator rose languidly. Lights flickered inside, and machinery made grinding noises as the car slowly climbed. Finally with a moment to breathe, Hayes looked down at Adbul in the arms of the soldiers. His friend was pale, ashen. Covered in blood. Not moving.

Mehdi caught Hayes's expression. "He is still breathing," he told Hayes. "Barely."

Hayes said nothing.

"You are still breathing, too," Mehdi continued. A pause. *"Barely."*

The elevator slowed. The doors dinged and opened. A long hallway, and at the other end, daylight. A window, a door, the roof.

"That way," Hayes told the soldiers. He tried to scoop up young Bilal into his arm, couldn't do it. Couldn't find the strength.

Zarah nudged him away. "It's okay," she said. "Just go."

So Hayes went. As fast as he could down the hall toward the light. Zarah ahead of him, pulling Bilal behind her. The soldiers behind him, carrying Abdul. The sound of the helicopter rotors loud now, like thunder. Somewhere directly above.

A face in the window. Silhouetted by daylight, but Hayes could tell it was the doctor with whom he'd left Payam and Freshta. Hayes watched the man's posture relax as he recognized Hayes. Watched him push open the door, relief evident on his face.

"Praise be to Allah," he shouted over the noise of the helicopter. "We thought for sure you were dead."

Beyond him, on the roof of the hotel, Hayes could see Freshta, her arm in a cast and a proper sling. Could see Payam on a stretcher, another doctor beside him, staring up at the sky. As Hayes stepped through the doorway he saw the UH-60 Black Hawk that Levi Shaw had procured dropping into a low hover just above the roof. And crouched in the open cargo door, beside a gunner manning the helo's M-240H, was Levi Shaw himself.

Hayes forced himself to ignore his old boss. Focused on rushing the Nassims to safety, gripping Payam's stretcher and pushing it across the concrete roof toward where the Black Hawk waited.

Ahead of him, Freshta shepherded Zarah and Bilal up into the arms of a combat medic, who sat them in the cargo bay before turning back to help the doctors load Payam aboard. Hayes met Levi Shaw's eyes. Shouted to be heard over the roar of the Black Hawk's turbine engine.

"There's bound to be more Taliban after us," he told Shaw. *"We can't leave these people."*

Shaw's eyes twinkled. *"That's what* they're *here for."*

He gestured skyward, and Hayes followed to where a second helicopter—a Bell AH-1Z Viper—stood overwatch, its triple-barrel M197 rotary cannon pointed directly at the hospital door.

"I have Marines on the way," Shaw continued, *"with orders to evacuate everyone from this hospital, including the sick and elderly. I just need one thing from you, Adam."*

Hayes looked at Shaw. The smirk on the older man's face. He hesitated. *"Thank you?"*

"Not quite," Shaw replied, holding up a hand to the doctors as they tried to help Hayes into the Black Hawk, Abdul Nassim and the others already safely aboard. *"I told you I'd call in that favor, didn't I?"*

Oh, shit, the voice said. *Oh no.*

Levi Shaw's smile widened. "Congratulations, Adam," he said. "You're coming back to Treadstone."

About the Author

JOSHUA HOOD is the author of *Robert Ludlum's The Treadstone Resurrection*, *Robert Ludlum's The Treadstone Exile*, *Robert Ludlum's The Treadstone Transgression*, *Warning Order* and *Clear by Fire*. He graduated from the University of Memphis before joining the military and spending five years in the 82nd Airborne Division. On his return to civilian life he became a sniper team leader on a full-time SWAT team in Memphis, where he was awarded the lifesaving medal. He is currently a full-time author living in Collierville, TN.

ROBERT LUDLUM was the author of twenty-seven novels, each one a *New York Times* bestseller. There are more than 225 million of his books in print, and they have been translated into thirty-two languages. He is the author of the Jason Bourne series – *The Bourne Identity*, *The Bourne Supremacy*, and *The Bourne Ultimatum* – among other novels. Mr Ludlum passed away in March 2001.